Ann
Greyson

Never-DEAD

Copyright © 2019 by Ann Greyson

Written by Ann Greyson

First Edition: December 2019

ISBN 978-0-578-58829-2
LCCN 2019915451

Printed in the United States of America

ACKNOWLEDGMENTS

The author wishes to thank Vivian Davis, Tutoring Art; Alexis Miller, founder of the Purple Shelf Club; and Meaghan D'Otazzo for their help in making this work of fiction ring true.

Never-DEAD

Prologue

A FRESH campsite lay thirty feet from the rapidly flowing Usumacinta River in the woodland of Chiapas, Mexico. The zippered-flap door of a blue tent was open. Inside the tent were two neatly arranged sleeping bags. Several feet away was an empty black Isuzu Rodeo SUV, with the words JUST MARRIED written in shaving cream on the windshield.

The bloodied, beaten body of a raccoon was lying on top of an extinguished campfire. A tire iron with blood and raccoon hair on it was lying on the ground a few feet away from the campfire. A few more steps away was the dead body of a woman lying on its left side and bent at an angle of about ninety degrees. Her neck was nearly severed by bites, head twisted at an unnatural angle. There was dried blood on her neck, chest, and a small puddle on the ground. There were scratches on her arms and chest, and her dead eyes were staring up at the sun.

From the near distance came the sound of loud barking from a lone bewildered golden retriever wading in the river. Now growling and showing his teeth, the canine didn't care for what he saw, a man hanging off a cliff, attempting to pull himself up.

The snarling man slowly inched his way up the rock until he stood on the mountain top. He was dressed in a black double-breasted suit, white shirt, and gold tie. There were dark stains of blood smudged on his shirt, and on the cuffs of his pants. On his right hand there were scratch marks and dried blood from a wound of an animal bite. He staggered slowly down the mountain toward the road.

The scared dog moved backwards. He whined softly with an expression of confusion on his face. The dog whimpered again, then traveled farther down the river.

Forty-five minutes later, the ghastly looking man was walking in the road, moving toward the town. Less than fifty feet away from him was a fruit stand on the side of the road. In the shade under a tarp, stood an elderly woman beside a table with mangos and bananas for sale. She had gray hair pulled in a tight bun and was wearing a shawl around her shoulders covering a white short-sleeved blouse, and a long maroon skirt. There was a small radio on the table tuned to a station playing Mexican music. The blasting song was preventing her from hearing the grunts of the man.

He was approaching her, and she didn't think much about it until he growled at her showing teeth like a mad dog. She also looked at him suspiciously because he smelled foul. When he surrounded her, raising his arms to grab her, a rush of fear shot up her spine. She jumped back on instinct, however not quick enough. He came in closer, got her by the shoulders, and took a bite into the side of her neck.

She screamed in Spanish, "Ayuda. Por favor. Ayuda."

The man got her again and bit into her arm. She pulled away and unraveled herself from his grasp, losing her shawl in the process. He was confused for only a moment, but then snarled and lurched toward her. She ran with all her might.

She screamed again, "Ayuda! Ayuda! Policia!"

She felt faint as she tried to run faster, and her ankle twisted and she fell to the ground. Her knees were scraped and hands bloody where she had tried to stop the fall. As she lay there with both hands on the dirt road, she tried to catch her breath.

Nearly a minute later, she turned her head to find the man had gained on her. She scrambled to get back up only to find the man standing behind her. The man reached out with his arms to grab her just as she started to run again.

Despite the blood gushing from her wounds, she had out run the mad man. She looked over her shoulder to see him trailing a long way behind. But she was tired and quit running because the dry heat and blazing sun were dehydrating her. While taking a couple of deep breaths, she turned to find the man was still stalking her. She sighed then started walking fast.

Five minutes later, a white Toyota Tundra pickup truck appeared on the road. The driver was listening to Mexican music on the radio.

The driver honked the horn and shouted out the window, "Muevete. Loco."

"Estupido," the driver yelled as the Toyota truck swerved to one side driving around the man.

Moments later, the woman saw the pickup truck, waved her arm and called out to him in a loud voice, "Ayuda. Por favor."

The driver saw the woman swaying around, blood dripping from her wounds. Something was going on. The Toyota truck skidded to a stop. The driver got out of the truck to help her. He had thick black hair and eyes, a muscular figure, and was wearing a navy T-shirt and faded blue jeans.

"Que paso, vieja? Cual es tu problema?" he asked.

The woman looked at the driver with despair, pleading with him in Spanish. She told him that she'd been assaulted and pointed to the man. The driver turned around to look at the man, who was closing in on them.

"Mi nombre es Roberto. Cual es su nombre?"

"Magdalena," she said in a soft voice.

He turned and hollered, "Loco."

Magdalena begged him to leave, pleaded with him to take her away. "Vamonos! Ahora mismo, Senor."

Instead, as the man approached, he helped her to sit on the ground. The man made a grunting noise and leaped at Roberto, grabbing him from behind biting him on the back of his shoulder. He pushed the man hard in the chest. The man faltered back a step, nearly fell over onto the ground, went for Roberto again, his left arm swinging around. He threw a quick punch that struck the man's cheek. Next, he kicked the man in the shin and kicked him much harder in the ribs. He snatched the man's left arm, twisted it behind him, hard enough to dislocate his arm. And lastly, he head-butted the man with all his strength. The man grunted as he fell on his side, landing hard on the ground. Roberto took a deep, satisfying breath.

After lying still for a couple of minutes, the man came to and was trying to get up. That did it. Roberto hurried to his truck and grabbed an L-shaped tire iron. The man growled, got to his feet and rushed him. His tire iron crashed into the man's knee. He was shocked that the man was not bleeding anywhere. The man's blood seemed, by all accounts, to be coagulated. Nevertheless, he was desperate to stop this mad man. He raised the tire iron again. This time he aimed for the man's head and swung the tire iron rendering the man unconscious.

Scratching his shoulder wound, he trudged back to the truck and tossed the tire iron into the back. Breathlessly, he rushed around to the passenger door and pulled it open. Then he went to check on Magdalena. As he helped her walk to the truck, it was clear to him that her condition had worsened.

"Descansar. Te voy a llevar a la hospital," Roberto said and lowered her into the seat.

She was half unconscious and didn't respond. He slammed the door shut, then ran around and slid into the driver's seat and started up the truck.

Little did they know they were both infected. This wasn't a random act of violence, but something much worse. Their attacker was the original carrier of a communicable disease that reanimates dead tissue. Now the virus would spread through Mexico. And one thing was for certain, there would be no celebrating this day of the dead.

The Toyota truck roared away driving by a sign that gave the distance to the city of Palenque, which had a site of stone carvings from the Maya. The year was 2012, and the Maya's Long Count calendar was coming to an end, just as a world changing pandemic was starting in Mexico.

Chapter 1

COASTAL AIRWAYS FLIGHT 238 was boarding at the Tucson International Airport on a sunlit morning in Arizona. At 8 a.m., Henry Winter sat in an aisle seat in business class, browsing his HTC smartphone. The middle-aged man had sandy hair, green eyes, and was wearing khakis, a blue polo shirt, and dress shoes. There were eight single seats by the window on the left and right sides, and one row of six, two-by-two seats in the middle, separated by two wide aisles.

A thirtyish man with dark hair and eyes, wearing a well-tailored gray suit, black tie, and a bandage around his hand, stepped onto the plane. He was looking and feeling groggy.

"Welcome to Coastal Airways. My name is Jacqueline. Enjoy the flight," the flight attendant said to him.

She was a tall, Hispanic woman. He barely smiled as he walked past her toward his seat.

"Good morning. Seat 4D. My name is Griffin by the way," he said.

"Henry. How do you do?"

He did his best to avoid eye contact, however Griffin hadn't done likewise. Winter was uninterested in the conversation and more concerned with whatever he was checking on his smartphone.

"Not too good. You're probably wondering what happened to my hand?" Griffin asked.

"Not at all. I didn't notice."

Winter stole a sidelong look at him as he lifted his wrapped hand. He wasn't thinking about what Griffin had just said to him. He was wondering instead if he could sit somewhere else.

Sweating profusely, Griffin loosened his tie, opened the top two buttons of his shirt, and said, "Well, it's the strangest thing. Just before daylight this morning, I was waiting in my hotel's driveway. Less than a minute later, a taxi pulled up alongside me. As I reached out to open the door, a woman came up, grabbed my hand and bit it hard."

Taking interest in what he was saying, Winter put away his phone and said, "Yes, that is strange."

"The woman who bit me looked like a vagrant. I pushed her away, opened the door of the cab, threw my suitcase inside and slid in behind it, then slammed the door shut. I told the driver to get a move on because I have a plane to catch. Which he did. Thank God."

Winter looked at his bandaged hand again and said, "You should have that looked at."

"No worries. I will. When I arrive in Albuquerque," Griffin said, without the slightest concern.

An announcement was made welcoming the passengers aboard and that the plane was about to depart. An attendant checked the seat belts and overhead compartments. The plane started down the runway and lifted off smoothly, climbing to cruising altitude.

Winter put on a headset, dialed up easy listening music, and leaned back in his plush seat. Griffin scratched at the bandage on his hand, where he felt an ache like an irritation, then he closed his eyes and dozed off.

Thirty minutes into the flight, Winter was waiting for another tune, when he heard the sound of heavy breathing. Griffin's body was leaning over to one side. He glanced over to Griffin, who was pale as a ghost, looking very sick now with beads of perspiration on his forehead streaming down his face. Winter looked at his bandaged hand and noticed that leaking through the gauze was blood.

He put away the headset, unfastened his belt, and stood abruptly from his chair. Hurriedly, he walked down the aisle till he found the flight attendant putting a tan blanket in the overhead compartment. It was Jacqueline.

"Excuse me, Miss. I'm sitting next to a man who looks ill," he said, out of breath, as he passed a hand through his hair.

"Take me to him," she said as she closed the compartment.

Jacqueline followed him to his seat. She looked Griffin over. There was a troubled look on her face as she tapped him on the shoulder.

"Sir are you all right?" she asked, getting no reaction.

"Did he mention anything to you?" she asked, turning to face Winter.

"He told me he had been bit in the hand by a vagrant woman," he said, with a puzzled look spread over his face like he didn't know what was happening.

"Let me take a look."

She leaned over him, took his hand and inspected the bandage more closely. Griffin's bloodshot eyes flew open wide, and he looked deranged. She noticed, pulled her hand away, and was going to say something. He was trying to stand up but couldn't do it because he was strapped in. Then he growled and bit her shoulder, his teeth tearing her flesh.

A moment's hesitation before she pushed him off. She ran down the aisle toward the rear of the plane. Winter stood there for a minute just looking at Griffin in a state of confusion. Then he followed after Jacqueline.

The flight attendant chime sounded in the cockpit.

"Captain, we have a medical emergency with one of our passengers."

The Captain's voice returned, "Jacqueline what's going on? Are you okay?"

"No, sir. The passenger bit my shoulder. He is a danger to others."

"Okay, Jacqueline. Stay where you are until further notice."

Henry Winter was standing by the bathrooms. Knowing that things were bad, he grabbed his cell phone and dialed his daughter Hannah. He told her there was a problem with a passenger, and that there might be an emergency landing. In the midst of the conversation, the signal was lost. He hung up.

Meanwhile, Griffin had ripped off his seat belt and was wrestling with a gangly, blond-haired, young man wearing a gray Puma T-shirt and jeans. He had attacked the passenger biting him on the forearm, causing blood to trickle onto his shirt sleeve.

"Get off me, you freak," the young man said, struggling to break his grip.

He elbowed Griffin in the ribs. Passengers got up from their seats to watch. A flight attendant was attempting to break them up, just as the young man wrapped a leg around the back of Griffin's ankle and tripped him, knocking him off balance. Griffin landed hard on his knees, but it was useless, because he stood up again just as the young man started running to the other side of the plane.

Then all panic broke loose. People, scared of being bitten, left their seats and were running down the aisle toward Henry Winter. Jacqueline saw the rushing crowd, hurried to the cockpit and banged on the door.

"Captain, it's Jacqueline. Please let me in! Hurry! It's an emergency!"

The copilot opened the door to let her in. The thickset black man slammed the door shut and locked it.

How could this be happening? Winter thought as he opened the bathroom door and locked himself inside. The screaming scared the daylights out of him.

After an additional fifteen minutes, Jacqueline convulsed and gasped for breath and was losing her balance. She collapsed onto the carpet, shaking and whimpering, then fell unconscious. The copilot hadn't seen her drop, but he had heard the sound of her reaching the floor. Quickly, he left his seat, crouched beside her and was able to roll her over.

A couple of more minutes passed, and Jacqueline was perspiring until her eyes opened suddenly. She snarled and bit the copilot's arm. Tense with fear, he pushed her down and stood up.

The Captain turned his head to see what was happening just as she raised from the floor, grabbed him from behind with both arms, and bit into his neck. The copilot tried to pull her off the Captain, who struggled to steer the plane into a descent, making a wide turn, as he tried to land from the east.

Winter was being shoved around in the bathroom by the plane's turbulence. The plane dropped, and the rumble was so loud from the jet's engines that he couldn't hear the passengers' screams anymore. He clapped his hands firmly over his ears. And then he lost it. His face filled with tears, as he drifted off into grief.

Ten minutes later, the plane lost control and went down, crashing in the Gila National Forest in Catron County, New Mexico.

Chapter 2

AT A LITTLE past eight o'clock in San Antonio, Texas, the temperature was a pleasant sixty-seven degrees. With the weather cool and breezy and no clouds to be seen, you could fool yourself that everything was right with the world, and that nothing bad could happen.

But peaceful looks could be deceiving. You would find out soon enough that it wasn't a picture-perfect December day after all. It looked like a normal morning, but nothing would be normal again. As the year was coming to a close, a change was coming about, and not a good one.

A good-looking man in his twenties, seated on a wooden bench at a bus stop near the corner of Babcock and Callaghan Roads, was about to get the shock of his life.

The young man wearing a loose dark-green T-shirt and dark blue jeans had jet black hair and an average build. He tapped his fingers lightly on the armrest of the bench, then looked down at his watch, growing impatient. Thirteen minutes after eight. He didn't look pleased.

From nowhere a Hispanic man in his early twenties came running on the sidewalk. He passed by the bus stop, moving at lightning speed.

"Esos locos estan muertos," he mumbled to himself, while looking at his scratched-up hand.

The Hispanic man looked as if he was escaping from someone or something. The young man sitting on the bench thought that he was running away from a crime scene because he behaved as if he just swiped a lady's pocketbook and was desperately trying to get away.

He pulled his cell phone from the leather case attached to the front of his belt. After that he dialed a number and waited.

"Hello Bobby. This is Kyle."

For a minute, he listened to the caller, then said, "No, I'm still at the bus stop. The bus is running late."

Another pause, then he said, "Yeah, okay. I'll call you back in thirty minutes."

He ended the call. For quite a long moment, he held the phone before he placed it back in its case.

Kyle glanced around, rather annoyed. Another Hispanic man standing in the middle of the sidewalk, caught his attention. The man's eyes fixed on the ground, his body swayed back and forth. And he was bleeding from a neck wound. In his early thirties, of average height and weight with dark brown hair, he wore jeans and a blue and white striped

T-shirt. Kyle stared openly at his wound a little longer, eventually losing interest. In his head he was thinking the Hispanic man might just be some weirdo.

There were some faint growls and grunts not far off, muted by the cars driving on the street. The noise was coming from the half a dozen living corpses slowly staggering around in the parking lot behind the bench. The sight was unimaginable, right out of a nightmare. They were not wearing costumes, because it wasn't Halloween. If you wanted to give them a name, you could call them zombies.

Kyle was not aware of them. But they had seen him. A zombie, thirsty for his blood, tripped over a rock, went down on one knee. Then it was up again. It was missing an eye and its skin was falling off its face.

The sound of screeching tires on asphalt, pulled Kyle out of his daydreaming. A blue Nissan Versa tore out of the parking lot at breakneck speed. The driver's side window of the hatchback was halfway down. The radio was playing the song "Wide Awake" by Katy Perry, loud enough for everyone in the vicinity to hear.

Driving rapidly, the person behind the wheel was obviously in a great hurry. Kyle was certain that the driver deliberately drove the Nissan over the curb and the sidewalk, turning left onto Babcock Road. All that he could see of the driver was that it was a young white woman with blond hair pulled into a ponytail. As she drove past him, he noticed that she kept checking her rearview mirrors. It was like she was looking at someone or something.

As she reached the intersection, she took one last look out the window at the parking lot behind the bus stop. Then she was gone. He believed she had gone through the red light, but it all happened so fast it would be hard to say for sure.

A gust of wind blew in his direction. He tilted his nose in the air, like he smelled something foul. It was then that he sensed that something wasn't right. The acrid smell alerted him to look over his shoulder.

Did he see what he thought he saw? He sprang from the bench and turned around to confirm what he was seeing. Could it be real? And, without a doubt, they were zombies. His jaw literally dropped, hardly able to believe his eyes.

For a fleeting moment, he was so stunned he didn't know what to do. Was this really happening? His face showed complete confusion, as the zombies growled and walked about. They were heading straight toward him.

As he tried to think things through, he heard muffled shouts somewhere in the distance. Waiting for the bus was not an option anymore. He needed to get out of there.

Kyle turned his attention now to a zombie who was fast approaching him. It opened its mouth slowly, showing rotten yellow teeth. Then it raised its arm trying to reach for him.

At that point, he started to run down the street. His thoughts were spinning as he passed a woman out of her car, yelling and fighting with two zombies. He didn't help her because she probably didn't have a chance, and neither did he. Even more aggressively, he sprinted for his life down Babcock Road.

When he saw a silver Honda sedan turning into the Starbucks parking lot directly in his path, he stopped. Exhausted from running, he tried to catch his breath while waiting for the car to enter the lot. But he was so tired, and consumed with thoughts about saving his own skin, he couldn't warn the female driver away.

Thinking to himself, he supposed he could have said something to her, should have said something. And if he did, what good would it have done? Instead, he convinced himself that it wouldn't matter because nothing he could do or say could help her or himself.

Glancing over his shoulder, he was relieved to see that the zombies were not chasing after him. He bent over, putting his hands on his knees, taking as many breaths as possible. By that time the Honda was out of the way, he started to run, turning left onto another road. He never stopped running till out of sight. And boy, did Kyle run.

Chapter 3

JENNA WINTER parked her car in the lot facing Babcock Road. She reached into the backseat for her backpack next to a large shopping bag loaded with Christmas presents. Slinging the backpack over her right shoulder, she slid her five-seven slender body out of the car and locked it. She wore black jeans, a black camisole top under a green jacket, and black Converse sneakers.

Earlier that morning, she had cleaned out her dormitory, and said good-bye to St. Mary's University. All the way across campus and through the student parking lot, she carried a box stuffed with her possessions. Eagerly, she had placed the box into the trunk of her silver color Honda Civic. She experienced an incredible feeling of relief, like a great weight had been lifted off her shoulders.

With her green eyes, and creamy white skin, she had a face that men said was intended for magazine covers, or possibly motion pictures. With dreams of being a fashion model, now she could do what she really wanted to do. But she didn't have a plan. For the time being, she had no intention of doing anything.

She pushed through the door of Starbucks. As she weaved through the customers in line, she came close to bumping into a man in a business suit, eyes down on his phone. There was nothing like the hustle and bustle of a coffee shop. She soaked up the aroma of coffee combined with the scent of baked goods. Gleefully, she took her place, last in line.

A loud sound of the impact of crashing metal, tore her away from the line. Jenna and others went to the window to check out the situation. She was sure it was an accident.

Sure enough a Metropolitan Transit bus traveling at warp speed, had plowed into her parked Honda Civic, which then slid sideways fifteen feet before overturning. The public transportation bus was stopped halfway in the driveway of the store and halfway on the street. The Honda was crushed.

"Oh my God, that's my car!" Jenna gasped out loud.

She watched a group of people running out of the damaged bus. The bus driver, a heavy-set Hispanic man, was struggling to get out, his left leg was broken. Just as the driver limped off of the bus, a zombie followed behind him, lifted his arms to grab him. It was a skinny black zombie with blood red eyes, sporting a head full of Buckwheat-like hair, wild and standing on end. The bus driver slipped and fell to the ground. A look of disbelief came over his face as the zombie fell to his knees and reached out with both arms to grab him. He yelled as the zombie picked at him, pulling at him, feeding on him. Though he struggled to get away, he knew he had no chance.

"Did you see that?" someone asked.

Jenna looked repulsed and stunned at the same time. She shook her head in disbelief, not knowing whether to move or stay put. Then her Samsung cell phone vibrated in her backpack from an incoming text message. She quickly pulled it out. Like most teenagers, the phone was within easy reach.

"Move out of my way!" someone yelled behind her.

She heard feet scampering. Someone was running for the door. Looking up from her phone, she saw only an upraised arm. She swung around, trying to get out of the way of whoever it was.

A fearful voice called out loudly, "Call nine-one-one!"

It was pandemonium as the people in the Starbucks panicked and pushed forward toward the door. A woman started screaming. She inched her way through the crowd near the door. More screaming. She tried to press her way forward against the fleeing crowd dropping her cell phone to the floor, which got stomped on by the people running.

A clerk and Jenna were the only ones left in the store because everyone else had left, including the store manager. They all jumped into their cars and sped off. The car doors slamming and engines roaring to life had gained the attention of the zombies. Now there were four zombies lurking outside the store, additional to the zombie that was still feeding on the bus driver. Jenna was going to have to wait it out, hoping the zombies would move on, that she wouldn't be discovered, standing well away from the window, out of sight.

The clerk came out from behind the counter. He was a tall, skinny, glasses wearing geeky-looking twentysomething, wearing a green apron over a blue T-shirt and threadbare jeans.

He locked the front door, and said frantically, "Don't worry. I called nine-one-one. Help is on the way."

With all the stuff going on, she had forgotten about her cell phone. Looking on the floor, she saw the front of the phone cracked in half and the screen shattered. She picked it up and it broke apart in two sections. There would be no way to fix it. She dropped the remains of the phone in the trash can.

"Looks like it's just the two of us," he said.

"That's just great," she said, thinking, trying to figure out what to do next, which was not easy as she felt a little anxious.

"This is a little awkward, don't you think?"

Suddenly a thought came to her. "While we're waiting, could I trouble you for a venti double-shot vanilla latte with soy milk? It might settle my nerves."

"Hmmm," he said, thinking it over, "I guess due to the circumstances. We might as well help ourselves."

He traveled behind the counter and began to make the drink. While waiting she grabbed two bottles of water from under the glass counter and placed them on the counter by the register. Five minutes later, he stood behind the register, handing her the drink..

"Never mind, I am not going to charge you."

"Are you sure it's okay to do that?" she asked with concern in her voice.

"Yeah. Don't sweat it. I doubt I'll get into trouble. And I don't care if I do," he said and laughed.

She smiled tensely. "I thank you kindly."

Then she put the bottles of water inside her backpack and took the latte with a trembling hand.

He left the counter, walked over to her, extended a hand, and said, "Name's Cory, by the way."

"Jenna," she replied a little unsteadily.

"Pleased to meet you," he said, greeting her with a firm handshake.

"Likewise," she said, released her hand, and took a sip of her latte.

His introduction was cut short by the ring of his cell phone. Immediately, he dug it out of his jeans pocket..

"Hello? Where are you right now?" he asked the person on the other end.

Neither the police nor the emergency medical services had arrived. Jenna had waited about ten minutes, not sure what to do. For several more seconds, she peeked out the window and watched a zombie at a reasonable distance away, the only one she could see anyway. The latte was finished. She tossed the empty cup into the trash can. There was no more thinking to be done.

"Okay. Bye," Cory said, then ended his call.

Next thing she knew, he was standing right next to her.

"That was my brother. He's coming here to get me."

She wasn't saying much, just listening.

He kept talking in a nervous chatter. "You could go out there now, but I think you should wait until the police get here."

Cory told her that she was wise to just stay put and see if

things improve. She happened to look out the window and saw that the nearest zombie was moving further away from the store. While he was still rambling on, lost in the moment, he never saw it coming. In the course of a few seconds, she unlocked the door and left.

"Hey, where are you going?" he asked.

Jenna didn't look back.

Chapter 4

SOMEWHAT traumatized, Jenna started walking fast down the sidewalk, not knowing where she was going, except in the opposite direction of her damaged Honda. Several of her personal effects, including clothing, were inside the car. She couldn't afford to think of that right now.

Howling sirens could be heard close by, as people scattered all over the place. Somewhere a woman screamed and there came the sound of a gunshot. She didn't look.

Just a little further down the sidewalk was a young black man not older than twenty, leaned up against a fire hydrant between two parked cars. He was propped up motionless, bleeding from his mouth and chest. She'd never seen a dead body before, so it was quite a shock. What stood out the most was that he was wearing brand-new Air Jordan sneakers. There wasn't a drop of blood on them. She suspected he was most likely infected, and not yet risen from the dead.

A wave of people were making their way down the street, and she made a run for it around the corner. That was when she saw a flicker of red and blue lights out of the corner of her eye. The police had arrived. She could just make out the voice of a man over a loudspeaker demanding the zombies to stand down.

"This is the police. Stop and put your hands where we can see them!" a voice yelled.

Stopping abruptly in the parking lot of a taco stand, she paused for a moment, catching her breath. Then she took cover behind a parked Toyota Sienna minivan nearby. She knew bullets were going to fly. The police were ready to have it out with the infected and she didn't want to get stuck in the middle of it. She crouched down lower to watch and wait.

A gnarly zombie with a shredded piece of torn skin hanging from its right arm, half of its right cheek gone, and shirt covered in blood was going after a police officer. The black, heavy-set cop in his thirties was panicking, desperately looking around for backup. The zombie lurched forward, snapping its mouth open and closed as its arms reached up.

"Hands in the air. I repeat, put your hands in the air. Don't come any closer. I said stop! Stop right there, or I'll shoot!" he demanded, eyes filled with rage.

He didn't wait for a response. The cop drew his Glock, with a round already chambered, leveling it at the zombie's chest. He fired off a shot. The bullet didn't even make it flinch as it was still headed directly for the cop.

Then at that moment, a stocky, square-jawed officer arrived on the scene to assist. "You! Down on the ground!"

But even then, the zombie didn't stop. It was much closer now. The officer fired three shots in a row, the sound splitting the air.

At the exact moment gunfire exploded, Jenna ducked even lower behind the vehicle. With each gunshot, her body jerked in terror. She held on to the side of the Toyota, shaking like a wet dog. Tears rolled down her cheeks. She felt desperate and started praying. What else could she do?

"Please, God. Make this stop," she said to herself.

She had never been so afraid in her entire life. She had never been so close to violence. How was a nineteen-year-old girl supposed to handle something like that?

One of the bullets had slammed into the zombie's head, dropping him to the ground. The black cop walked over and kicked it to make sure it was dead.

"Jesus!" the cop exclaimed.

When the cop realized that a blow to the head kills the infected, he turned around and shouted, "Aim for their heads. Shoot them in the head."

After a short while longer, the gunshots thinned out. Jenna took a quick look around from her hiding place. Just when she thought it was safe to leave, she heard someone running up behind her. She shot an apprehensive glance over her shoulder. It was a police officer hurrying by, his hand on his holster. The officer in his early twenties hesitated, looking uncertain and scared. He had a hard time walking over the bodies of the infected that had been shot down.

"Keep going," a voice demanded.

Following behind the young officer, came three uniformed officers taking their pistols out of their holsters, all petrified. While Jenna flicked a glance at a team of heavily armed police entering a building across the street.

When a blue Hyundai Sonata came racing down the street and slammed into the curb, she saw her opportunity. That was when she decided to make a run for it. It was imperative that she get out of there before it got any worse. She looked over the hood of the minivan, and beside her. While dozens of officers scrambled to the area, she took off fast enough that no zombie could catch her. Quickly glancing over her shoulder, she could see that the Sonata had caught fire.

Further down the street, she heard the sound of a helicopter clattering overhead. A news helicopter drew nearer, circled low, swerving between skyscrapers. A cameraman was trying to get closeup shots of the scene, trying to film it all. She kept her distance, walking at a faster pace.

The helicopter tilted to the left, then lifted with a zombie clinging to the open door. It was after the cameraman. The engine hummed and the flying machine lowered. The zombie dangled from the aircraft then lost its grip and fell through the air and onto the street. The cameraman looked relieved. The helicopter sped along the street, picked up speed as it headed northwest, then lifted gracefully into the sky.

She walked through the underpass of the interstate. Five police cars were parked here and there along the curb and intersecting roadways of Babcock and Northwest Loop 410. It was cordoned off. Near the sidewalk, were three police officers using an overturned pickup truck for cover. They were gearing up for battle. She did her best to navigate past them, because she knew what was going to happen next.

The officers had drawn their guns. A fat, topless, middle-aged, infected Chinese woman, missing an arm and part of her lower jaw, staggered toward them. A half-dozen zombies were twenty yards behind her, and another dozen infected were coming in behind them. To say the San Antonio Police were outnumbered by a large number of infected was an understatement.

She turned, stopped for a minute and stared at the infected, her green eyes wide and scared. It was about to get really ugly. She looked down one side of the street, and then looked up the other street.

Her mind was made up. She started to go down the street to her right. Nothing at all seemed familiar. How confused and lost she felt. She had no phone to call anybody. But then, who could she call? Inwardly she was quaking. Her thoughts were racing madly about all the horrible things that could happen to her as she was close to panic.

To ease her nerves, she stopped walking and took a couple of deep breaths. Then she glanced around in all directions, looking for a way to escape safely.

A minute later, the gunshots started going off. Looking to her left she saw an empty street. She ran for it. Turning right, she ran through a parking lot and almost smashed into a car that was pulling out of the lot. Luckily, she had stopped herself in time. As a result, she found herself turning onto a street that led right back to Babcock Road.

Jenna was sure, that she'd quit smoking cigarettes the minute she got out of this alive. It was almost beyond belief to her that she would be making a pact with herself. She would use this experience as motivation to stop smoking for the rest of her life. After some reconsideration, she thought probably not.

Chapter 5

FRIDAY, DECEMBER 21, 2012, I was lying in bed thinking that my life was like a fairy tale. In the almost three years I had worked as the head of the information technology department for Biogenetics & Disease Control, I was the happiest I had ever been in my life. My formal job description entailed making sure the latest medical information was accessible for research by managing data storage. Additionally, the software systems needed to be carefully maintained, among a slew of other things.

You must pardon my ego, but many people would say that I was a cutting-edge computer scientist. It just so happened that I was good with computers, better than most people would assume. Although, me being the computer geek with no direct responsibility for any medical breakthroughs, I still felt I played a big part in technology shaping our world.

I hoped to find a well-paying job after earning my Bachelor of Science degree from the University of California, Los Angeles. It was just my luck that I was hired by the BDC. It was a great opportunity for someone who was young and single like myself, having just recently turned twenty-six.

Because the BDC utilized research methods classified to the general public, I had to sign a non-disclosure agreement form when I accepted the job. I put down my John Hancock, and in so many words said, "I, Hannah Winter, do solemnly swear to keep my mouth shut."

I considered it a privilege to work here because the BDC was at the center of disease research and prevention in the United States. There was a direct link between the BDC and the administering of influenza shots and other yearly vaccinations. Intense research and tests on West Nile virus and Lyme disease were among the most recently conducted.

I sat up in bed, swung my legs over, put my bare feet on the carpet. As I looked around for the cat, I maneuvered my way over to the closet and swung it open to pick out my clothes for the day. Searching my closet for something comfortable, yet professional looking, I pulled out a short-sleeved pink blouse and tan-colored pants and laid them out on the bed. And still I wondered where the cat was; I hadn't seen her at all.

After undressing, I walked into the bathroom for a shower. While the water splashed against my body, it dawned on me that I might be a workaholic. It wasn't so much that I didn't care about anything other than my job. I would like to have a relationship, but simply didn't think I was cut out for one at the present time. These days, I wasn't going anywhere with anyone. I didn't have time for romance. That was what I often told myself. And I wasn't unhappy either. Yes, it was possible to be happy being single, no kids, minus a boyfriend.

It wasn't easy to meet people due to the fact that I rarely ventured outside. This made sense if you took into consideration that I lived and worked in a secure facility deep underground beneath the city of Dulce, New Mexico all year round along with over one hundred technicians, scientists, and support staff. And I always felt relaxed here, far away from the troubles of the outside world.

Living in a small, furnished, one-bedroom unit, with one full bathroom, kitchen, and living room was actually rather cozy. And I wasn't lonely because for the last eleven months I'd shared the place with the cutest little Siamese cat. I got her when she was a kitten, at eight weeks old. Small and tan with black fur on the tips of her ears and feet, she was named Mim short for Miriam, after the woman who donated a basket full of kittens to the pet store in Albuquerque where I bought her.

Back in the bedroom getting dressed, I just saw Mim running toward the living room. And I meant running. She was full of energy this morning. Earlier I'd been wondering where she had gone off to, thinking I didn't want to leave her alone on Christmas Eve and Christmas Day. But what choice did I have? I planned to put out a two-day supply of food and water. She plays all day long, so she probably wouldn't even notice I was gone.

Already I had finished my Christmas shopping weeks ago. And, in a couple of days from now, I would be celebrating the holiday season with my sister Jenna and my dad at his home in Albuquerque.

I had just come to terms with my sister dropping out of college at the end of her semester and returning to live with our father. I admit I wasn't thrilled at first. But I understood she was too much of a free spirit. At school, she felt bogged down with assignments. Not necessarily in those words, but that was what she'd tried to say.

When I was putting on my shoes, the thought of Jenna returning to live again in New Mexico triggered a feeling that something was out of place. But I knew she was okay. I couldn't figure out what else could have made me think along these lines. Maybe I had contracted a case of the holiday jitters.

Were my suspicions, paranoia, being fueled by long term confinement? Maybe deep down inside, I was longing for some fresh air and a change of scenery. I rarely went outside on weekdays, whereas I spent a lot of weekends on shopping expeditions in the city of Dulce or surrounding neighborhoods. But oddly enough I didn't go out last weekend.

For reasons beyond me, I couldn't stop thinking about it either. Going on thirteen days straight without a glimpse outside, I swear, I was feeling confined. It was the only logical explanation, right? I should go out this weekend. Or, better yet, tomorrow, I would take the elevator to the parking garage, hop into my car and go out for a spin. And I would feel all right again.

Or, on the other hand, I might be having a premonition. Yet, I didn't notice anything out of the ordinary. All I knew was that if there was something coming, I was not prepared for it. I entertained the idea for a handful of seconds, then shook off the thought.

I had to leave now if I wanted to grab breakfast. I put cat food and water in the cat's dishes. She ignored me, apparently not yet hungry, and was completely involved scratching up the sofa. I grabbed my purse, and phone and saw there were a few text messages from Jenna. I read the texts Jenna had sent me as I grabbed the keys and walked out the door.

Chapter 6

WHEN I walked into the cafeteria, there were a small number of people standing around engaged in conversations on their cell phones. I stood there a moment wondering why a bunch more people were glued to the television. Last Tuesday I was here having dinner and the television was tuned to a Denver Nuggets vs. San Antonio Spurs NBA game. This time it wasn't a basketball game because chatter rolled through the room as people tried to get their heads around what was being said. I knew something was up, and I didn't like it. In that instant, I forgot why I was there.

The television monitor on the wall told the story: Live-action footage was running on the network. My brown eyes fixed on the screen to a broadcast already in progress. The reporter, a black man in his mid-forties, was standing outside a building in El Paso, Texas.

He pressed his earpiece and said, "What's occurring here is that infected people are attacking everyone, acting like rabid animals."

The network's anchor, Catherine Vargas, a light-skinned Hispanic in her early thirties, appeared on the set and pressed for details. "Davis, have the police been able to control the situation?"

"Catherine, police officers are responding to reports of attacks by those in a zombie state. But they can't keep it under control everywhere, at the same time. It has gotten out of hand."

I looked around the cafeteria and saw that everyone was in a state of awe because the television news footage was horrifying. There were ambulances and police vehicles racing on the streets. Panic stricken people were abandoning their cars and running onto the streets. Kids were hurling rocks and bottles at the infected. Police were clubbing infected people with their batons and hurling tear-gas grenades into crowds of infected. A police officer wrestling with an infected, knocked it down, his baton pressed to its neck. And finally, a closeup of an infected woman trying to grab a young man, who was trying his best to push her away.

And just like that, things changed. I heard the words. However, they didn't sound believable. Still unable to accept it, shaking my head, I was as stunned as everyone else. Could all this be true? For a few seconds I couldn't wrap my brain around the concept, trying to find my way through what they were telling us. I watched closely to see what happened next.

"Do we know anything about the virus or how it's contracted?" Catherine Vargas asked.

"So far, we know little about it, beyond the fact that the disease is transmitted through saliva and the virus reanimates dead tissue. Those infected are alive and dead at the same time. They're never dead and spread the disease to anyone they bite. We've never seen anything quite like this before. Government officials are urging people not to have any contact with the infected and to stay in their homes because the streets are dangerous."

Catherine Vargas went on. "Back to our studios in Washington, DC for commentary as we continue to update our viewers on this story."

Almost a half hour later, I had seen and heard enough to get the gist of what was going on. A viral plague that brought the dead back to life? One we had never seen before? Never dead. That was what the reporter called the infected.

It had only just occurred to me that the Mayan calendar had ended with a world changing disease. People around the world were preparing for the coming apocalypse based on the Mayan predictions. However, I, along with many other people, believed that the well-publicized doomsday predictions was a lot of hype about nothing, all the anxiety had been for nothing. Now, with this outbreak spreading so rapidly, I question whether there was any truth to the doomsday prophecy that had been circulating all year. After all, the year was 2012, and it was very possible the world could end soon.

There was no way I was prepared for this. I was just

starting to get over the shock of singer and actress Whitney Houston being found dead of a drug overdose in the bathtub of a Beverly Hilton hotel room earlier this year. My late mother had all of her albums and was a huge fan of her music, which was popular the year I was born, 1986. "How Will I Know" was my favorite song of hers.

My phone rang, shaking me back to the present. I reached in my purse, found my LG phone and looked at the caller ID. It was my father.

I answered on the third ring. "Dad, I'm so relieved to hear from you. Have you heard the news?"

"Hannah, I'm in the air. I'm on the flight back to Albuquerque. There is a problem with a passenger," he said, sounding stressed.

"Dad! Are you all right?" I demanded.

"The aircraft may have to make…," he said.

Static came on the line.

"Just a minute. I'm losing reception," I said, as I walked out of the door of the cafeteria.

Within seconds the reception was clear again, so I continued talking. "Right now, I'm really starting to worry about you."

"There is no need to worry. I must go. I'll call you back…," my father said, before the connection failed.

"Dad, you're breaking up. Hello? Please repeat the last…," I said, a bit hysterically, but the line was cut off.

The call had lasted less than three minutes. I tried to call him back right there and then, but the call was directed to voicemail.

Just then I remembered my father had been at a legal conference in Tucson with a colleague of his who had graduated from Tulane University, his alma mater. He was coming back to Albuquerque today in time for the holiday season.

As I put my cell phone in my purse, a horrible thought came into my mind. What if that passenger that had a problem, was actually infected? It was giving me a sick feeling. I was desperately worried about my father.

As it turned out, the trauma wasn't over. I still had no word from Jenna. Meanwhile, I dialed her number from my phone. It rang four times, then went to voicemail. I left her a message.

"Jenna. It's Hannah. It's important that you call me. It's very urgent."

I hung up thinking there had to be someone who knew where she was. There had to be a way to find her. I tried to think who she might be with and all I knew was her boyfriend, Kevin. And of course I didn't have his phone number.

As I put my phone away again, I was left with a number of questions. First, I asked myself, why didn't Jenna answer her phone? Second, and perhaps the most important, why hadn't she called me? I also knew that she had already left the university. This morning she texted she was in her car in the university's parking lot about to leave. The last thing she told me by text message was that she was going to drive to Albuquerque. She could be anywhere at this point. I would feel better when I heard her voice.

I shrugged to myself, walked to the elevator, pushed the button on the wall and waited. I didn't remember much about the following ten minutes, the time it took for the elevator to arrive, only that my mind was all over the place. Trying to process it all. I was worried about my co-workers, the world itself, and most of all worried that my father and sister were right in the thick of it. It was unreal. I hated feeling like the world was caving in on me and that I couldn't do anything but wait. Then I thought how lucky I was to be in a secure facility, far below the turmoil.

When the elevator door opened, a handful of people spilled out. I got into the elevator still thinking about that phone call from my father. My dad's voice in my head, as if he was standing right next to me. Just hearing his voice, reminded me of when we saw each other last at his house a few weeks ago. He was all I could think of. Then, as the elevator door closed, it just struck me that I hadn't had any breakfast, not even any coffee.

Chapter 7

AN HOUR LATER, Jenna was still walking on Babcock Road. She was very thankful to God to have escaped the madness. The last hour repeated over and over through her mind, the sounds of gunshots and people screaming. She was in a state of disbelief, from everything that had just happened.

She spotted a café called Suzy Bubble Tea in a small shopping plaza, coming up on the left. It looked to her like the infection had not yet reached this area, so she hoped. The café appeared safe enough to hide in, which is what she wanted to do more than anything.

A bell above the glass door chimed as she pushed her way through the entrance. From what she could tell, the store had been abandoned. She looked around, didn't see anyone. Then she found a hiding place behind a corner table with a good view of the entrance, so she could look out the window.

Suddenly, a Chinese girl with jet black shoulder-length hair parted in the middle, raised up from behind the counter.

Jenna wasn't alone after all, but she didn't notice until she spoke from behind the register. "Welcome. I'm Grace. What can I get for you today?"

Grace didn't appear to have a care in the world. Surprisingly, she had no idea what was happening.

"Wait a minute. You haven't the foggiest idea about what's going on?" Jenna asked looking at her as if she were clueless.

"No. What? Just come out with it," Grace demanded to know.

"There are dead people walking everywhere outside and eating people," Jenna said in a nervous tone.

Grace shot her a double take as she thought about it for a couple of seconds. The look on her face made it clear she was hearing this news for the first time. Now she squinted at Jenna like she hadn't heard right, and as though she didn't believe a word she'd said.

"Is there more?" Grace asked, peering at her.

"Isn't that enough?"

"Are you kidding me? Do you think I am so dumb?"

Jenna was surprised that she didn't believe her. She believed she came across as sincere. So, she thought.

"I hate to break it to you, but I am not joking. I'm saying exactly what you think I'm saying."

"And what are you saying? You're going to have to refresh my memory," Grace asked coldly.

Grace was not convinced and fired back with attitude. She was not taking it as gospel. Yes, she heard what Jenna said, but it was preposterous, so she asked her to say it again.

"You're not listening to me. Didn't you hear a word I said? The recently deceased have been somehow returned to life and are attacking the living," Jenna said matter-of-factly.

Grace was frustrated with the conversation. She walked down the counter to get a closer look at Jenna. Then she looked out the window.

"I don't see anything outside."

"They're not here yet," Jenna said, stating the obvious, "but they will come."

"Great. Can't hardly wait," Grace muttered with sarcasm.

Grace's expression went from irritated to confused. She walked closer to Jenna, then stopped.

Putting her hands on her hips, Grace scowled at her, and shook her head. "Are you serious? I find it impossible to believe. We're done here."

Grace was having none of it. She turned away from Jenna and walked over to the register.

"Think whatever you want," Jenna said before turning back to the window, hiding and watching.

"Excuse me. Are you going to order something or not? Bubble Tea. All flavors," Grace asked in a frustrating tone.

Jenna wasn't looking at her. She ignored her, keeping her eyes on the window. Thinking it was best not to say anymore. At least she was trying not to.

By then Grace was tired of it. She came out from behind the counter, walked over and tapped her on the shoulder. Jenna turned away from the window, looked at her.

She pointed her finger at the window. "I've heard enough. I don't need to spell it out, do I? Time to move on."

"Are you asking me to leave? Because, I can't go out there right now," Jenna insisted.

Grace was upset, and demanded, "I'll try this again. Let me put this in a way you will understand. Do me a favor and move on. Else, I'm going to call the police."

"But you have to believe it. I'm telling you the truth."

She rolled her eyes as if Jenna were crazy. "Yeah, right. I'm so sure."

"Fine. Don't believe me."

The girls were at it long enough not to see a zombie walking unsteadily near the store making its way to the door. When Grace casually turned toward the window, she looked absolutely stunned for a moment. In the space of a couple of seconds, she quit listening to Jenna and kept her eyes on the zombie that slammed its grisly hand on the glass and snarled. Seeing the zombie at the door shocked her, so much that her right eye began to twitch a little.

"I...I believe you," Grace stammered, barely able to speak.

Jenna's head snapped around to face the door. Neither of them said a word. Only a minute had passed, though it felt longer.

Finally, Jenna turned to her, and blurted out, "Does this place have a back exit?"

Grace was too dumbfounded to say anything more. When the zombie looked directly at her, opened its bloody mouth, and growled, she turned away from her long stare, ready to bolt out of there.

It took a couple of extra seconds to put her words together, but finally Grace said, "Yes. Let's get out of here."

She turned and started to run with Jenna following closely behind.

Abruptly, Grace stopped near the register. "Wait. I need to get my purse with my cell phone inside."

Jenna ran ahead, then stopped, and looked at her. "There's no time. Hurry up. We have to get out of here now."

As Grace ran behind the counter and grabbed her purse, the zombie slowly pulled the door open, and he wasn't alone. Three zombies had joined behind him.

"Come on, let's go," Grace said, and they took off.

Grace was not paying attention when she opened the back door. She ran straight into a zombie, almost knocking him over. He was a teenager with bloody blond hair and one eye missing. Everything happened so fast. The zombie grabbed her by the arms and panic swept over her. She gave him two Kung-Fu slaps in the face. One thing was for sure, there was no way she was giving up without a fight.

Just then Jenna came out the door. She just stood there, shocked, trying to figure out a way to help. But it looked like Grace had it under control.

Grace kept slapping the zombie until he finally released her. By a miracle, she escaped without a scratch, or a bite. She broke into a run with Jenna dashing after her. They were running alongside each other for a block. Then Grace inched herself forward, ahead of Jenna.

"Do you have a car?" Jenna asked breathlessly, trying to keep up with her.

"No, I take the bus," Grace said and turned to run in a different direction.

Jenna stopped to catch her breath, turned around and yelled, "Stop! Don't go that way!"

Grace didn't stop, there was no stopping her. She was too far ahead and going the wrong way. She either didn't hear Jenna or just didn't care. There was no mistaking her fear.

Jenna wasn't going to follow her. She knew the sheer madness that lay in that direction. Turning back to Babcock Road, she continued in the same direction before she'd turned into the shopping plaza. Just for the sake of it, she looked back for Grace, but she was long gone.

She began to think about where to go and what to do next. Nothing came to her. She had no idea and figured something would come to her eventually.

Chapter 8

WRESTLING WITH ALL OF IT, I came into the department and saw something that didn't look right about my co-worker Vivian Wheeler. She was in her office standing with her back to me, as if hiding something. I could tell that she knew I was there, but she didn't look my way.

"Are you making any sense of this?" I asked in a subtle tone.

Vivian put a cell phone in the top drawer of her desk and looked at me. I took a few more steps closer to her. For long seconds we shared a worried look, waiting for the other to speak. It was pretty intense.

The silence was broken when she said, "I dialed my husband's cell and waited for him to answer. Direct to voicemail. I tried two more times, and then left a message. I can't reach him on the phone."

Vivian tried to look calm and in control. She was neither of these. Given the news earlier, she was taking it rather badly. I didn't know what she was going to do next. And I hoped she wouldn't do anything drastic, like go outside.

She was talking again. "I'm afraid. I can't bear the thought of losing my kids. I don't know what to do, Hannah?"

There was a pause, as both of us attempted to remove all thoughts from our minds that were too awful to imagine. She erupted into tears, and I realized the full extent of her fear. Then she put her hand to her eyes, turned away, and wiped her eyes with a tissue. It was terrible to see her in this state.

"You've got to hang in there. There is still so much that we don't know," I said.

A petite African American, no more than five two, and physically fit, Vivian was very dependable, my go-to person for backing up computer systems. Most often she had a bubbly and outgoing personality. But circumstances had changed all that. I had a feeling that rebooting frozen computer screens was off the table for her today and perhaps all of next week.

Three minutes later, she had regained her composure. She turned her face to mine. Feeling I had to do something, I came around the desk to comfort her. Even though I wondered if there was any comfort possible. I stretched out my arms to her. We hugged for a long minute.

"You're safe here," I said in a soothing tone with the intention of encouraging her to stay.

She nodded her head. "Thank you."

It was for her own good to stay. I knew better than to suggest she take the day off. Even if she could use the time off. With the way she felt, if she had time on her hands, she was capable of leaving the facility. And that could be deadly for her. None of us could leave the BDC, at least not now.

All she could do was wait. Her family needed her to be strong. I decided I would give her time to work through this emotionally. Besides, I needed the time myself because I still had not accepted that I just lost my father. I wanted to tell her, yet at the same time I didn't want her to know. For a few reasons, I didn't tell Vivian or anyone else. As far as I was concerned, she had her own family to worry about. I didn't want to make her feel worse than she already did. And I didn't want any pity.

I stayed with her a bit longer. As she settled into her chair, she wasn't speaking anymore. She was returning to her duties, staying busy, filling her mind with work. It was all she could do to hold herself together.

As soon as I got to my desk and sat down in my chair, I picked up the telephone and called my sister's cell phone. I had to try again. Would she answer her phone? Unfortunately the phone rang four times before going to voicemail. A robotic voice instructed me to leave a message after the beep. I did precisely that.

"Hi, it's your sister Hannah. Call me as soon as you can. I really need to talk to you. Please. It's important."

I placed the telephone receiver, back into its cradle, wondering again why she hadn't answered my calls.

After booting up the computer, I went to the Coastal Airways website. There were no status updates for flight number 238 from Tucson to Albuquerque, nor a single mention of any planes crashing. Not more than sixty seconds later, James Stebbins came into the room carrying a stack of papers that he distributed to the various desks, including mine. He was wearing dark gray chinos, and a beige shirt under his lab coat. It was a rare sight to see him performing the duties of a messenger. The thirtyish, smart, and well-trained lab technician spent most of his time peering into microscopes. But it was apparent to me that he was doing his best to pitch in wherever needed.

The all-staff memo James put on my desk, to my surprise, wasn't the almost monthly announcements about another employee being promoted to a Vice President position. Even if it was just in name, the fact remains that this company had many vice presidents. Rather, this memo informed me that I was required to attend a mandatory meeting at eleven o'clock. Dan Saunders, the Chief Executive Officer of the BDC, summoned the heads of the departments to a conference room.

It was obvious I was going to be briefed by management about this fast-spreading plague. What else would it be about? Maybe they would be able to shed some light on why this was happening. I put the document on my desk thinking I was still in the dark about so many things.

Although I wasn't clear on everything that was happening, one thing I knew for certain was I was working on an empty stomach. With some time to kill before the meeting, I decided to grab a coffee before heading to the conference room.

I got up from my chair and headed toward the break room. Just as I suspected, there was no fresh pot of coffee waiting for me. It should be no surprise, after all, we were in the middle of a viral outbreak. At that point, I put several scoops of Café Bustelo in the filter, shut it, rinsed the glass pot, and refilled the machine with fresh water. After pushing a few buttons, the red light flickered, and the coffee maker started percolating. The aroma of fresh brewed coffee in the air was fantastic.

As I waited, my eyes wandered to the Christmas tree that had been set up in the corner of the room. The lights from the Christmas tree lent a soft ambience to the room, glimmering off the sparkling glass ornaments—gold and red—hung on the tree's branches. I admired the wrapped presents under the tree. There was a present addressed to Vivian, but none addressed to me. I wasn't upset about it. I imagine that now, with the pandemic, this year's Christmas festivities would be canceled anyway.

My coffee was ready. I poured myself a cup and added three hazelnut-flavored liquid nondairy creamers, which had plenty of sugar. I enjoyed a few sips—oh, yeah, it was good. Then I saw a bunch of bananas on the counter, and I helped myself to one.

Time moved faster than I'd realized it could. The meeting was starting soon and I wanted to get there in time, so I gulped down the rest of the coffee. As I was about to leave, Vivian came through the doorway of the break room. I had nothing but sympathy for her. If only there was something I could say, something to ease her pain. But there wasn't. Words never said enough. I thought small talk would be good, best to keep it simple.

"Hello, Vivian," I said.

"Goodness. Hi," she said, as if she had been thinking about something else, "I was just going to get some coffee."

Another pause, then she swept past me. I stared back at her for a moment, then turned away and left.

Chapter 9

MINUTES LATER, there I sat in one of the eight swivel chairs, along with all the other employees, who all looked distressed by the news which we received earlier today. Nobody was talking as I scanned the faces around the walnut conference table.

Dan Saunders sat at the far end of the table, arms folded across his chest, head resting against the back of the chair. On his left were two empty chairs. The seats were being saved for Thomas Bauer, the President of the BDC, and Ken Langtry, the head of the security operations. Saunders was unnerved and not his usual charming self. The irritated expression on his face gave the impression that he was waiting impatiently for Langtry to arrive. The last thing we needed was a stressed-out Chief Executive Officer.

Next to Saunders was someone whom I had never met before. Sandra Ortiz, a tall, self-confident Hispanic with smooth skin in her late thirties, worked as Saunders' assistant, serving as his eyes and ears. Every day she fielded telephone calls, e-mails, and faxes for him.

Next to me sat Dr. Julie Mehta, who runs the BDC's state of the art laboratory. She was born in India and came to live in the States after getting her undergrad degree. Her department just happened to be right next door to my department. Out of everyone in the room, I knew her the best. At thirty-three, she was one of the smartest people the BDC could hire.

Five minutes later, Thomas Bauer entered the conference room. Bauer was all business all the time. He looked in charge, and not alarmed by the gravity of the situation. I suppose, he was somewhere in his early fifties. He had commanding blue eyes, a small chin, thinning blond hair, and a slim build. The double-breasted tan suit and Ferragamo shoes he had on, would eat up my whole paycheck.

He approached Saunders and asked, "How bad is it?"

Saunders shifted in his chair, leaned in closer to him, and murmured, "It's bad."

Bauer leaned in to whisper something that no one but Saunders heard. Afterward, Bauer checked out the room, looking at all the people and made a point of checking his watch. He shook his head as though he was annoyed, just before he settled himself in the second chair near Saunders.

Just as the meeting was about to start, Ken Langtry walked through the door. Langtry, a stocky man with big shoulders and dark sandy hair, in his mid-forties, was a former lieutenant with the Boston Police Department. He pulled out a chair next to

Saunders and dropped into it. He took a breath, gathering himself, then poured a glass of water from a chrome pitcher on the table.

"It's about time. I was starting to think you left," Saunders bellowed.

"I got here as soon as I could," Langtry said.

"Don't bother making any excuses. It doesn't make a difference."

After Saunders said that he gave him a scathing look, but Langtry didn't catch it, didn't answer back. Saunders could throw a fit when he wanted to. The rumor was that Saunders was next in line for the president's job. And Saunders was certain he'd run the BDC one day. Langtry had his own troubles and wasn't at all concerned about it.

"Let's get on with it, Thomas," Saunders said, waving a hand at him.

Before Bauer spoke, he swept his eyes around the table, seeing that everyone was present and seated. "Welcome, ladies and gentlemen. I thank you for coming, considering the state of affairs. By now everyone should be aware of the disease that is tearing through our communities. As of an hour ago, our board of directors has made their position very clear. The development of a vaccine is their highest priority. Our Chief Executive Officer, Dan Saunders will provide further details."

Bauer nodded toward Saunders, who sat quietly for ten seconds, then got out of his chair and walked around the table.

"Well, at the present time, without testing samples, we don't have anything to go on. We don't know what we are dealing with yet. All we know is that the virus is perhaps the most horrible threat to humanity," he said slightly agitated.

I wondered what else Saunders knew, because he always knew more than he let on.

Julie looked at him carefully, concern on her face, then leaned forward, and asked in her British accent, "How may I be of assistance?"

Saunders sat back down into his chair. He instructed Julie to report all important findings to him, or to Sandra who would relay the message to him.

"Report back when you have something. I want you to keep me in the loop."

"I understand. I will do so. Do you know where and when it started?" Julie asked.

"I can say for certain the infection originated somewhere in Mexico. As to when, I guess about fourteen days back."

Julie relaxed back into her seat, running a hand through her hair and watching Saunders as he stood up from the table again and started pacing the conference room, an act that made everyone stiffen up nervously.

He turned to Langtry and asked, "Ken, can you give us an update on security?"

"Dan, my department is prepared for all kinds of emergencies. Our mission is to protect every employee of the BDC. A team of well-trained, armed security guards patrol the gates of the complex on a twenty-four-hour schedule. If the infection makes it to the area, we will handle it," Langtry said and cleared his throat.

After listening to him, Saunders said, "Just keep me posted on any developments."

Bauer stood up looking at Saunders before he went to stand at the entrance. "Well, then, this concludes our meeting. You all carry on with your duties and thanks for your time."

I could see everyone racking their brains over what seemed like a pointless meeting as they got up from their chairs to leave. Perhaps the controlling force of the BDC wanted us to know they were on top of things.

Langtry sprang from his seat and bolted for the door. He couldn't get out of the room fast enough. I left the conference room feeling more edgy than before the meeting.

It was late afternoon when I returned to my desk. *What should I do now?* I thought. I was having a hard time accepting this apocalyptic shift, which got me thinking of the Maya prophecy of 2012. The doom seemed to be coming true. A new world had begun. A zombie world. Was it real? Or, was this some kind of hoax being perpetrated by the powers that be?

Glancing at the clock, I noticed that I had been sitting at my desk for almost twenty minutes. I had spent most of the time staring blankly at the computer. There were too many thoughts in my head. My father's sudden death had left me distressed. And only God knew where my sister was. I shook my head and tried to concentrate.

As I moved about the chair, trying to get comfortable, I realized it was useless trying. Too much nervous energy was racing through me to stay seated. I decided that my best move was to get out of the office because I needed to get my feelings under control. I knew I wouldn't lose my job by leaving early.

Before exiting the elevator on my floor, I thought about what I knew so far, until it was all too much to think about.

I slipped my key into the lock of my apartment door. When I opened the door and stepped inside, Mim ran from the living room and threw herself at me. I bent down, gave my cat a pat on the head, then put away my keys and purse. Mim was always so happy to see me.

She followed me into the kitchen, where I grabbed a bottle of water from the refrigerator for a quick sip. I became aware of Mim, who was rubbing against my legs.

"You're so cute," I told her.

I picked up Mim, carried her into the living room, and set her down on the sofa. Then I plopped down next to her, petting her. Within seconds, she began to purr. It was something she did when she was happy.

My focus shifted to a photograph in a frame on the end table, positioned next to "Insurgent" by Veronica Roth, a paperback science fiction novel I'd been reading. It showed my father smiling, standing in between his two daughters in front of a Christmas tree in his home. I had on a dress. One of the few times in my life I'd worn a dress.

The thought of never seeing him again sent a chill down my spine. My eyes welled up. I wiped away a tear. I cried, for the first time in my adult life. Flooded with images from my childhood and showing up on weekends at his house in Albuquerque.

I readjusted my sitting position. However, I kept staring at the photograph until I felt tired. I stretched out on the sofa and fell fast asleep.

Chapter 10

AFTER TWO MORE HOURS of walking on Babcock Road, Jenna's legs were feeling tired. She'd never walked so much in her life. For a quick minute, she stopped to get her bearings. Turning for a moment of uncertainty, she looked around, wondering where she could go. This was a challenge since she wanted to leave San Antonio, but she believed it wasn't possible to take a plane, train, or bus.

The idea came to get a hotel room for one night, hoping that by morning she would have a fresh angle on the situation. Turning left on Danville, she walked through the Hillcrest neighborhood, heading toward Spencer Lane. Not far off, she could see a hotel. To get there, she walked through an underpass just as two police cars flew past her and turned on Frontage Road in the Balcones Heights area of San Antonio.

The infection was spreading faster than she had anticipated.

Twenty feet above her, six police cars blocked a lane of traffic on Interstate 10. Two lanes of traffic were moving slower than Jenna could walk and the other three lanes of traffic backed up for over a mile. The air split with distant sirens. People who were tired of waiting, abandoned their vehicles. Impatient drivers honked on their horns and yelled out their car windows. They were terrified of the infected getting them because they could not get through the roadblocks.

She walked the last couple of yards to the front entrance of the Comfort Inn & Suites. A security guard opened the door for her to enter the two-story hotel. There were a dozen guests in the lobby. Standing beside the ATM machine against the wall near the elevators, was a fortyish Hispanic maid, dressed in a tan and black uniform, looking as if she didn't know what to do next. Jenna quickly walked over to the ATM and inserted her Wells Fargo VISA debit card. She withdrew one hundred and eighty dollars, her entire savings, but she wanted to have extra money on hand. She took a fifty-dollar bill, folded it neatly, slipped it behind her driver's license in her wallet and put the rest of the money in a zippered pouch of her wallet. Then she walked into the lobby and waited in line to check in.

The front desk clerk signaled her forward. "Hello. Hi. Welcome. My name is Brad."

Brad had a thick head of blond hair, bright blue eyes, and a long thin neck. The earring in his right ear, which in the eighties would have meant he was gay, matched his perky personality. He told her that the management had instructed him to tell guests that if the situation worsened, nobody would work in the hotel anymore. And that the hotel was expected to close within days, indefinitely. She understood and plunked down her credit card for the one-night stay.

Brad smiled, handed her a plastic key card, and said, "I regret to inform you that there is no housekeeping or room service. Enjoy your stay here."

She left the front desk and walked straight to the elevator at the east end of the lobby. When she reached the floor, she stopped to look at the sign showing which rooms were in which direction, right or left. Her room was to the left. Next she eyed the vending machines around the corner. She bought two bags of barbecue potato chips, two bags of peanut M&M's, three candy bars, and three bottles of ginger ale, and put the lot in her backpack and swung it over her shoulder.

Jenna inserted the key card into the lock, a little green light blinked, and the door clicked. She went inside quickly, shut the door behind her, and kept the lights off. After taking a settling breath, she grabbed the telephone from the small bedside table and called her soon-to-be-ex-boyfriend. The phone rang four times, and voicemail answered.

"Hello, this is Kevin Flannery. I'm not available right now, however leave a message, and I'll get back to you as soon as possible. Thank you."

"Kevin, it's Jenna. Where are you? I'm staying at a Comfort Inn near IHOP. I'll try to call you again later."

Her father had been away on business in Tucson and was returning to Albuquerque today. She tried calling him and got his voicemail too.

"Dad, it's Jenna. I want you to know I'm okay. I really need your help."

Despite the fact she was scared, she had tried to sound like she wasn't. After she hung up, she thought about her father and sister, that she didn't want them to worry about her. She could manage without a cell phone, but how could she get out of San Antonio without a car? She needed help.

She called her sister Hannah. After a loud sigh of relief, she got her up to date on all that had happened in the last nine hours. Then Hannah told her that their father was most likely dead. She was devastated. After hanging up, she laid down on the bed, closed her eyes and felt both upset about losing her father and relieved she had talked to her sister.

Now she set aside the horrors of the day and started thinking about her father, Henry, whom she loved best in all the world. Tears streamed down her cheeks. He had been a private practice lawyer in Albuquerque. Her best memory of him was the day he showed her around his office. She was eight and couldn't be any prouder of him. Now he was gone.

Since she was in a state of grief, she needed to talk to someone. Only one person sprang to mind, as there was only one person other than Hannah that she would ever confide in. She sat up, pulled the telephone onto the bed and called Kevin once more. No Answer.

Lying back on the bed, she thought about the last time she saw him. True, it had been days ago, but it was fresh in her memory — she wasn't coming back to school next semester and wanted to talk with him about it before telling anyone else.

"Jenna, what happened?" Kevin asked.

And she told him she was not getting enough out of the relationship. So she was going to stay in her father's home in

Albuquerque. She wasn't sure that came out the way she intended. And she sensed it wasn't the answer he expected, or the answer he wanted to hear. But it was the only answer she could give.

"You have to choose what is more important to you," he said, and left it at that.

She sighed deeply and replied, "I think I know what's best for me."

It was evident from the expression on her face at that time. Even though she hadn't actually said the words. She knew what he was thinking because she was thinking the same thing. It was as if they were breaking up yet couldn't find the right words to say it. In her heart, she knew it was going to happen.

They had continued talking for another ten minutes, but when she left Kevin, there was a terrible feeling inside her about what had just taken place.

The last thing he said before he left was, "I hope it works out for you, Jenna."

She didn't tell Kevin that they could stay friends. She had no idea how to resolve it with him. It was hard for her to face the fact that they wanted different things. They had only known each other for a little over fifteen months, which seemed like much longer — maybe because they'd been together all the time.

That seemed like so long ago. Everything now changed. She had changed. And she was sure that her relationship with Kevin had come to an end. And to make things worse, she had lost her father that morning.

Around five minutes later, she brought her thoughts back to the present. She sat up, grabbed the remote control, and turned on the flat-screen television. After cranking down the volume, she flipped through the channels searching for CNN until she found it. Next to the CNN logo were two words. BREAKING NEWS.

She spent the next hour planted in front of the TV listening to developments till she had seen enough of it. The viral pandemic, as the news reporter called it, was spreading rapidly throughout the northern hemisphere. It was worse than she could have imagined.

After turning off the TV, she felt somewhat hungry. She walked across the room and checked the contents of the minibar. She grabbed a small bag of almonds and a bottle of Perrier sparkling water. When she finished eating, she got undressed, locked the bathroom door and spent the next twenty minutes in the shower.

When she came back into the room wrapped in a towel and began dressing, for a handful of seconds, a sudden flash of red lights lit the room from wall to wall as a fire truck roared by outside. The siren disappeared, but it was replaced by screaming, followed by three gunshots, which tore through the building. Her eyes turned to the door, reminding herself it was double-locked.

Fully dressed, she slid down the wall to sit on the floor. For the next thirty minutes, she stayed sitting in a corner of the room, her back to the wall, with her arms holding her knees tucked up under her chin, listening to heavy gunfire echoing in the hallway. The fear was so great she couldn't move, could not think, and all she could do was sit there.

For the first time in her life, Jenna Winter was on her own and was crying nervously. She took a breath and wiped the tears from her eyes. When the halls were quiet, she fell asleep sitting against the wall.

Chapter 11

JENNA called around five o'clock - six o'clock her time. Almost two hours had passed when I startled awake from a dead sleep on the sofa, by the sound of my cell phone ringing. I didn't recognize the number on my caller ID, but I answered anyway, still half asleep.

"Hello," I said with a sigh.

"Hannah, it's me."

Immediately I recognized her voice. I jumped up from the sofa, nearly knocking over a vase on the coffee table. I was so happy she called. Swept away in the moment, I started talking right away.

"I have been trying to reach you all day. Are you all right?"

Jenna's voice exploded in my ear. "I'm okay. Hannah, it's awful. I'm really worried about Kevin. He's not answering his phone. I keep getting his voicemail."

She was talking a hundred words a minute. The fear in her voice was clear. I could only imagine what horrors she had gone through over the past several hours.

When I could get a few words in, I told her, "Slow down."

At which point she stopped, took in a breath, and slowly began to explain what had happened. She said she didn't have her cell phone because it was broken beyond repair and no way to get a new one. Her Honda Civic had been struck by a bus. And lastly, she had been outrunning zombies since the early morning hours.

After listening to everything she had to say, I paused in my pacing around the living room. "Where are you?"

"I'm in a hotel room in San Antonio. Tell me what to do."

"I will. But first I have something else to tell you," I said, sounding a little more emotional than I'd intended and sat back on the sofa.

"What is it?" Jenna wanted to know.

A moment passed before I said, "I'm sorry to have to tell you this. I'm pretty sure Dad is dead."

When I had said that, my voice was about to crack. I had covered my mouth with my hand to prevent her from hearing that. The grief snuck up on me. Tears were streaming down my face, and I palmed them away.

"Are you sure? How do you know?" she asked frantically.

I told her everything I knew, trying to keep emotion out of my voice. "Dad called me from his flight and told me there was trouble with a passenger. And I haven't heard from him since. I think the plane crashed."

The line went quiet for a minute. She fully understood what I was saying.

"How can you be so sure?" she asked.

"I know it's difficult to believe. I'm speculating, Jenna, but it makes sense," I said, undoubtedly.

Then I heard sobs. Now she was crying and couldn't help it. Next came a deep sigh, then a pause at the other end of the line. Emotionally I could feel her pain. It was best to let her get it out of her system. It was the hardest conversation I'd ever had with her.

"Jenna are you still there?"

A solemn pause and total silence.

"Yes, I'm here," she said, her voice dropping to barely more than a whisper.

"I want you to come to Dulce, New Mexico. The BDC is secure. You can stay with me in my apartment, till all this is over. Really. There is plenty of food to go around." I stopped, took a deep breath before continuing. "I think it's your best option. How fast do you think you can get here?"

My emotions were running high. Maybe I was asking for the impossible. But the situation was impossible. What else could I tell her? I didn't want her to die. She had to come here. I wanted her here. With me. Safe.

"I plan to as soon as I can. I mean that, Hannah. I promise," she said with a sniffle.

"I believe you can do it," I said confidently, wanting to instill hope in her.

Instantly I heard her crying cease. And it hit me that I was actually doing that. Instilling hope. She sounded much stronger. Maybe she had a plan after all. I was sure she would find a way.

"I know Dad would have wanted us to be together. It's hard to be on your own, but try to be strong," I added, when she didn't speak.

"I'll do my best," she said, thinking it through.

"No matter what happens don't give up. I'll be here, waiting, however long it takes. And please be careful," I said, sounding like an overly concerned sister.

There was no mistaking the sincerity in my voice. I meant every word of it.

"Don't worry. I will be very careful," she said, reassuring me that she was all right and ended the call.

I placed the phone on the coffee table and reflected on the conversation I'd just had with Jenna. Just hearing her voice, I felt such a sense of relief. Outside of text messaging, it was the first time I'd spoken to her in almost a week. And to be honest, I was upset by her dropping out of the university. But, right now, that was irrelevant.

So, now all I could do was wait and pray.

Still, I couldn't figure out if I was protecting her or if I was putting her at risk by asking her to come to New Mexico. Her life was in danger no matter where she went. Because the infection was out there, just about everywhere. And with the way things were going, I was so grateful she was alive. At least one good thing happened today.

The other thing that happened was losing my father. It was devastating to me. Though it was hard on me, it had also been hard on Jenna. It was something we were going to have to come to terms with.

"I wondered where you were," I said to Mim, who came running into the room.

Mim meowed in response. I stood up. She came closer to me, meowing pathetically. I gathered that she was hungry. I walked toward the kitchen with Mim following behind me, tail up.

"Okay, time to eat," I said to her excitedly, "and that goes for both of us."

Once I put food in the cat's bowl, she chowed down. While watching her eat, I suddenly knew exactly what I wanted. I grabbed a pint of Ben & Jerry's chocolate fudge brownie I had stashed days earlier in the freezer. During these troubled times, I wanted to reward myself with a sugary treat to soothe my nerves.

I sat at the kitchen table eating my ice cream, enjoying every bite. After Mim ate, she took off again. Could you imagine what it must be like to be a cat? No worries in the world. Life couldn't be any easier.

All this thinking made me tired. I couldn't eat anything else. I tossed the empty carton in the wastebasket. Then I headed for the bathroom to wash up.

When I turned the corner to walk down the hallway, the cat appeared out of nowhere, screeching by me. You could say that she startled me. But I could handle her faux pas, because she was the sweetest little creature in the world. And I was sure she would settle down as soon as I killed the lights and hopped into bed. Which would be in about ten minutes, give or take a few seconds.

Chapter 12

HEARING MY SISTER'S VOICE yesterday, helped me wake up feeling better about the day ahead. For a brief moment, I sat at the edge of the bed watching Mim, the cat. She was curled up near the pillow, sleeping. It was an adorable sight.

Carefully, I got out of bed, reluctant to make a sound that would wake her. She was asleep all the while I showered and dressed.

After locking up, I headed straight to the cafeteria to get some breakfast. A good cup of coffee would make a world of a difference. I was doing the best I could to maintain some normalcy in my life. Like going back to work today, despite the traumatic loss of my father.

While I was riding in the elevator, I realized that it was foolish to think that the world was coming to an end. And that this wouldn't last long. It would all be over soon. A girl could hope, anyway. Like many people, I just wanted to go back to the way things were before.

Once I stepped into the cafeteria, I looked around. At first glance, nothing seemed out of the ordinary. The exception being that many people were glued to the TV watching the news coverage. It was starting to become the norm around here.

Following the smell of coffee, I moved through the food line, grabbing a banana and a yogurt. Vivian saw me and came over.

"Good morning, Hannah," she said.

I looked over my shoulder. "Vivian, it's so nice to see you. How are you this morning?"

"I'm managing. Thanks for asking. When you're done, please, come sit at my table."

Vivian, who looked like she hadn't slept much, walked away just as the woman behind the serving counter asked what I wanted. I told her scrambled eggs, wheat toast, and home fries. She handed me a plate full of food and it smelled fantastic. I grabbed a mug of coffee, mixed in cream and sugar, and went to the register to pay.

"Any good news?" I asked hopefully, as I was putting my tray on the table.

As I dropped into the chair opposite of Vivian, I noticed her attention fixed on the television as though she couldn't get enough of it. The twenty-four-hour news rotation was all zombies, all the time. It was the same story as yesterday, and they didn't have anything new to report. She tried to maintain a calm expression as she processed the information.

Looking worried, she gazed at me for a long moment, shook her head, then said, "It's a lot worse. It's much worse than you can imagine."

I noticed she had barely touched her breakfast. Things were not right with her. From what I could grasp, she suspected much, but knew nothing about her family. It was a difficult time for her.

"I don't believe this is happening," she said, for the third or fourth time, then placed an elbow on the table and massaged her forehead, "I don't believe it."

You could make that five or six times.

"Yeah," I said in agreement after a moment's consideration, "I'm with you on that."

She gasped and clasped a hand over her mouth. Then she looked off into space like she was waiting for the news reporter to say everything was going to be all right, desperately seeking some glimmer of hope, but not getting it. I stopped talking because she was no longer listening. I told myself that she needed to find some purpose for the day, or she was going to drive herself crazy.

Only barely listening, but half watching, the television, too, I slowly sipped my coffee. It was the same report about the infected wreaking havoc in neighborhood after neighborhood. Vivian and I saw TV footage of people fighting zombies, people running from zombies, and people shooting at zombies.

His name was Davis something. The same reporter from yesterday was speaking live from a road in El Paso, Texas. He stated that the only way you could stop the never dead, was to shoot them in the head. Once again, the reporter called them "never dead."

"It is essential to disable the brain. Apparently, their brain is still working, so you have to destroy the brain itself," Davis said.

That was when I took an interest and started watching more intently. As I listened, questions flowed through my mind. I started to speculate that if things got any worse, high-ranking government officials might choose to use weapons of mass destruction. What would happen if a missile with a nuclear warhead was launched in a zombie-infested city? I thought that was possible. It was the most awful thing that could happen. Or even worse. What if I woke up tomorrow and found myself living in a post-apocalyptic world where zombies outnumbered the living? How could I carry on living if I was the last woman on earth? Maybe this was a lot worse than I thought earlier.

I heard Vivian's voice calling my name.

"Hannah," she said, shaking me out of my trance.

I looked at her. "Yes?"

"I'm finished. I'm heading to my office."

I'd lost track of the time, and needed to finish eating. That was what I got for watching the news.

"Right, then, I'll see you there in ten minutes," I told her.

"See you at work."

Before getting up to leave, she looked around in bewilderment. She looked like she was lost and trying to find her way back. Moments later, she stood up, grabbed her tray, and left.

Instantly, I went back to eating my breakfast. I wasn't watching TV anymore.

A little while later, I was back in the office. After the computer booted up, I started typing on the keyboard, pouring over data, and analyzing the computer-generated reports. I went right back to filling my head with information relevant to my job. After all, it was my responsibility to oversee and manage the millions of dollars' worth of computer equipment in the facility. Plus, it was keeping my mind off the bad things and made me feel useful.

Around one-thirty, and just before I left for lunch, I was handed a memo from James Stebbins. The memo was directed to all BDC personnel. It had been marked urgent and all staff must read immediately. In essence, it stated that all BDC personnel were to stay in the facility, and they were not to leave, for any reason, until further notice. The BDC's security level had been raised due to the infected lingering around the gated entrance, and in the vicinity.

In addition, the memo stated that "Readmittance would not be guaranteed to those who left. Anyone approaching the entrance of the facility would be detained and quarantined on arrival and required to have a medical evaluation by a resident physician in accordance with guidelines of the BDC. Infected individuals would be turned away or disposed of as deemed fit by the BDC."

I understood what they meant by disposed. In other words, killed. It was the absolute truth explained in black and white. Given the present circumstances, the BDC took no chances.

Going outside would be dangerous. They didn't have to worry about me, because I wasn't planning to leave. The fact was that I was going to stay and do my part. I wanted to feel good about it, even though a small part of me was worried about my sister. It would continue to be that way, until I could see her again. So I kept telling myself, "Jenna would get here."

Chapter 13

DR. JULIE MEHTA dove into research as early as yesterday afternoon. She'd wasted no time getting started. Day two, she came into the office at eight this morning ready to tackle the challenges ahead.

The first thing she saw on her desk was a memo from the president stating that she should strictly work for the development of an antidote to the virus, effective immediately. This implied that all the work she had been doing before was now on hold, indefinitely. She understood well what was going on. There would be no argument from her. So, right now, her number one priority, was finding a cure to the plague of the century.

Sitting down at her computer, she stared at her in-box, which was full of e-mails, many unread. In the past few hours, quite a few had come from panic-stricken parents and siblings in India concerned about her welfare. It took her nearly thirty minutes to respond to her family and clear her in-box.

Taking into consideration that this zombie virus makes people rabid, she started examining the database containing rabies cases for information that could be useful. Over the past years, Biogenetics & Disease Control had collected plenty of data on rabies, and other diseases affecting the central nervous system, from research and tests. She entertained the possibility that a rabies-related virus strain might be at work in this case. Those infected displayed many of the same symptoms of madness, agitation, and delirium, with death occurring within a few days. Additionally, rabies was transferred through saliva entering the body through a bite or scratch from a rabid animal, such as a dog or a raccoon.

A couple of minutes into it, she stopped typing, and read over the notes she had taken. After cracking her knuckles, she shifted her mouse, opened the browser, then hit some keys on her computer. She searched the Net for reports out of Mexico before December twenty-one, something that would explain the cause of the infection, such as the point of origin. It was more than likely that the answer was somewhere out there. But would she find it? Desperate to find something, anything, she even checked social media, but she didn't see anything that jumped out at her.

After googling for over an hour, she turned her attention to sources outside of the BDC. The first place she thought of was the Pasteur Institute in Paris, France, founded to treat diseases, specifically infectious. It was named after Louis Pasteur, a French chemist and microbiologist, and the first to develop a rabies vaccine. She had met Sophie Dupond, a biologist who worked there, in November at the 28th World Vaccines & Immunization Congress held at the Georgia World Congress Center in Atlanta, Georgia. They had attended a presentation on the subject of vaccine preventable diseases. Barely a week ago, she had communicated with her through e-mail, about the Ebola virus. But she didn't save Sophie's e-mail address in her address book.

She typed a few words into the search bar: Sophie Dupond Pasteur Institute. Immediately after she tapped the enter key. Eight matches appeared on the screen. Her name was listed with the website of the Pasteur Institute in Paris, France. She tapped a couple of more keys then clicked on a link and the screen showed a biography page. Scrolling down the page, she found an e-mail contact. She tore a page from her notepad and wrote the e-mail address in the middle of the page. After that, she closed the web page and opened her work e-mail. She flexed her fingers and typed.

Dear Sophie, I write you on a matter of great importance. It's good to know you are still working for the Pasteur Institute. I am going to bring you up to date about the viral outbreak that is infecting so many in Mexico, the United States and Canada. I am in New Mexico, a place where the infection is spreading the fastest. It is, as you will understand, very serious, and it's contagious. As you may know, the BDC facility headquarters in New Mexico is a place secure underground. I am safe at the present moment. Are there any reports of infection in France or other countries in Europe? Perhaps we can collaborate? This situation is having a devastating effect on the planet. I would sincerely appreciate to hear the news from your side of the world. Sincerely, Dr. Julie Mehta.

She read it over a few times and sent the e-mail. It was worth a try. All she could do was wait for a response.

Within a minute or two, she checked her in-box and found that the e-mail was returned "undeliverable." The e-mail was not accepted by the Pasteur Institute's mail server. It was possible their communication systems were down. There was no point in trying again.

After thinking things through, she required blood and brain tissue samples from infected individuals. The blood was needed for chemical analysis. She was interested in studying the response in infection of the cytolytic T-cell, a T lymphocyte and type of white blood cell that kills cancer cells and was a component of the protective response to the rabies virus. She was curious to know if the cytolytic T-cell response might be suppressed in the infection. And she wanted to examine the brain of the infected to understand why it was able to continue its functions after death, as if it was running on electricity.

She needed to talk to Dan Saunders. Picking up her desk phone, she began dialing his number. He answered after the first ring.

"Dan, this is Julie."

"What may I help you with today?"

"I hope you can. It may not be easy, but it is crucial to my work."

"Simply tell me, and I will help you. But spare me the technical jargon," he said, sounding a little annoyed.

Saunders wasn't much of a conversationalist.

"No matter what I ask for?"

"Whatever you need, Julie."

"Are you certain?"

"Please don't ask that again, Julie."

"I need whole brain specimens from the infected, both male and female. And, I require blood samples."

"Done. It shouldn't be difficult. I hear there are infected hanging around the gate outside."

Saunders would make sure that she got everything she needed.

"You could've cruised over to my office and asked me, you know?" he added.

"I know. Thanks Dan," she said, and hung up the telephone.

Leaning her left elbow on the desk, she rested her chin on the palm of her hand. Craving a cup of tea, she resigned to herself that she needed a break. So, she stood up, turned, stepped out of the office and headed for the break room.

The break room was empty. She went to the sink, put a mug under the faucet, turned on the cold water and filled it.

In the middle of walking over to the microwave, she stopped to admire the Christmas tree in the corner of the room. Looking at the wrapped presents under the tree, there was one addressed to her.

After putting the mug of water into the microwave, she

scooped up the wrapped gift. It was heavy, like it was a lead crystal vase or bowl. The gift wrapped in red foil paper with a fancy gold ribbon was from James Stebbins. What a nice gesture she thought, even though he celebrated Hanukkah.

Just then the microwave beeped.

She grabbed the mug from the microwave. Then she poured in three packets of sugar and a little milk from the carton she took out of the refrigerator. She left the Darjeeling black tea bag in the mug and took a quick sip.

Her only Christmas present was lying on top of her desk. Sitting in her chair and sipping tea, she felt her brain coming back to life. The tea was exactly what she needed.

She turned to the computer and started reading about lymphocytes and cytolytic T-cells important to immune defense against viruses. There was more data than she had anticipated. She paused and took a sip of tea. Then she grabbed her notepad and jotted down the essentials.

By the time her mug was empty, she was ready for lunch. She exited from a screen on the computer. Before she logged off, she pulled up her e-mail in-box one last time. Nothing there. After organizing her notes, she placed them on the left side of the desk. She got up and headed for the cafeteria.

Chapter 14

SITTING ALONE at a table in the cafeteria, where everyone could see me, I was trying to rip open a bag of potato chips. A moment later, I finally opened the bag, twitching my elbow on the table, knocking a spoon to the floor. I reached underneath the table and picked it up.

As I looked up, I saw Julie coming through the room. She was wearing yesterday's brown trousers, a wrinkled cream-colored silk blouse, and a lab coat. Her dark brown hair was pulled back into a loose ponytail rather than neatly coiled in a bun, how she usually had it. I knew that she had been working tirelessly for the last twenty-four hours. Seeing her here was good, because she had earned a much-needed break.

After filling her tray, she slid it along the metal bars toward the register and paid. As she carried her tray looking for a place to sit, she looked in my direction and saw me. I was pleased to see her smile at me and waved her over to my table.

She approached me and asked, "Hannah, it's good to find you here. May I join you?"

"Of course, Julie," I said with a warm smile.

She put her tray on the table and took a seat. All the while I was munching on potato chips. She didn't say anything more, as if her mind was somewhere else. I guessed that she must not have been eating much lately because she immediately tore into her lunch. After many bites of her tuna sandwich, she took a few sips of her iced tea. Perhaps this was not a good time to ask her how things were going in the lab.

Evidently, she was under pressure from her supervisors who expect so much of her. They believed if anybody could find a cure for this deadly virus, she would probably discover it. So, I chose to stay quiet, assuming she would talk when she was ready. But for now, she ate silently. That was the case until five minutes later when she broke the silence and opened up.

Between spoonfuls of her potato salad she politely asked, "How are things in your office?"

Lately, her mind was strictly on business.

"Now that you mention it, it hasn't been that busy," I answered, as I took a quick sip of my coffee.

Her eyebrow shot up as her mouth was chewing. She seemed surprised. But what I had said wasn't far from the truth. My department wasn't affected by the outbreak.

Then I told her, "Since the attention of the BDC has been directed toward facilitating the development of an antidote to cure the never dead, I haven't had many requests for software updates and malware scans."

At that moment, she became very interested in the conversation. She gazed at me, somewhat surprised by what she'd heard, mulling it over in her head.

"Never dead. Never dead. Never dead?" she repeated several times, "I have to ask. Never dead? Can you elaborate more, Hannah?"

She acted as if she didn't know what I was talking about. And she probably didn't either. Putting down her spoon, she anxiously waited to hear what else I had to say.

"Yes, I've been saying that ever since I heard it mentioned on the news. The TV news reporter named Davis something, referred to the infected as quote, "never dead," I said.

I made air quotes with my fingers when I said the words "never dead." It wasn't my intention to exaggerate. I was just trying to be matter-of-fact and I wondered if it came across that way. But it didn't matter, because she was all ears, listening quite intently. After thinking about it for a few seconds she apparently had taken a liking to it.

"That's an interesting name for them," she said.

"I agree Julie."

"It's rather catchy."

"If you think about it, calling them "Never Dead" really makes sense," I said, making air quotes again.

"And appropriate, too."

"Before long, everyone will be calling the infected people, never dead."

"Word of mouth can travel fast."

"It's contagious," I said lastly.

Then we both laughed a little, which made the situation more comfortable for me. I was not meaning to be funny right from the start of the conversation, but somehow it ended up that way. And it was worth it to see her smile.

I grabbed my mug for a sip of coffee and couldn't help wondering if she thought I was wired from too many cups, perhaps a little high-strung. Thinking I'd sounded over-enthusiastic, I quieted down a little after that. That was the moment when I decided not to drink any more coffee today.

Her cell phone went off in her lab-coat pocket. Instantly she fished it out. Her expression turned serious when she looked at the caller ID, showing no interest in talking. But for reasons unknown to me, she couldn't ignore the call.

"So much for a quiet moment," she said dryly, staring at her phone.

I simply shrugged in agreement.

"You'll have to excuse me. This could be urgent," she said, answering on the third ring.

"Go ahead," I said.

She spoke into the phone, her voice without emotion. "I'm in the middle of lunch. Can I call you back later?"

Julie was looking rather tense. Her shoulders slumped and her voice dropped because she didn't want her call to be overheard. I could barely hear the conversation, but it seemed she was discussing something about her research. And by the look on her face you could tell she wasn't pleased. The little she got out sounded discouraging.

Why was it top secret? Why not inform people about it? How could a person get the answers they needed to their questions about the pandemic? But that was life at the BDC. *There was no point in asking Julie such questions*, I thought. The fact was, there was little known about this virus, except that it brought the dead back to life. And nothing was known about how to treat it. She would tell me that the secrecy was meant for the good of the people. The BDC would prefer not to get anyone's hopes up or give the impression that the situation was hopeless.

"There may be something I can try," she said, louder as she got more frustrated.

She listened for thirty seconds, her expression not once changing. Grabbing a pen from her pocket, she scribbled something on a napkin. Afterward she took the napkin and shoved it in her pocket.

"I'll be there within the hour. Okay, thank you. Talk soon," she said into the phone and hung up.

Although she didn't say anything about the call, I was certain that she was thinking of it while she scarfed down the rest of her sandwich, hurrying through her lunch.

After another minute, she smiled slightly and said, "I have work to get back to. It was a pleasure having lunch with you. Let's catch up soon."

"I agree. Have a nice day," I said.

She downed the last of her iced tea. Two minutes later, she got up from the table with her tray in hand and put it away. And with that, the busy doctor walked out the door.

There was still time left on my lunch hour. And I didn't have any pressing matters that needed to be handled back at the office. Plus, I was still drinking my coffee. There was no reason to let it go to waste, despite the amount of energy I was wielding.

Chapter 15

SOMETIME NEAR three a.m., Jenna had gotten up from the floor and got into the bed. Now, hours later, she was sitting up in bed dialing her ex-boyfriend on the telephone for a third time. Frustratingly, she listened to Kevin's phone ring four times then go to voicemail. After leaving a message, she worried about why he didn't answer the phone last night or this morning. What could be the reason he hadn't called? Was he okay? Maybe he didn't check his voicemail.

She went to the bathroom briefly then returned and sat on the bed. Ten minutes became fifteen, and he didn't call her back.

For almost fifteen hours, tucked away in the Comfort Inn, she couldn't wait any longer. Food was becoming a worry now. She had to make a decision.

After getting out of bed, she walked to the window of her room, and looked out through the narrow space between the curtain and the wall. The sun had just come up, and the infected were nowhere as far as the eye could see. It was unmistakably clear that she wanted to go.

She quickly put on her socks and sneakers, and snatched her backpack. Pressing her ear up against the door, she didn't hear anything. A deep breath released from her chest as she eased out the door.

Making her way down the hallway, she stopped when she heard something. The sound was weak, but it was definitely there. Some more steps and she had tracked the sound from something moving toward her in the darkness, with only the sliver of glowing red from an emergency exit sign nearby to light the hallway. It looked to her like a man with a blanket around his shoulders.

Her feet were frozen on the brown carpet, while her mind quickly ran through the options. Heart pounding in her chest, she tried to remain calm when she saw drops of blood on the hallway carpet near the door of a room that had a Do Not Disturb sign hanging on it.

Closer now to her, it was an old man bleeding from cuts on his arms. He appeared disorientated, most likely infected.

Forget about the elevator. There was no way she was going out the front door of the hotel. Her best option was the back stairway of the building. So, she turned, opened the emergency exit door, and went down the two flights of stairs. Fortunately, she made it to the bottom without incident.

She burst through the door to the outside and immediately heard sirens screaming in the distance. At the same time, sunlight spilled into her eyes, half blinding her for a minute.

Scanning the vicinity, she saw a Circle K store on Vance Jackson Road, just down the road from the hotel. After checking the street one final time to confirm there were no zombies, she felt it was safe to walk the block to the store.

Seconds after she entered the parking lot, she stopped when she saw a man pointing a rifle at two zombies. He was six one, with brown eyes, and thick brown hair tucked through a Houston Astros baseball cap. She was astonished when the man pulled the trigger. The blast of the rifle so close to her left a ringing in her ear.

Jenna watched as the bullet hit the zombie in the left shoulder. It shook at the impact, but it didn't die. The zombie with sunken eyes, a half ripped off chin and bruises on its arms, was still moving.

For a long moment, all she could do was stand there, motionless, frozen in time and space as if her feet were nailed to the ground. Fear was building up inside of her as the man raised the rifle to his shoulder and fired. Another bang. A small piece of brain flew out the back of the zombie's skull, as he slammed onto the ground. Coagulated blood leaked from the head wound onto the ground. He swung the rifle around at mind-boggling speed for the next one coming. The rifle kicked against his shoulder as he shot the zombie in the head at close range. The head of the zombie blew open. It collapsed to the ground. The man replaced the empty cartridges in the rifle with loaded ones. When he was finished, he wiped the sweat from his brow and breathed a deep sigh as he looked Jenna over.

"You just made my day. But your timing sucks," he said, with a suggestion of a bad-boy smile.

The dead zombies lay just feet away from her. Bits and chunks of their brains were splattered across the ground. She stood there looking at the corpses, knowing she'd been changed. She didn't feel like the same person who'd left the university the day before.

Trying to hide her nerves, she produced a smile, not to make it obvious. "Well done."

She wanted to act tough, but he could see the fear in her face.

"I can't help it. I just have no respect for the dead," he said.

"Well, nice chatting with you, but I have to run," she said and turned away, hoping to discourage any further conversation.

He tipped his hat back and smiled at her. "What a shame you're not running my way."

She ignored the comment. Keeping her head down, she kept walking toward the store. She was used to getting hit on, used to being told she was beautiful and things like that. It wasn't the time or the place for it.

The convenience store was empty, from what she could see through the dirty windows, there was no movement inside. Before walking in, she stopped on the doorstep and took a deep breath. She pushed open the door and stuck her head in to confirm no one was there.

When she stepped inside, she smelled blood. In another corner, on the opposite side of the store, she saw blood on the linoleum floor. It was wet and looked fresh. She wasn't going to waste any time on it. She grabbed a map of Texas from the counter and shoved it into her backpack. As she passed the counter, she heard a sound. She froze and waited. It was a cat scurrying away to the back exit.

On the way to the fridge filled with soft drinks, she saw a cell phone on the floor. Unzipping her jacket pocket, she picked it up, and put it inside. From the fridge, she grabbed a can of Sprite, dug her middle fingernail under the tab, pried it up, and took a big, satisfying sip.

A gunshot echoed outside. It was probably the rifleman. There was no doubt the man knew how to handle a weapon. Another shot followed, as she opened the fridge door again. She grabbed four bottles of water and placed them in her backpack. Having made a quick scan of all the aisles, she filled her backpack with chocolate bars, granola bars, and bags of potato chips.

Just when she believed things couldn't get any worse, somehow they always did. Before she made it to the door, she caught movement in the corner of her eye. Zombies! They were outside and hadn't seen her. She took cover in an aisle and flicked her eyes toward them.

Where was the rifleman? She didn't see him anywhere, until she looked to the ground. He was swarmed by four zombies chomping on his arms, and blood gurgled from his lips. The sight was gruesome, even from where she was standing. His rifle lay seven feet from him. Logically, she suspected he had been overrun by them.

Jenna was worried that she might be trapped. Then she remembered the back exit. Earlier, she hadn't seen any zombies on that side of the Circle K. There was a chance she wouldn't find them there.

She seized her moment. While the zombies gave all their attention to the rifleman, she raced out the back door. And just as she thought, no one was around. She ran heading east, turned left on an empty street, and began walking.

Remembering the cell phone in her pocket, she lowered her head and dug it out. She tinkered around with the phone and turned it on. The battery still had half a charge. She dialed a number. No service. She believed that the telephone lines were down. As if things weren't bad enough already, no way to communicate with anyone now. Disappointedly, she dropped the phone on the side of the road.

Chapter 16

TWENTY MINUTES LATER, Jenna was in an area unfamiliar to her. She didn't know San Antonio well enough to recognize anything. After slowing down, her head darted from side to side, her eyes looking everywhere, as she tried to determine where in the world she was.

It wasn't like she had a phone to call or text anyone. There was no service anyway. Though it didn't make a difference because she didn't have any acquaintances, much less friends, other than Kevin who she'd met in an Astronomy class, given the short time frame she attended St. Mary's University. More often than not, she'd hung out with him and his friends at the shopping mall and the movie theatre. But for the most part, she had stayed in the dorm on campus. Now, more than ever, she needed the help of her ex-boyfriend, who was a native of San Antonio and knew the neighborhoods well.

Jenna was lost in suburbia, armed only with a map to guide her. She was headed for Abilene, assuming she hadn't misread the map and its directions. As she turned right onto the next street, she heard shouts ahead.

"Go away. Please. Stop it," a woman's voice cried out.

She didn't look back. Then came the alarming sound of a slap.

"Hello, you over there? Please help me," the same voice yelled out again.

The voice calling out to her, prompted her to stop. She turned to look behind her. Forty feet away, was an elderly woman who looked to be in her mid-sixties, with white hair piled on top of her head, dressed in denim capri pants and a white long-sleeved shirt. She was trying to open the door of a bronze Toyota Camry parked in the driveway of a house. A zombie, shuffling about on clearly a broken ankle, was trying to grab her.

The woman flinched as the zombie grabbed her wrist. Her eyes widened, and she hit it with her pocketbook. Then her eyes went wild when she shouted to Jenna or anyone around to offer assistance.

"Let go of me," yelled the woman as she fought off her attacker.

From what Jenna could tell, the woman was not infected. She looked around and saw that there was nobody in sight. Just then, something occurred to her. Maybe, just maybe, they could help each other out. Most important, the woman had a vehicle. That was precisely what Jenna wanted.

She needed to create some sort of diversion, something to distract the zombie long enough, that the woman could get into her car. Then the woman would offer her a ride. She thought it would be better if the woman let her drive the car, because she was ready to burn some rubber.

"I'll help you," Jenna said eagerly.

After she picked up a rock, she flung it at the zombie. The rock collided with the back of its head interrupting its attack on the woman. This was good because she had bought the woman a couple of minutes. Trying to save this woman's life was the most daring thing she'd ever done.

The zombie spun around and growled when she saw Jenna standing there, which just went to show how very startled she was. The zombie had stopped pursuing the woman and was shuffling toward her. Looking closely at the zombie, Jenna thought she was an awful sight. She had blood red eyes, stringy and greasy hair, a bloody banged up ankle, and a terrible smell of rotting flesh.

"That's right. Over here. Come and get me," she yelled.

Jenna formed a pistol with her index finger and thumb. *If only it was real*, she thought. She aimed the imaginary gun at the zombie and in one motion of her finger she pretended to shoot by squeezing an imaginary trigger.

"Bang, you are dead. Oh, my mistake. You're already dead," she said amusingly.

To further emphasize her point, she blew on her finger like she was blowing the smoke off the barrel. Next, she holstered her hand, shaped like a gun, at her hip. Perhaps she carried the joke too far, where it wasn't funny anymore, but she didn't care.

For no reason that she could understand, the zombie stopped dead in its tracks, as if collecting its thoughts. It snarled a couple of times, lifted its nose up in the air, sniffing several times as if it was smelling something. The zombie shook its head in confusion, then started rocking back and forth. Then, it looked at her intensely, as if it understood all that had transpired.

Jenna just couldn't believe what she was seeing. Her brow wrinkled while her mind tried to make out what it was doing. This zombie certainly was more lifelike and didn't appear to be so dead in the brain like the others she'd seen before. Did it have the ability to reason and learn? Could it really be thinking? *Fat chance*, she thought, that it was likely acting on instinct, driven like a shark to kill and devour all in its path. When she heard the car door open, she immediately turned her attention back to the old woman, who was climbing inside her car.

"Thanks a bunch," the woman said before she slammed the door shut with a bang.

"Wait. You can't just drive away. Can I have a ride?" Jenna yelled, watching her start up the car.

The woman might or might not have heard her. She didn't respond, didn't look toward Jenna. She backed out of the driveway, and just like that, she was gone.

"You're welcome," Jenna said halfheartedly.

Not until now, had she been interested in helping anyone and she did not regret doing it. Down in her heart, she knew she'd done the right thing. It was just one of life's lessons that she had to learn about being a good Samaritan. That good deeds weren't always rewarded.

The sound of hissing made her look back at the zombie. Her fear increased when she saw the limping zombie was closing in on her. At the last possible moment, Jenna stepped away from her, feeling she was about to bite her. She turned and ran fast down the street.

With some distance between her and the zombie, she slowed to a jog, then stopped. She turned around and saw the zombie in a stance looking sad. Her red eyes now had tears in them. She whimpered when she saw Jenna staring back at her. Instead of fear, Jenna could almost feel sorry for her. It was the strangest zombie she had ever seen, and she had seen many strange zombies. Did she still have basic human emotions and needs? Maybe she was upset because she couldn't feast on Jenna. Who could say for sure?

She turned her eyes forward, made a left, and started walking at a regular pace. There was no need to run. And she still didn't know where she was.

Chapter 17

BY THE TIME Jenna entered a neighborhood where the virus was raging through, she was worn out from walking. There were people everywhere fighting with zombies. She needed to get out of there and stay out of sight of the zombies.

She started running and dodged around a zombie charging a man on the lawn of a house. The man was holding a 9mm Beretta. Without the slightest bit of hesitation, he raised his pistol to point-blank range and shot the zombie in the head.

Quickly, she took cover in a narrow walkway between two houses. The rest was good. She hunkered down just in case anyone was looking her way.

Peeking from the corner of the house, she watched a teenager with a rifle standing in the yard of a house. His friend was using his smartphone to snap photos of a zombie approaching them. It was a teenage girl with black hair hanging straight down to her shoulders, scratches and bruises on her legs, wearing a white button-down shirt and short plaid skirt. There was dried blood caked on her chest.

The boy holding the rifle in his hands took a deep breath to calm himself, and felt a wave of peace sweep through him. He raised the rifle, aimed, fired, and prepared the next round. The zombie was hit in the head and dropped to the ground instantly.

Suddenly, the boy with the rifle found himself staring in shock at a zombie at the house across the street.

"Oh, no. Jeff, you're not going to like this," he said, stuttering over the words.

"What is it Cameron?" Jeff asked, stopped taking pictures and nudged him on the shoulder.

Cameron lifted his arm and pointed. "Is that your brother?"

Jeff turned to look at the zombie. When he saw his brother, tears came into his eyes.

"What happened to you, Scott?" Jeff yelled at him.

Scott, the zombie, began walking toward them. Cameron adjusted his grip on the rifle and lined up the shot. He placed his finger over the trigger.

"Can I shoot him?" Cameron asked.

At this point, Jenna felt she had rested long enough. So, she turned and went down the walkway. She moved quietly toward the street on the other side of the neighborhood, hoping that the zombies didn't hear her. Concentrating once again on keeping herself out of sight, she crept behind a line of bushes that hid her. She waited and carefully looked around the street.

She saw a boy and his father fighting with a zombie in the driveway of a house. The zombie was over six feet tall and heavyset, wearing a kippah on his head, dressed in a navy suit with a white shirt covered in dried blood, and bite marks on his neck. The boy, in his late teens, elbowed him in the back of the neck, causing the zombie to falter to one side.

"Get him, dad!" he yelled to his father.

The zombie made a clicking noise with his teeth before going after the boy. The father was fast approaching the zombie. On instinct, the zombie turned around and caught the father charging him.

"Dad, watch out," the boy shouted.

The father smashed his weight into the zombie's rib cage. The impact knocked the zombie off his feet. The zombie was face down on the ground with the father on top of him. The father grabbed the zombie's head and twisted it, breaking his neck.

"Kill him dad, kill him!" the boy hollered.

Jenna had been crouched down for quite a while. She raised up and poked her head out of the bushes. No movement. She ducked back, just in case that the zombies might cast a glance in her direction. Then she moved through the shrubs, found an opening, and took off.

As she walked down the street, she tried to convince herself that she wasn't crazy. Her mind was set on finding an empty house. But which one? The thought of being an uninvited house guest didn't disturb her. Because of the insane circumstances, it was the only sensible option.

She walked another two blocks until she saw what she was looking for. There was a house with its front door standing partially open, broken glass on the ground. The house was completely still and appeared vacant.

Cautiously, she moved forward a few steps, passing trash spilled out of a black plastic bag resting against an olive-green garbage can at the curb in the front of the house. She wrinkled her nose because the garbage stunk to high heaven. Staying far from the door, she listened for sounds from the house, but couldn't hear anything.

When she was five feet from the door, she hesitated again, sure she couldn't go through with it. A strange feeling came over her that she shouldn't be doing this. She didn't want to get caught breaking and entering. Left to her own devices, she had no clue how to navigate this walking dead nightmare.

She spent the next five minutes studying the door, trying to muster up the courage. Afterward, she stepped forward into the doorway. Gazing inside the house, she had to risk it.

"Please let there be no one there," she muttered to herself.

As silently as she could, she slipped into the house, closing and locking the door behind her. Her eyes shot right, left, and all over the place until they landed on the door to a bedroom. It was closed.

Disconcerted, she walked over to it. Fearful about what she might find, her hands shook when she twisted the doorknob. Nobody was there. She let out a sigh of relief.

To confirm she was, in fact, alone, she took a quick, thorough look around the house. Anxiously and nervously, she was waiting for a sound, to let her know someone was there. But there was only silence. She was alone in every sense of the word.

With nervous haste, she made sure all of the doors and windows were closed and locked tight. And she checked that all the window curtains were closed, and no lights were on. Once she felt she was secure, she turned the corner and headed toward the bedroom at the end of the hallway.

The bedroom had a bathroom and a double window, large enough for her to fit through, if she needed to escape. She flopped the backpack down on the neatly made king-size bed and made a swift turn into the bathroom. She kept lights off, with the exception of the bathroom. After washing her face, she took a quick shower, which she desperately needed.

It was pure chance that the house was empty. She believed that, in all likelihood, probably the reason the house had been abandoned was the people who owned the house were dead or had fled from the zombies. Most people left, most likely to find some safe shelter, and planned that when the epidemic was over, they would return to their homes. That seemed the most plausible explanation.

Back in the room, she dressed. Fully clothed, shoes and all, in case she had to make a quick escape, she fell onto the bed.

Laying there in silence, she started to think about the circumstances that brought her to where she was now. She had come to accept that this was the only way she could survive. Her mind was drifting to the Maya prophecy, so widely publicized, but not accepted or taken seriously. Was this the end of the world? Could this be the beginning of a new way of living? Would she ever see her sister again? She had to. She wanted to be optimistic about her future, but she was also a realist. After a few more moments, and some more racing thoughts, she fell asleep, completely exhausted.

Chapter 18

THE NIGHTMARES were a result of finding out the infected had reached the gate outside. Or so I believed. Coworkers often shared the office gossip in the cafeteria. I had heard much about the horde of zombies camped outside but had yet to see them myself. Just knowing they were out there was sufficient enough to cause a bad dream.

It was nearly eight-thirty, thirty minutes later than I usually woke up. Mim was curled up at the foot of the bed, sound asleep. Staring blankly into space without moving an inch, I listened to the soft drone of the five-blade ceiling fan whirling overhead. Yawning, I felt as tired as when I had gone to bed. Despite the clock ticking away, I rolled over, fluffed my pillow, and lay there for a few peaceful moments reflecting on last night's dream.

The dream began with me walking down a hallway. There

was smoke coming from under a door. Behind the door was an armless zombie sitting in a chair. Her eyes were black, and the side of her face was smeared with blood. She slowly rose her head up as she growled. When the door flung open, I awoke with my heart racing, and fear in a corner of my mind.

I'd also been dreaming about my sister, making a brief cameo appearance. A different scene with her in a hotel room talking on the phone. It was this part that moved my thought, that made me think, because I last spoke to her on the phone when she was in a hotel room. The next thing that happened in the dream was that she was smoking a cigarette and dancing to songs from the radio. I couldn't figure out that part yet.

Jenna started smoking at the age of sixteen. The smell of tobacco reminded her of our late mother. She first tried smoking when she was nine after stealing one of mom's cigarettes. I knew because I caught her doing it. It was a secret between sisters.

If my mother were still alive, she would not approve of Jenna smoking. She died of lung cancer during my senior year in high school. In actuality, she passed away nearly one year to the day of her diagnosis of cancer. When she went into the hospital, I knew she wouldn't be coming home again. I flashed on the image of my sister as an upset eleven-year-old trying to understand why her mother had died. It was the worst day of Jenna's life.

Would I ever see Jenna again? Was she dead? But I couldn't let myself think along those lines. I prayed that she was safe. She just had to be.

I looked up at the painting hanging on the wall and thought of my dear departed father. His spirit was alive and well in my memory. The image of a boat with blue and white sails on a sea of green, made me think of how he loved sailing. It was his way to escape the drudgery of everyday life. He was at peace with the wind in his sails and his hand on the helm. In my mind, I pictured him on a yacht far out to sea, existing somewhere in space and time, as if in another dimension. And he was happy and watching over me.

"What do I do now? I know nothing of Jenna. I don't know if I'm strong enough to handle this completely alone," I asked him.

My eyes watered. There I went again, I scolded myself. I had done pretty well up to that moment. I wiped my eyes and refused to think anymore about it. This was not the way I expected to start my day.

As I took a breath, I thought about what I needed to do. The first thing that came to mind was get up out of bed, that which I did. Otherwise I might be late for work. I passed by Mim on the way to the bathroom. She yawned, but didn't open her eyes or get up. She looked so cute sleeping.

After quickly getting dressed, I left the apartment. There was no time for my usual breakfast in the cafeteria. Making it with a minute to spare, I flopped down in the chair at my desk. Because I had a minute, I went to the break room for a cup of coffee then headed back to my desk.

I found a memo dated from the day before next to the computer. What could it be now? It must have been placed there yesterday after I left the office.

It stated that "The bottommost floor of the facility has been turned into a temporary shelter. It contains fifty cubicles, each equipped with a cot bed. These accommodations have been made for family members of the BDC employees, and any others."

By 'others', they meant that the helicopters picked up people occasionally when they were out getting supplies for the facility. And there was a chance that some people would follow the helicopters to the gated entrance. Additionally, I knew that the employee's friends were allowed entrance into the facility. Thomas Bauer's and Dan Saunders' wives and children arrived at the facility the first day it all started, December 21. Rumor had it that their families were airlifted by helicopter and flown here. In this business, it was all about who you knew.

When I finished reading the memo, I was out of coffee. Maybe I drank it too fast? I really wanted more coffee, but it would have to wait, because I was ready for my first task of the day. At least, I thought I was. I picked up the phone at my desk to call Vivian and listened to dead air. To add to the drama, the telephone lines were not working.

With the way I was feeling earlier, I knew something was coming. It was as if I had a premonition. As ridiculous as this might sound, it was as if something was trying to tell me all communication systems were severed. I had yet to receive a memo about it. But I was sure I would soon.

Not to worry, I thought, waiting for the computer to boot up. I had to know if the Internet was working — and yet somewhere in the back of my mind, my unconscious mind knew that it wasn't. After logging into the system, I clicked on the Internet Explorer icon. Just as I thought, no Internet connection. This also meant there would be no e-mail communication. Who was to say what could happen next?

No phone system to communicate with my sister, my coworkers or the outside world? With communication systems down, things would slow down around here. Now was the time to tear myself up inside trying to understand why all of this was happening.

How come no one had told me? Apparently, it was every man for himself around here now. I wanted to know what happened but wasn't sure who to ask. The only way I could find anything out was to walk over to someone's office to ask something rather than calling or e-mailing the person. Only one person came to mind.

So, I got up from my desk and headed over to Vivian's office to find out what she knew about the telephone lines. Then, I stopped halfway there. What if she didn't know? Should I tell her? I didn't want to upset her further. Then I reassured myself that she would find out eventually, best I tell her. Before I did that, I was heading to the break room, feeling like I was going in circles. This was a good time to get a second cup of coffee.

Chapter 19

"SHE NEEDS EVERY BIT of support that we can give her," Saunders told Langtry, when he asked him to secure a brain specimen for Dr. Julie Mehta that morning. Standing twenty feet from the gate, Langtry pulled out a pair of high-powered Nikon binoculars, scanning the scene. He watched a black Bell helicopter, about a mile way, in the desert. The chopper was searching for a lone infected.

He lowered the binoculars, grabbed his walkie-talkie, and adjusted it to the correct frequency. "Lucas, this is Ken. Do you copy?"

"Copy, Ken," Lucas called over the radio.

Lucas Rawlett and Stewart Cabrera were positioned on each open side of the helicopter. They wore black bodysuits and were holding Century Arms AK assault rifles. James Stebbins, dressed in a hazardous materials suit, sat next to Lucas, the mission's team leader. Lucas was five eight, with thick, sandy-blond hair, blue eyes, a square jaw, broad shoulders, and an average build.

"Zombie. Southwest, fifty degrees," Lucas said to the pilot.

The pilot was a tall man with dark hair, and a five o'clock shadow. He looked across the cockpit at Lucas with his sharp green eyes. Judging by the expression on his face, you would assume he got it.

"Ken, I've got an infected male. His head looks good," the pilot told him.

Langtry raised his radio to his mouth and demanded, "No one move till I say. Can you get him safely, Lucas?"

"He is isolated. There is no sign of any other infected within a mile's radius. We are in position," Lucas replied.

"Take him," Langtry ordered, then said to the pilot, "At the first sign of trouble, you pull them back up."

"We're going down! Take us down, Chris," Lucas said eagerly to the pilot.

A nervous expression flashed across Stebbins' face as the helicopter went into a steep dive toward the ground. The noise of the engines, reverberating through the aircraft, made him nauseous. Whereas Stewart, a medium-height Hispanic in his mid-to-late twenties, with brown hair and eyes, and a slim build, was ecstatic as the chopper lowered.

"Stay alert," Langtry spoke into a walkie-talkie.

His concern for their safety was evident. Langtry brought up his binoculars and proceeded to keep a watchful eye on everything transpiring.

Stebbins and the two guards spilled out of the helicopter.

Stewart had a shovel fastened across his back. Stebbins carried an insulated medical cooler. And Lucas wielded a machete. Lucas and Stewart encircled the zombie while Stebbins, stayed off to the side, watching and waiting. Chris Nevins, the pilot, switched off the chopper's engines and powered down his craft. Then he kept his eyes on the men while he sat in the helicopter.

The zombie was anxious to attack but couldn't decide which of the men to grab. His grunts and growling noises grew louder by the second. Stebbins stepped back further, clearly terrified. The zombie was not a pretty sight. It was about his age — thirtyish — with swollen arms, rotting skin, and baring its greenish teeth as it growled and hissed at them.

Lucas stepped back and swung the machete that came crashing against its neck. The blade sliced the zombie's head clean off with one swipe. Its head just rolled off its shoulders onto the ground. While the zombie's body fell to the ground.

Stebbins ran over to the body. He took a syringe out of his backpack. He clasped it in his hand and inserted it into the arm of the body. The coagulated blood was difficult to extract. With applied pressure on the syringe, the blood was slowly moving.

Stewart was digging a hole, while Lucas reached into a pocket and pulled out a muzzle. He walked over to the head and placed it over the mouth. Then he pulled out a net from his pocket and threw it over the head. When the net was secure, Lucas put the head in the medical cooler on the ground next to Stebbins.

By this time, fifteen minutes had passed and four vials of blood had been extracted. Stebbins put the tubes of blood securely in his backpack. Stewart and Lucas carried the body to the ditch. Then Stewart started shoveling dirt onto the grave, while Lucas signaled to Chris, who in turn gave him a thumbs-up. It was time to go.

The helicopter started up as the three men loaded and the door was closed. Chris flew the helicopter due west toward the BDC facility. Stebbins made a face, as he was still uncomfortable riding in a helicopter.

"Ken, we are coming in."

"Roger that, Lucas," Langtry's voice crackled over the radio again.

When the men dropped out of the helicopter, Langtry greeted them by saying, "That was a job well done. Keep in mind that Dr. Mehta requires a specimen of a female infected too."

Lucas and Stewart looked at each other bewildered, exchanging uncertain glances with one another. They would have to do it again. This news took them by surprise.

Langtry turned to Stewart. "Stand over there and don't do anything till I tell you to."

Stewart stood where he was told to stand and waited for further instructions.

Then Langtry saw Stebbins walking away carrying the medical cooler. "Hold on a minute, James."

Stebbins stopped and turned toward him. "What is it?"

"Lucas will go with you to collect the remains to be incinerated," Langtry said, looked at his second-in-command, and waved him over.

"Okay, fine by me," Stebbins said, giving him a nod.

"Lucas report back to me when you're done," Langtry said.

"Yes, sir."

"Oh, and one more thing," said Langtry, before his radio interrupted.

"Chris, the pilot of the chopper, wants to know whether he can leave," the voice on the other end said.

"Affirmative. Move out. Now," Langtry ordered into his walkie-talkie, then turned to Stebbins and said, "Be careful with it. The specimen must be contained. The brain could still be functioning. Is that clear?"

"Yes. Of course, I will be very careful. Let's go, Lucas," Stebbins said.

"Yes, sir," Lucas said again.

As they walked away, Langtry said, "Stewart, I think we have some things to discuss."

Lucas was standing guard by the door of the surgical room. Inside the room, Stebbins wore protective goggles, and latex gloves. The zombie's head was on a steel table. He started to cut away the net with scissors, and left the muzzle on the mouth. With an electric saw, he began slicing through skin and bone. He removed a cap-shaped piece of skull. Then he reached in with both hands and gently lifted the brain from the skull. Holding it near his face, he almost gagged from the odor.

Stebbins placed the brain in a glass box filled with liquid to keep it preserved. The muzzle, skin, skull, and bone fragments were placed into a red plastic bag marked with a biohazard symbol. He stripped off his latex gloves and tossed them into the bag. Once the bag was sealed, he immediately washed his hands in the sink and pulled on a pair of sterile gloves. After spraying the table with disinfectant, he grabbed the specimen, the bag, and his backpack. When he walked out of the room, he was greeted by Lucas.

"All done?" Lucas asked.

"Yes. Please burn this. I've got to deliver this box to Dr. Mehta."

Stebbins handed him the red biohazard bag, turned in another direction and began walking.

Chapter 20

IN THE LAB, Dr. Julie Mehta was staring down at an infected human brain in a large stainless-steel surgical bowl. She carefully slid her gloved hands under the brain and began to examine the foramen magnum, the opening where the spinal cord entered the skull. Then she looked at the nerves and muscles for manifestations of the disease.

The macroscopic examination revealed the white matter of the brain was enlarged and swollen, with the accumulation of fluid, and three small patches of a bright yellow discoloration on the right frontal lobe. Disease was indicated by the discoloration possibly from the accumulation of bilirubin, a neurotoxic that binds lipids in the brain and damages mitochondria, affecting cellular respiration. There was a yellow discoloration in the cerebrospinal fluid, flowing in and around the brain, important in determining the time of the cerebral damage.

She put on her protective goggles and picked up a handheld ultraviolet lamp. Flicking off the lights, she snapped on the lamp and ran it over the brain. When exposed to an ultraviolet light, the cerebral cortex showed some softening.

These observations showed that there was inflammation caused by the virus, which might easily be mistaken for encephalitis, as the symptoms were genuinely similar.

She put the lights back on and removed her goggles with a sigh. Next, she scooped the brain up and placed it onto the scale. The weight was two pounds more than normal. She was now going to photograph the brain with the magnetic resonance imaging machine. The MRI scans might show brain swelling and identify structural pathology.

The computed tomography scans of the brain were displayed on the high-resolution monitor. She studied the CT images which had her thinking all kinds of things. The longer she looked the more confused she felt she was becoming. It might be a good idea to discuss it with James Stebbins. A second opinion couldn't hurt.

No time like the present, she thought as she stripped off her gloves. She walked over to the biohazard waste disposal can, stepped on the foot pedal raising the lid, and threw them inside. Then she left the laboratory heading for his office.

Peering into his office, she saw him sitting at his desk. She wondered if he had been sleeping with his head cradled in his arms on the desk because there were swollen bags under his eyes, a faint crease mark along the side of his face, and his blond hair was a mess.

"James."

He looked up from his computer screen, swiveled his chair to face her, and said, "Good afternoon, Julie."

"Can you come to the lab a minute? I'd like you to see the CT scans."

"Sure."

He tapped a key on his computer to activate the screensaver, then stood up to follow her. Once in the lab, he looked at the scans for a few long minutes with his hands jammed into his pants pockets under his lab coat. He was puzzled by them, maybe more than she was.

"It makes no sense to me either. But this infection has sent our minds spinning," he said.

"As you can see here, the infection is apparent," she said, and pointed to an area in the image, "but there is no real indication that it is anything other than just something white and cloudy."

"I agree, Julie. Anyway, it looks like a good place to cut into and dissect."

"Thanks for the suggestion. I will start there."

"Okay, I'll be going. I know you have a lot of work to do," he said.

"Before you go, I'll give you one vial of the infected blood to run some tests," she said, and walked over and opened the refrigerator door.

Julie pulled out a vial of infected blood and handed it to him.

"I'd like a complete blood count performed, a white blood cell differential test, and lastly, a sedimentation rate blood test to determine inflammatory activity," she said as he looked it over.

"I'll get to it right away. And I will get back to you with the results of the blood tests sometime tomorrow."

"Oh, there's more."

"Sure, tell me."

"I am compiling a report for upper management. If you don't mind, I would appreciate if you would come back here at the end of the day, so I can show you some of the results of the analysis of the infected brain tissue."

"Sure, I'll stop by. For the duration of the day, I'll be at my desk retrieving file data from the computer's hard disk," he said, before he turned and left the laboratory.

Briefly, she reviewed the CT images again to determine which piece of the brain she would need to cut off for examination. Using a small surgical knife, she sliced off a piece. She placed the tissue in a petri dish. Following that, she cut out three more pieces of tissue and put them into petri dishes.

While, she waited for a machine to prepare a brain tissue sample, she wrapped the brain and put it in the refrigerator. Soon afterwards, she took out a vial of infected blood and placed it on the counter.

It didn't take her long to put on a hazmat suit, a necessary attire for where she was going. She walked down a hallway to a steel door, entered a code into a keypad on the wall for the door to open. As she entered, the door closed with an electronic click.

The room had three cages of white mice. They were curled asleep, nestled in a bed of cedar chips. She opened a cage and grabbed one. It yawned in her hand, still more than half-asleep. She gently put it in an empty cage, separating it from the others. Because mice had genes that were more than eighty percent identical to humans, she believed that she could learn how to treat or cure the disease from their response of being exposed to the infected blood.

She took the vial of infected blood and ran water over it at the sink, gradually increasing the temperature. A couple of minutes after, she picked up a syringe, removed the cap from the needle, inserted it into the vial, and removed a small amount of blood. She injected the isolated mouse. The syringe was put into the biohazard waste can. Then she set up the video camera to record the affects the infected blood would have on the mouse. She would come back later for the results.

She walked over to a stainless-steel tank and twisted the latch open. After pulling out a steel tray, she put the vial inside and sealed the tank shut. After a quick look around, she left the same way she came in.

When she returned to the main room of the laboratory, she took off the hazmat suit. The timer had beeped, and she opened the machine. She retrieved the brain tissue sample embedded within a small rectangular block, which she took to another machine that cut slices off. The slices were stained and put on slides. She put a slide under the microscope. Looking through the eyepiece, she adjusted it, zooming in on a cell. After careful study, she saw something quite similar to rabies.

Chapter 21

THAT NIGHT JENNA had nightmares. At two a.m. she woke up trembling and in a cold sweat, not certain where she was. All she could remember about the dream was that she was walking in the hallway of the Comfort Inn and there was a zombie coming toward her.

She got off the bed and splashed cold water on her face in the bathroom. Feeling refreshed, she came back to the bed, placed her head down on the pillow and closed her eyes. No longer concerned about the dream, she dismissed it as coincidence and closed her eyes. Not even a second later, her eyes flew open to stare at the ceiling until she fell asleep.

A few minutes before six a.m., she jumped awake from yet another nightmare. Alone in the quiet room, resting on the pillow, she was thankful the bad dream was over. Tensely, she shifted around to get more comfortable, turning over on her side.

Not a second later, she just lay there, her extremely vivid dream still niggling at her mind. She was watching the rifleman with the baseball cap on the ground surrounded by flesh-eating zombies. Next, she was shouting at the top of her lungs for him to get off the ground, desperately trying to get his attention.

Abruptly, the dream changed, and she saw herself sleeping in the bed. A moment later, footsteps announced someone approaching. There was someone in the room with her. She studied the dark shape as it drew closer.

"Who in the world are you? Why are you in my house?" asked the figure of a woman at the foot of the bed.

With that she'd woken up. Now she was wondering if she was infected. She couldn't be. The intense dreams were probably stress induced. Still tired, she lay there trying to calm herself to sleep. Thirty minutes later, she was dozing.

Around nine o'clock in the morning, she woke again. While rubbing the sleep from her eyes, she swung her feet off the bed and headed for the bathroom, where she undressed for a shower. Even though she took one the night before, she felt she needed another shower because she didn't know when she would have the chance to take another one.

She stepped into the tub and closed the curtain, letting the hot water revive her. While in the shower, she started thinking about where she could go next. It wouldn't be wise to walk through the city. She knew things were escalating. It might be more sensible to travel through the suburbs.

After she dressed, she looked over the map to confirm directions. Everything looked okay, but she still had a long way to go.

She carefully opened the bedroom door. The house was quiet. She darted to the kitchen and grabbed three cans of Diet Coke from the refrigerator. Thirsty as she was, she opened a can and gulped it down. Then she opened another and drank it nonstop, while putting the last can in her backpack. Searching the cabinets, she found a box of Cheerios cereal, and helped herself to nine handfuls. When she finished eating, she washed her hands in the sink.

Moving quietly. she walked to the window closest to the front door. Only God knew how many zombies were out there. She had no interest in finding out, but needed to know if the coast was clear.

Peeking around the curtain, she didn't see anyone from the window, but she was most certain that she heard something coming from somewhere outside. She kept scanning the street until a scraggly zombie stumbled into view, coming from behind a house. He had wandered forward not even looking as he crossed the street. She watched the zombie lurk around and turn to walk in another direction. He didn't see her. She was brave enough to hide and outrun him. Or so she was planning.

As she slowly opened the door, a woman zombie came from out of nowhere and was walking toward the house. The sound of the door opening caused her to look toward Jenna. The zombie went lunging for her, growling like an animal. She slammed the door shut, locked it, and moved back.

She didn't turn and run, not right away. Momentarily, she was unable to move. Facing the door, she wasn't sure what she was going to do. Listening to the zombie pound on the door, she felt a sinking sensation in the bottom of her stomach.

Movement and shadows rushed by the window. Then a zombie hit the window. It was all happening much too fast for her taste.

Without wasting one more second, she ran into the bedroom. She closed the door, locking it behind her, and raced to the window. Looking outside, she didn't see any zombies on this side of the house. If she was going to go, it would have to be now because in a few more seconds the zombies would find her for sure.

As quietly as possible, she opened the window and climbed out. She ran to the walkway on the side of the house that led to the backyard. Trying not to make a sound, she slowly opened the chain-link gate. She went down the walkway between the houses, through the backyard, and entered another walkway that led to the front of another house.

From the side of a house, she peeked around the corner. As quick as she could, she hustled across the street. The zombies never saw her, at least she hoped not. She turned left and walked three blocks.

Two minutes after, a gray Lexus RX 350 flew past her. The SUV drove into a zombie that had been walking in the middle of the street. The zombie went flying and landed on the other side of the street, while the speeding vehicle jumped over the curb and smashed into a stop sign. Jenna stepped off of the sidewalk and into the street to get a better look.

The driver's door opened, and music blasted from the car stereo. A man in the driver's seat crawled out of the Lexus and collapsed to the ground. He was about forty, with light brown hair and a face that was twisted into an expression of agony.

The lower right pant leg of his blue jeans was soaked in blood, and more blood pooled under his nose. He lay there, struggling to breathe.

A woman came out of the passenger door. Her blond hair was stained with red from blood, there was a two-inch laceration across her scalp, and her eyeglasses were broken. Placing her hands on the hood for a few moments to catch her balance, she couldn't see anything. She wiped the blood from her face with the sleeve of her shirt. Her eyes turned to the man lying on the ground at her feet. She ran around the front of the Lexus to help him.

"Hang on. I'll get help," she said, as she knelt down and gently cradled his head in her arms.

She waited for him to speak. He tried to speak, but didn't utter a word. The only sound that came out of his mouth was a moan, but she knew he heard her.

The woman raised her head to look around and spent a few seconds racking her brain for ideas. When she saw four people a block away walking down the street, she left the man and ran toward them.

Fifteen feet away, she stopped and yelled, "Hello. Excuse me. Can you help us? We've been in…"

Before she could finish the last sentence, they slowly turned their heads to face her and their bodies followed after. They all had turned around at the same time, but in slow motion. It was like something out of a horror movie. All the while, "Another Brick in the Wall, Pt. 2" by Pink Floyd was playing at a maximum volume on the stereo of the SUV.

Because of the broken eyeglasses, she couldn't see well from a distance, but up close, she saw that they were zombies. Her mouth opened, in shock. She turned around and started running.

"Don't worry sweetie. I'll come back with help," she yelled, as she ran past the man on the ground.

When she came near Jenna, she said, "I wouldn't go that way if I were you!"

"Don't worry, I won't." Jenna said softly to herself.

Just as Jenna was turning a different direction, she saw the zombies stop pursuing the woman and start going after the man on the ground lying by the Lexus. By the time, he'd regained consciousness and tried to stand, they had surrounded him and he couldn't escape.

The very moment the zombies began feeding on him, she broke into a run. She pelted down the road and didn't stop running until she was too tired to go on. That was when she paused for a beat, took in a breath, another one, and another, then began walking.

Chapter 22

LESS THAN AN HOUR LATER, Jenna ended up in the inner city in Bexar county on the northwest side of San Antonio. As she heard screams somewhere off to her right, she glanced around the neighborhood, looking right and left. Then she stopped, trying to remember which direction she came from. Most of the streets looked the same to her.

On a hunch, she turned and started walking west. As she rounded a corner, she felt the presence of someone or something behind her. She paused and turned to face whatever it was. Her eyes widened with panic at the sight of a zombie coming toward her. One minute she was alone and the next she was being trailed. *Zombies in the ghetto*, she thought. She was sick of them already.

"Give me a break," she said under her breath as she listened to the low moaning sound coming from it.

The zombie was getting too close for comfort, much faster than she thought possible. She backed away a few steps, about to flee from it. Panic beat at her, as she frantically tried to decide which direction to take. She tried not to look at the black woman with a dangling eye, a bloody grin, extending her right hand with its bleeding stump where a finger should have been.

There would be no more thinking about it. She turned and started running up the road as fast as her legs would carry her. It was no exaggeration that she moved with determination as she dashed around a corner and into a dead-end alley. There she paused to catch her breath, leaning against a wall. Until she felt something slimy on the wall was dripping down the sleeve of her jacket. It was some sort of grease. She wiped most of it off with her shirt.

The dark alley smelled like garbage and urine. She searched for something to use as a weapon, but found nothing. Her chances of making it through the day were not looking very good. Clearly, hiding was her only option, something she was becoming good at.

With a step, she backed further into the alley. A rat scurried out of her way as she took shelter, crouching in the black shadow of a stinky dumpster. Hidden in the shadows, she could see out, but nobody could see her, making her practically invisible.

Since she had no plan, no idea what she was going to do, she thought, perhaps it was best to stay put for a while. She just looked around, checking things out in what otherwise would normally be a lively, low-income neighborhood.

Right away she saw a young, thin, black man with short dyed blond hair in cornrows, wearing jeans hung loosely at his hips revealing his blue and gray striped boxer shorts, running at top speed across the street. He was looking over his shoulder, nearly tripping over his own feet, as he retreated from the following zombies.

Out in the distance, a zombie was turning the corner at the same time an old black woman, with pink plastic curlers in her hair, was walking nearby. She hit it in the head with a cast iron frying pan, knocking it out cold. The zombie, a twentyish black man with a shaved head and skin that was yellowish brown, lay face-down, sprawled on the sidewalk.

"Take that, you demon!" she said, with satisfaction.

A few moments later, the zombie started wriggling on the ground trying to get up. Undoubtedly, there was no other alternative for her. She had to do something about it. Quick. With both hands gripped tightly to the handle of the frying pan, she smacked it on the head, harder than before. It slumped to the ground, with a gash on its head, blood streaming down the side of its face. This time, it didn't move. Not a single muscle twitched.

"Oh, goodness me. May the Lord have mercy on my soul. God knows things as they are is unbearable. Is this what the world has come to?" the woman exclaimed.

She shrugged to herself and let it be. After looking up and down the street, she turned to her right, and began walking.

A big black guy in an African skull cap said with a ghetto accent, "Right on, big mama. You tell 'em. Leon Valley is my neighborhood."

The six-foot-one man with a muscular body, was carrying a Louisville Slugger smeared with blood over his right shoulder to bop zombies in the head. He wore a green camouflage T-shirt that was splattered with blood, tan cargo pants and black combat boots. Apparently, he had been walking the streets in the neighborhood, swinging his bat at the infected, ridding them from the neighborhood.

It wasn't long before a foul zombie with one arm severed at the elbow, crept up near him. The black guy was all too ready and more than fired up.

"Well, I'll show you a thing or two. You want a piece of this?" he yelled, holding the bat in a swinging position, "I got some for you!"

He swung the bat hard at its head knocking the zombie off balance and to the ground. After staring at it for a good minute, he noticed it didn't move an inch. It was down for good and the man with the bat breathed out a loud sigh. He paused to gather his strength, lowered the bat to the ground and leaned it against his leg.

A short moment later, as he started walking away, he yelled, "You want some more? Come on and get it!"

He moved through the street slowly, appearing tired. Clearly, he'd been at this a long time. Jenna watched him as he turned left into another street disappearing from her view.

At long last, she saw what could be a miracle. She could see the back of a police car parked under a broken streetlight. The driver's door hung open a crack. And that was all it took for the girl with no plan to step out from behind the dumpster. She glanced around the street not seeing the police around.

Seconds later, she ran toward the driver's side of the car, looked inside. Fortunately, the keys were still in the ignition. But there was blood on the seat and just about everywhere else in the car. Yet, she refused to stick around any longer.

Just bloody well grin and bear it, she told herself as she climbed inside, despite the blood and smell. There just wasn't enough time to clean the blood off the seat. She slipped her backpack off her shoulder and dropped it in the passenger seat. As she turned the key in the ignition of the Dodge Charger, she prayed to God that it would start. But if it didn't, she was prepared to bolt out of there.

"I really need a miracle here," Jenna said to herself.

No sooner she said that, she saw a zombie some yards away. To make matters worse, the engine cranked but didn't start up. It failed to catch. Maybe the battery was dead? She prayed to God once more and cranked the key one last time.

When the engine roared to life, she breathed a sigh of relief. Quickly, she closed the car door, checked that the windows were sealed tight, and made sure all the doors were locked. She pulled the seat belt across her body with her right hand, clicked it into place, then checked the rearview mirror. She saw a zombie reaching for the car door handle and three zombies following behind it. Her eyebrows came together in a dissatisfied frown

She took her eyes off the rearview mirror and slammed the accelerator to the floor, taking off at top speed just as a zombie stumbled, fell against and over the hood. The speedometer hit fifty-five, then sixty-five.

Swerving around a truck in the middle of the street, she missed it by inches. As the Charger raced along, the speedometer was pushing seventy. And she kept driving fast until she made it out of the neighborhood safely. She liked the feel of the car, her first-time riding in a police car.

Chapter 23

TRUCKLOADS of zombies were clinging to the gate, hissing, and moaning. You couldn't go anywhere near the main gate of Biogenetics & Disease Control without being growled at by them. In just a few days' time, nearly sixty of them had shown up.

Ken Langtry didn't find the infected crowd the least bit interesting to listen to. He suspected the zombies had followed the mumbling drone of the helicopters, which came and went quite regularly. Earlier in the day, he had commanded a mission that secured a specimen from an infected for Dr. Julie Mehta. He didn't remember seeing so many. Dozens more had arrived in the past four hours, and more kept coming.

Meantime, more supplies were coming in. Anxiously awaiting a delivery, he stood watching from the entrance. The thumping of the low-flying helicopter overhead was inciting the crowd of zombies. They growled louder and pushed harder against the gate. He wanted the infected that were closest to the gate to settle down. But it was only wishful thinking on his part. They couldn't be predicted and they couldn't be controlled. The virus had made them mindless.

Into his walkie-talkie, he said, "Chris. What's your twenty?"

"Ken, we're one mile out. We're coming in hot," the pilot reported.

"We'll be ready for you."

He lowered the walkie-talkie and gave the "ready" signal to Lucas, who led the security team to ensure safety of the delivery.

"Move into position. Watch the corners and set a perimeter," Lucas spoke into his mic.

Stewart and three other men were in a wedge formation. All of the men, outfitted in black bodysuits, used hand and arm signals as they flanked out to the right and left. The instant they came near the gate, they raised their rifles.

Langtry watched the helicopter land on the helipad. He appointed Stewart and three others to unload the aircraft while Lucas stood near the gate.

Nearly an hour later, the helicopter's rotor blades started to turn. Chris Nevins waved goodbye from the cockpit. Langtry nodded, returning the gesture as the helicopter took off. At less than a mile away, Chris spotted a man carrying a woman in his arms. The man had dark hair and eyes, and looked to be in his late twenties. He was wearing mirrored sunglasses, a white button-down sleeveless shirt tucked into jeans, and tan cowboy boots. The woman appeared unconscious, probably infected.

"Check him out. It looks like he's carrying an infected and walking in the direction of the BDC. I wonder how he knows about us?" Chris mentioned to the copilot.

The copilot picked up a pair of binoculars for a closer look. "The woman is definitely infected. Her arm is bleeding profusely from a bite."

"I'm calling it in. Let's see what the boss has to say about this," Chris told him, then spoke into his radio, "Ken. We've got a survivor. He's carrying a woman. She's limp, most likely infected. But he looks fine. Do you want us to pick him up?"

Sweeping the desert with his binoculars, Langtry found the man. He took a step closer, and zoomed in on the woman in his arms. For the most part he was not pleased with what he saw. Lowering the binoculars, he wanted to think about it some more.

In all honesty, he did not want to answer Chris, though he already knew what he had to do. Unfortunately, at this stage, he would have to say no. Because he knew that Dan Saunders would not allow the rescue of an infected person. The risk was too great. He could only assume that the man was infected too.

Langtry went for his radio. "Negative. I repeat, that's a negative! Do not pick him up."

"Got it," came Chris' voice over the radio.

"Maintain your course and altitude as directed. Do you understand that?"

"It's just ... Scratch that. Either way, it's not my business anyway."

"Don't trouble yourself anymore about it, Chris. If he reaches the gate, we'll let him in. Then we'll evaluate to see if he is infected. A physician will check him over."

"Sure thing, sir."

As the man holding the woman looked up, the helicopter flew past him. He shouted for help, but it was too late. The chopper turned, rose higher and moved across the desert. He didn't understand why he hadn't been rescued, until he looked at the woman in his arms. Her condition had worsened. Her face was very pale and her long brown hair was wet from perspiration.

The helicopter was long gone now. The man lugging the woman was a little over one hundred feet from the entrance gate. Not soon enough did a zombie near the gate stir and fuss. After that, the rest of the infected were riled up and switched their attention to the man.

The man saw the zombies coming and began to run with all his might, his sunglasses falling off as he did so. The woman's weight slowed his pace. He had no chance, as there were too many of them.

One of the zombies grabbed him from behind and bit him in the neck, causing him to stumble to the ground, releasing his hold on the woman, his butt suddenly hot with pain. The unconscious woman was grabbed by the lot of them. They lifted her body up and held her. It was as if they knew, sensed, she was infected, becoming just like them.

"You brainless monsters. Let her go," said the man on the ground.

With all the strength the man had left, he got up from the ground. He pushed the zombies out of the way and tried to fight them off to get to the woman. But he was bitten multiple times and fell to the ground again.

He had fought as hard as he could, but the zombies infested on him. There was nothing he could do but lie there and take it. He wanted to kick himself free, but his legs were pinned down. His face was now covered in blood. He was bleeding out all over the ground and his eyes started to flutter closed.

The zombies placed the woman on the ground. Just that quickly, her grayish eyes opened. Not soon after that, came a look of hunger on her face. She crawled over to the man in the cowboy boots and took a bite out of his arm.

Langtry had been watching the horror scene unfold through the binoculars, in disbelief, as the infection spread right before his eyes. He'd never felt so useless in his entire life. The rage built up inside him. It wasn't his fault, but that didn't stop him from wanting to slam his walkie-talkie up against the wall and watch it shatter.

Obviously, he was upset by what had just transpired. And there wasn't anything he could do about it. He was obligated to protect the people he worked with. The safety of the BDC came first and foremost.

After another hour, he brought his binoculars up for one last sweep of the desert. All he could see was zombies.

Killing them and leaving their corpses to rot on the ground would be a biohazard. He needed to think up a plan. For the time being, he had to perform security checks around the facility that required his immediate attention.

Before leaving, he took one more look at the gate. *Too many zombies*, he thought.

Chapter 24

SOME MINUTES LATER, Jenna reached the multi-lane highway. There was no traffic, a small number of abandoned and damaged vehicles, and the best chance to avoid the zombies. Driving along at sixty-five miles an hour, she was determined to get to Abilene as fast as possible.

A little while into the drive, she was passing through the wide-open space of Texas, full of dry land and where you could see everything from the highway. She rolled the window halfway down and let the breeze blow through. Mixed scents of hyacinth and horse manure came in on the breeze, not like the usual stink of death. She just couldn't ever get used to that smell.

"What the heck?" she said.

She could hardly believe her eyes when she saw a protester camped out on the side of the road. It was a gaunt-faced man with tattoos on his arms, wearing an olive-green T-shirt, cut-off jeans and sandals on his feet. His brown, ragged, hair kept getting into his eyes every time the wind blew. With his left hand, he was holding up a neatly lettered sign on a wooden stick that read:

THE END OF THE WORLD IS HERE.

"Repent. We are in the last days. Doom is upon us all," he shouted to anyone who would listen.

As she came closer, she could see that he seemed oblivious to the commotion he was causing. She was surprised he hadn't been attacked by a bunch of zombies. Fortunately for him, there were no infected around. The question she had to ask herself was, what in the world was he doing there? Since he wasn't asking for money or a ride, why bother preaching? She couldn't understand the point he was trying to make.

"They are all demons. Jesus, did not raise them from the dead. The end is near," he shouted as Jenna drove past him.

"Yeah. I heard you," she said smiling and waving at him.

"God bless you, lady," he yelled at her.

"Maybe he's right. Given the way things have been, it feels like the end of the world," she babbled to herself.

When she pulled down the visor to shield her eyes from the sun, it came to her that she should monitor the situation. She turned on the police-band radio, flipping through the channels, anything to make the time move faster for the ride ahead of her.

Some voices crackled over the radio. Not able to make out

much, she kept scanning until she came to a channel that was clear. She turned up the volume and listened to police officers trying to push back the crowd of infected surrounding a hospital. It sounded like a war zone as officers were shooting at the infected.

Gunfire exploded over the radio, followed by shouts from different voices, and then a voice announced, "We have a situation at the emergency entrance."

"The infected are in motion."

"Take cover! I repeat, take cover."

"There have been casualties."

"Get out of there! Retreat."

Almost an hour later, she turned off the police band and went to an all-talk station, all about the infection. She listened closely. News on the radio reported infected in widespread areas. Emergency responders were working nonstop. And neighborhoods were being evacuated where the dead were outnumbering the living. It was a bombardment of bad news. The talk did nothing to instill hope to anyone listening.

A dark brown horse came trotting along the right shoulder of the highway about fifty feet away. She turned off the radio, thinking it probably belonged to someone around, and just strayed away. She wanted to jump onto the horse's back, and gallop away to never-never land.

The horse looked healthy and strong. Until now, it never occurred to her that she hadn't seen any animals showing signs of infection. Most likely the infected hadn't been attacking animals, but if they had, so far, the virus hadn't affected them.

To prevent the horse from stepping on the highway, she flipped on the siren, wanting to scare it away. Sure enough, the startled horse galloped away. Shortly afterward, she turned the siren off, careful not to attract any attention. After all, it was a hot car.

Roughly three hours later, she was a distance of approximately one mile from an off-ramp exit for Abilene, Texas. She'd driven the whole time without stopping, not even for gas. It was not a wise thing to do. An unhappy look crossed her face, because she could tell from the chugging sound of the engine, that it was out of gas. The tank was definitely empty. The needle on the gas gauge pointed to E.

Slowing down, she steered to the shoulder, and threw the Charger in park. After dusting off her hands, she climbed out of the car. Back on her feet, looking around, she had no idea where she might be, and it didn't matter to her. She was grateful to be alive, and a little closer to New Mexico.

She began walking toward the exit of the highway. As darkness closed in, she knew she had to find shelter fast. The only place in sight was a liquor store up ahead on Farm to Market Road 1750. RICHBURN LIQUORS, said the sign out front. If she had her way, she would be spending the night in a store, her first time doing that. As far as she was concerned, she was so tired that it really didn't matter where she slept.

Her eyes looked all around as she walked toward it. After opening the glass door, she didn't see anyone, living or dead. The store reeked of wine and spirits. From the doorway, she leaned forward and took a fast peek at the mess of broken bottles on the floor. As far as she could see, there was no one stirring about, so she stepped inside.

Jenna walked to the back and stopped at a door marked STOREROOM. The door had a latch with an open padlock hanging from it. She removed the padlock, put it on the floor, and opened the door. With her right hand, she felt the wall for a light switch. When she finally found it, she flipped it and light from the overhead fixture flooded the small supply room.

Without further ado, she entered and did a quick search of the place. There was a wool blanket on the floor by a bathroom. Across the room and up against the wall was a two-door metal utility cabinet. She opened the cabinet doors expecting to see shelves of cleaning supplies, but found a red-and-black checkered flannel shirt. By this point, she was satisfied that the place was empty.

She hurried back to the front of the store and locked the door. Then she pushed a small metal shelf from the room against the door. It was better to be safe than dead, more specifically, walking dead. And who could blame her for being afraid? She couldn't help but feel edgy. Though she was safe, a lingering fear hovered in her mind.

The store had little left on its shelves, but she managed to find a few things. She took two small bags of potato chips, three bags of M&Ms, two packs of Dentyne gum, and three bottles of Pepsi from the cooler. It wasn't much but it would sustain her for a little while. She stuffed the whole lot of it inside her backpack. Before returning to the back storeroom, she killed the light.

Once inside the room, she closed the door behind her and set her backpack down. She was very aware of the fact that she'd been wearing the same shirt for the past three days. Now, she had a chance to change it. She pulled the flannel shirt from the cabinet, disappeared into the bathroom, and closed the door. Looking in the bathroom mirror above the sink, she saw blood smeared on her clothes. It had come from the seat of the Dodge Charger. All she wanted to do was to get the smell of death from her clothes, and off her skin. She washed up and cleaned some of the blood off her clothes. Removing her jacket, she took off her shirt, discarding it on the floor and put on the flannel shirt.

When she came in the storeroom, all she wanted to do was eat and sleep. She laid out the blanket on the floor, sat on it, and began pigging out. After eating all she was able, she lay on the blanket with her backpack for a pillow, and used her jacket for a cover. She thought that for some time to come, sleep would be her only relief from the living nightmare of the walking dead. On that note, her eyes began to flutter shut. She yawned and was soon asleep.

Chapter 25

AT AROUND four o'clock, James Stebbins was sitting at his desk reviewing blood test data on the computer. He looked at the clock on the wall and suddenly remembered how Julie had told him to stop by the lab and provide his impressions and so forth on results from tests on the infected brain tissue. She was preparing a report for upper management, meaning Dan Saunders and Thomas Bauer.

Stebbins closed out a file on his computer. He rubbed his eyes, yawned, got up from his desk. and headed straight for the laboratory. And there she was, hunched over a microscope, exactly where he expected to find her after opening the door. She was preoccupied with what she was looking at and didn't appear to notice him.

A short moment passed before she detected him, raised her head, and slid her wheel-based chair to the table.

"Hello, Julie," he said.

"Thank you for coming, James."

"How can I be of service?" he asked, wondering what, if anything, she had discovered.

She filled him in on the last couple of hours she'd spent dissecting brain tissue from the infected. In great detail, she described to him her hypothesis about the virus derived from studying brain cells. And that her opinions were from a virology point of view. Perhaps when he looked at the tissue and cell samples, he might reach similar or other conclusions.

"I can show you what I have so far," she told him.

"I'm game. Let's see it," he said as he put on gloves.

"Look at this," she said, handing him a petri dish, "and tell me what you think."

He looked at it intently, scrutinized it carefully, and then he pointed to the counter on the left. "Will you hand me that magnifying glass?"

"Sure James," she nodded, picked it up, handed it to him for a closer look, and said, "I have three more to show you."

He grabbed a petri dish, among those she'd just put on the table, and then another, studying each one with the magnifying glass and a frown. His impression was that they were quite out of the ordinary for brain tissue, rather toxic.

"Gee, these are fascinating. Two of the samples are darker than the others," he said.

"Could this be due to exposure to a strain of rabies?" she asked.

"Yeah, that's actually what I was thinking. It might be possible, because rabies causes inflammation of the brain and spinal cord. The organisms responsible for this type of infection are variable and rooted in the brain. I can see the similarities."

"So, you can't say without a doubt. Or can you?"

"I would like to place them under the microscope for a better look," he said, and placed the petri dish on the table.

"I made slides from the samples. I'll put one in the microscope for you to examine."

"Just a minute," he said, as he leaned into the eyepiece.

First, he shifted the microscope, then increased its magnification, refocusing on the cells. He peered into the eyepiece for a second time. Looking at the cells, he tried to determine if an animal borne illness was present.

Not a moment sooner, he lifted his head and said, "You're right. I'm convinced that it is a mutation of the rabies virus. My impression is that the rabies virus changed the way it delivers its genes to human cells in a pathogenic manner becoming a genetically altered virus evolved to carry human DNA."

"James, I see where you're going with this, and I feel the same about it. Although there are still many more tests to do. Thank you," she said with a sense of relief.

"Anytime Julie, anytime. Glad I could help. Is there any other assistance I can offer?"

She nodded her head. "If anything springs to mind, I'll find you."

"All right, then. I'm heading out. Until tomorrow," he said, before he walked out the door.

While it was fresh on her mind, she wanted another look, and went right back at it. She grabbed a petri dish, opened it, tore off a piece of the brain tissue with a tong-like instrument, and placed it on a glass slab and stuck it under the microscope. Looking into the eyepiece, she moved the glass slab beneath the thick lens of the microscope. Then she tossed the glass slab into the biohazard waste disposal can.

Her eyes were getting weary. For too long, she had been studying brain cells. She leaned back in her chair, rested her eyes for a minute, and let her mind wander. Her thoughts led to how humans had always found a way to survive. She was hopeful and believed the solution was somewhere out there for her to find, yet to be discovered.

Thinking it was not all doom and gloom, reminded her of the 2012 prophecy that the world as we knew it would cease to exist. The theory, in part, stemmed from the ancient Maya civilization. And she would be correct in saying that the virus was changing the world. Was the epidemic a coincidence? The thought came into her head, that it didn't feel like one.

She knew that the Maya believed there was a link between disease outbreaks and solar cycles resulting in the downfall of civilizations. Solar activity was the magnetic cycles of the Sun which produce sunspots and solar flares. The first carrier of the disease might have had a vitamin D deficiency, which left his or her body vulnerable to the rabies infection when exposed during increased solar activity. This quite plausible theory fascinated her.

Her thoughts came back to the here and now. At this stage in the day, there was nothing more she could do. She yanked her lab coat off and hung it on the back of her chair. A long night's sleep was what the doctor would order for herself, and then start all over again the next day. Sluggishly, she left the laboratory.

Chapter 26

THE MOMENT I woke up, I wasn't sure where I was. I had dreamt that everything was again as it had been, as it should be, before the outbreak of the virus. A girl could fantasize, right? But I was a long way from believing that I had spent the last few days sleeping. In the back of my mind, I knew I was dreaming while I was dreaming.

The events of the past days came flooding back as Mim's purring echoed in my head, snapping me back to reality. The little fur ball was sleeping peacefully next to me, her head on my left shoulder. It was the cutest sight.

While gazing at the ceiling fan whirring overhead, I thought about what to do next. After sleeping till ten this morning, I had no real plans for the day at all. It was Christmas Eve and I took today and tomorrow off. My position at the BDC was not crucial to developing the antivirus. Therefore, I decided I might as well have a day or two off, preferably two.

I sat up, and hopped out of bed wearing a pink V-neck T-shirt and burgundy pajama bottoms purchased from Victoria's Secret. The outfit was my early Christmas gift to myself. I couldn't wait to put it on. Besides, I had nothing else to wear because I hadn't had a chance to do the laundry. Now that I thought of it, I just walked by the plastic laundry basket, overflowing with unwashed clothes on my way toward my bedroom closet. Like I needed to be reminded. And that was the moment I knew what I would do the first thing after breakfast.

"So, what am I going to wear today?" I asked myself.

I put clothes against my body, looking at myself in the mirror hanging from the inside of the closet door. It was difficult for me to decide because I didn't like anything. I went through every piece of clothing I had dumped on the bed that I had taken from the dresser drawers. Mim didn't do anything, she just lay there sleeping. So cute, I thought of her like family. After searching here and there, I had put together an outfit consisting of a KISS T-shirt with three-quarter sleeves, jean shorts and my trusty sneakers. Perhaps it was not the most glamorous outfit, but there was no need to dress up to go to the laundry room. But most important to me was that it was comfortable and easy to put on.

When I came out of the bathroom from a quick shower with a towel around my body, I saw that Mim was wide awake and sitting on the bed. She was all bright-eyed and bushy-tailed, literally, so to speak, watching me dress and playful.

After getting dressed, I quickly went into the kitchen and prepared myself coffee, toast, and grabbed a yogurt from the refrigerator. Mim came running in, probably because of the aroma of the coffee. The smell reminded her of food. So, I put food and water in her bowl.

After breakfast, I put the last of the litter in Mim's box. Before the end of the day, I definitely needed to make a shopping run at Lotte Market, the store on the eighth floor of the facility. Resembling a 7-Eleven, it was fully stocked at all times. Despite the circumstances as they were, the helicopters were delivering food and supplies to the facility regularly.

Later, in the laundry room, I was sitting alone on the floor next to the dryer. The thing that really stuck in my mind was that I should document my experiences of this epidemic. So, I came to the decision to create a video diary. While waiting for my clothes to dry, I was writing my thoughts in my, *The Hunger Games* movie composition book, preparing what I was going to say on camera. Jenna and I both liked *The Hunger Games*. It was probably the most popular film of the year.

Just then I saw a light flickering from the corner of the ceiling. It was the little green light on the video surveillance camera. Apparently, I was being watched. Welcome to BDC's headquarters at Dulce, New Mexico, where there were video cameras everywhere, recording everything.

This seemed as good a time as any for me to go on camera. I placed the digital camcorder on the table. It might be amateurish, but I didn't mind the sound of the dryer in the background. It wasn't too loud and should go unnoticed. The bright lighting was good and would make all the difference. After pushing the Record button, I spoke directly to the camera.

My name is Hannah Winter. I work for Biogenetics & Disease Control, a medical research company located below the city of Dulce, New Mexico. I am the head of information technology. Whatever you know about me will come from these files, my video journal. Everything I say will be true.

This is where it started for me, December 21, 2012, I watched a television news report about a virus reanimating dead cells that has brought the dead back to life. This deadly disease was greeted with confusion and disbelief by everyone, including me. Police and emergency medical responders were overwhelmed by the number of dead victims returning to life, multiplying at a fast rate.

Violent zombie attacks are on the news every day now. Currently, the infection is spreading rapidly throughout the northern hemisphere. It is being called the worst environmental disaster in history.

This is what I can tell you about it, my recap of the news stories, what I have come to call the virus of the never dead. The virus attacks nerve cells, reaches the spinal column, travels to the brain and spreads all through the body. The neuroinflammation causes dementia and hallucinations. The infected person slips into a coma and dies. In a short time, the virus reanimates dead cells returning the person to life in a zombie state with a desire for blood.

My sister Jenna is out there somewhere. I anxiously wait for her to get here. And, that's all I have for today, the day before Christmas. Signing off.

I stopped the recording, rewound it, and watched it on the LCD view screen of the camcorder. A thought hit me. What if the virus spread farther across the continent? What if we at the BDC were the only ones left? No one to watch these recordings. How much longer could I do this? I was just full of drama and not in the holiday spirit.

The dryer made a beeping sound when it had finished its cycle. I gathered all my clothes and left the room. As I carried the bulging laundry bag and camcorder with me toward the elevator, I caught a reflection on the vending machine. It scared me for a second there, till I realized it was my own. Maybe that was what all this talk of the zombies did to me. I put coins in the machine and got a bottle of Fuze tea.

When I came in the apartment, I placed the camcorder on a bookshelf. Mim came running, meowing to greet me, followed me into the bedroom, and watched me drop the laundry bag. It looked like I wasn't the only one interested in having lunch. Hopefully, I could whip something up for us, because guess who hadn't been to the store yet?

Chapter 27

KEN LANGTRY hadn't had a break since God knows when. If he didn't drink something soon, he would pass out from dehydration. When he got off the elevator on the eighth floor, he walked up to the soda machine down the hall from Lotte Market. He slid coins into the slot, pressed the button labeled "Diet Coke," and a bottle dropped down. He grabbed it, wandered around the machine, and leaned against the wall. Twisting the top off the bottle, he tilted his head slightly and took a gulp.

With a quiet moment to himself, he was worried about so many things. But the thing that troubled him the most was the whereabouts of his daughter Dana. Was there anything worse than losing a child? This was something he was still trying to come to terms with. For far too long, he'd pushed the thought out of his mind.

He felt that he had let her down and hated it. And that he

abandoned her by not going out to find her. If he just knew where she was, he could rescue her. But where would he start? The phone lines were down, and even when they were working, he couldn't reach her.

Twice he'd talked to her on the phone about a plan to extract her from El Paso. He told her to wait on the roof of her apartment building. It had been arranged between the pilot and himself, for the BDC to send a helicopter to pick her up. It all sounded so easy when he talked about it, even though somewhere deep inside, it scared him thinking about how many ways it could go wrong.

What he didn't know at the time was that the city of El Paso was hit the hardest by the epidemic. Being so close to Mexico, the infection spread like a tidal wave, to drown them all. And his daughter Dana was right in the heart of it.

His last conversation with her ran through his mind over and over again.

"Dana, I'm going to be there to pick you up with a chopper. Don't you worry no more about it."

"I love you dad," she said, sounding like she was crying.

"Do as I tell you. Stay on that roof and wait for my call."

"I'm not sure. Yes, I hear you. I will."

He would never forget the last words he said to her. "I love you, too, sweetheart. See you soon."

She didn't sound right to him, possibly scared, and talking slightly incoherent. Now that he had time to think about it, he suspected that she might have been infected. Either she didn't know, or didn't want to tell him that she was. Now, it didn't matter. Probably he would never know for certain.

Looking back on that most awful day he was set to retrieve his daughter, Chris Nevins was in the helicopter waiting for him. Then he was handed a memorandum from James Stebbins to attend a meeting in the conference room. Still, he had planned to get a recap of the meeting from Dan Saunders, upon his return with his daughter. It wasn't until, a minute or two later, when his cell phone buzzed in his pocket. It was Saunders. He shouldn't have answered the call.

"Listen Ken, we all have people that we are worried about. You have an obligation to the people you work for. I'm not telling you not to go get your daughter, because you can, and you have the right to do so. But I'd like you to wait till after the meeting," he told him sternly.

The phone was silent on Langtry's end for about twenty seconds. His brow wrinkled in thought. Then, he made a tough decision that he really didn't want to make.

"Sure, Dan. I'll be there. But just for an hour. Then I'm out of there," Langtry said in a weary voice.

"That's all I am asking," Saunders said and hung up.

Right after the call, he dialed his daughter's cell phone number, listened to the ringing, and then to her recorded voice directing him to leave a message. He didn't say anything and simply dialed her cell phone again. This time he left a message.

"Dana, it's your father. I'll be leaving soon. I'm a little delayed. I will arrive about one hour later than expected. Please call me."

At the time, it didn't occur to him that something might be wrong until she never called him back. Because of the widespread outbreak in El Paso, he didn't want to risk a trip up there, not knowing for sure where she was. And he had to consider the possibility that she might be infected.

He tossed the empty bottle into the trash can, inhaled deeply. Then he exhaled, feeling gripped suddenly by the fear that he'd lost his daughter for good. He was almost shaking when he pressed the button for the elevator. When the elevator arrived, he rode down to the security level.

But such emotions subsided when he came out of the elevator. He moved down the hallway toward the security room, a darkened room that contained a bank of twenty CCTV screens set into the wall in banks of four above a desk. Each screen showed a different feed from security cameras. Lucas Rawlett, an expert at surveillance, was seated behind the desk, watching the wall of monitors connected to security cameras located at various strategic points around the facility, inside and outside. This was where Langtry spent most of his time.

Upon entering, he noticed that Lucas was gazing at the monitor with a view of the laundry room where Hannah Winter was sitting next to a dryer. As was his personality, Langtry would have been annoyed, but being that it was Christmas Eve, he just ignored it.

Lucas pressed some keys on a keyboard, then turned his head over his shoulder. "How goes it, Ken?"

"Fine. Thanks for asking. Anything to report?"

Lucas pushed his hair out of his eyes. "No, sir."

Langtry turned right and walked to his office. He dropped

a walkie-talkie on his desk and looked over a clipboard. Then he left his office and went to stand by Lucas.

Immersed in deep thought, he looked at the monitors. One screen caught his attention. It showed a swarm of zombies clinging at the gate. He reached across the desk and tapped a button on the keyboard while Lucas sat quietly. The CCTV camera zoomed out and panned over to one side.

Langtry moved himself closer to the screen. "What do you think? There has to be more than seventy of them."

"I think you are right Ken. And it's only been a few days."

"Yes, surprisingly so."

"Can't we do something about it?"

"I'll be making a decision about it very soon. I'll tell you about it once I clear it with Dan Saunders."

"Okay, Ken."

Without another word, Langtry pressed another button and the camera zoomed in for a close-up of the vicious and foul zombies. A couple of them had their mouths open, displaying a combination of saliva and blood. After a good long look, he tapped a button, bringing the camera back to its original position.

So far, he had been able to keep the facility safe. But for how much longer? He had to do something soon. Executing them and leaving them to rot on the ground would contaminate the area for months releasing airborne bacteria, causing a hazardous environment, which would increase the risk of infection.

Another minute went by as he thought about it some more.

And then another couple of minutes passed before he walked back into his office. He opened the small refrigerator behind his desk and pulled out a bottle of water, twisted off the top, and took a couple of gulps. Putting the top back on the bottle, he carried it with him, grabbed his walkie-talkie from his desk, and exited his office.

Before leaving the room, he glanced at the screens and back at Lucas.

"Carry on," he said, and walked out of the room.

Chapter 28

JUST BEFORE NOON, Jenna woke up hungry. For some time, she lay awake thinking about the dream that she had last night. The most prominent image in her thoughts was that she had been sitting on the floor of her dorm room at St. Mary's University when a middle-aged man in a Domino's Pizza hat came through the door carrying a large pizza. Considering her present situation, she wouldn't be having a hot meal anytime soon. In times like this, so many things she'd taken for granted filled her mind.

With a degree of effort, she got up from the thin blanket on the floor. She stretched out her arms and shook her legs to loosen them up. Still, she could think of worse things than a few stiff muscles.

She quickly went to the bathroom. Checking herself in the mirror, she flipped a long strand of light-brown hair out of her face and tucked it behind her ear before returning to the storeroom where she gathered her belongings into her backpack.

As quietly as she could, she slipped back into the store. For more than a minute or two, she looked out the glass door. Seemingly satisfied that no zombie was around, she moved the small metal shelf out of the way, and walked out the door. To make certain that no zombie was in the vicinity, she circled the building and didn't see any of them.

Leaning against the wall of the liquor store, she searched her backpack for a bag of potato chips to snack on. Once she found it, she ripped it open and shoved a few chips in her mouth. She couldn't be any hungrier. It wasn't pizza, and it was a poor substitute for a good meal, but it was far better than nothing. Searching her bag again, she grabbed a Pepsi, opened it, lifted the bottle up, and took a few chugs.

Not long after eating, she desperately wanted to smoke. She took a pack of Marlboro Lights from the breast pocket of her khaki jacket, shook one out, slipped the cigarette between her lips, and lit it. With great deliberation, she took long drags from her cigarette, making every puff count, blowing clouds of cigarette smoke over her shoulder.

As she took one last pull on the cigarette, she heard a gunshot go off. She put the cigarette out on the bottom of her sneaker. Then, the sound of hooting and hollering reached her ears, which came from the direction of the front of the store.

She ran in a crouch position and took cover at the side wall, out of sight. A silver Nissan Titan pickup truck came roaring by. From her hiding spot, she saw two Hispanic men standing in the truck bed holding double barreled shotguns. The rowdy men were laughing and high-fiving one another, most likely drunk. She had no intention of hitching a ride with them. Watching them drive off, she smiled happily to herself as she left, walking in the opposite direction.

While walking down Clark Road, she squinted against the sun's rays rising from the east into her eyes. There was a mixture of sun and clouds across the sky and the temperature felt like high sixties. As she made a right on Bacacita Farms Road, the sun fell behind the clouds.

More than a half hour had passed since she began walking and she reached Maple Street with an urge to go to the bathroom. She was twenty yards from a Sunoco gas station and convenience store off of Industrial Blvd. Hurrying to the store, she neglected to check her surroundings before opening the door. From the state she was in, she didn't care if any zombie was following her. Yet, not sensing movement inside, she headed to the bathroom in the back of the store.

Once inside, she was upset by the foul smell of stale urine. She wasn't surprised because most gas station bathrooms were stinky and dirty. But she would have to push it out of her mind, since she wouldn't be there too long.

When she was done, she washed up in the sink. When she opened the door a split second later, she took a deep breath of air and let it out with a sigh. She was glad to be out of the smelly bathroom.

While in the store, she looked around for anything of interest, perusing the shelves. All she could take was a bag of pretzels and three bottles of Sierra Mist from the cooler.

She loaded it all into her backpack and stepped outside, fairly confident that no one was about. But that wasn't the case.

As she started to walk away, she sensed a presence. She was sure it was nearby because she smelled rotting flesh, hovering around her like a cloud. She hated to think she was capable of recognizing it.

She turned around, and low and behold, there was a zombie directly ahead of her, moving in the opposite direction. His back was toward her and she felt he didn't hear her; maybe didn't even know she was there. From what she could gather, he was headed elsewhere.

If it was not for his slow movements and faint groans, she would have thought he was a normal living person. She couldn't see his face, only that he was tall with no visible injuries or scars on his body. But she knew he was a zombie, even if he didn't look like a zombie.

"Thank God, he didn't see me," she spoke softly to herself.

Practically on her tiptoes, she quietly walked around the curve of the building. She believed she'd gone unnoticed by the infected man. Yet, when she peeked around the side of the building, the zombie wasn't where she expected him to be. Maybe it was too soon to call, but she didn't see him anywhere. Until she heard feet tramping toward her.

She swung around. The zombie was headed straight toward her. He came out of nowhere and had gotten behind her. Her bad, he had seen her after all.

She thought he looked relatively normal, except for the deathly white skin, the sunken, bloodshot eyes and the occasional growl he made. As the zombie came closer to her, his growls turned into blood-curdling sounds, sending a shiver of fear down her spine.

When she went to move past him, he blocked her path. She was fairly certain he outweighed her by fifty pounds. Terror filled her eyes as he was directly in front of her, fast approaching. Her fists were clenched because she had to fight.

The moment he raised an arm against her, grabbing her sleeve, she pulled her sleeve from his hand and punched the zombie in the solar plexus, pushing him backwards, and for a moment he was thrown off balance. Still, he lunged at her trying for her sleeve again. But when his hand rose, she stepped away, punching him in the windpipe. Hard. The zombie staggered, dropping to his knees, choking, resembling a living human reaction.

She ran toward the road. But despite her best efforts, she couldn't resist turning her head to look at the zombie. She wanted to make sure she wasn't being followed. She wasn't. When she saw the zombie still struggling to stand up, she breathed out a sigh.

She didn't know she had it in her to be so cunning and chocked it up to some Aikido, which she had learned from her former boyfriend Kevin, who had a black belt in the martial art. By chance, she happened to remember the moves he had taught her. She'd never physically hit anyone in her life, until now, because her survival required it.

And for that brief moment, she felt like she was in *The Hunger Games*. She thought it was a fantastic movie. One could easily compare her situation to the story. But she didn't like living that way. Hoping she would never have to fight like that again, she reminded herself she was lucky this time. She had to be extra careful, and always pay attention to her surroundings because she had no intention of being caught off guard like that again.

Chapter 29

IF SOMEBODY didn't do something about the virus, in a matter of time, every living thing on the planet would die from it. That was what Julie Mehta kept thinking as she sat behind her desk. She wasn't going to give up that easily. Already she was typing data into the fields on the computer screen. It was Christmas Eve, but that didn't stop her, because she was Hindu and would not celebrate Christmas. This morning she almost didn't bother to unwrap the gift from James, but curiosity got the best of her. The exquisitely cut lead crystal vase was now on her office bookshelf. She hadn't had the time to look for him and planned to thank him later.

Somewhat later, she clicked open a folder with files about rabies. She had to investigate it. Little did she know that she would spend the next hour combing through a large pool of data on the subject.

The file about the rabies vaccine, which was prepared through the chemical inactivation of virions grown in human diploid tissue culture cells, interested her the most. She grabbed a pen and notepad from her desk and wrote down a few details.

By now she was concerned about her experiment from yesterday. She wanted to check on the mouse she had injected with the infected blood. She rose from her chair and left the office, heading for the laboratory.

After scrubbing her hands with soap and water and putting on gloves, she put on a hazmat suit. At the steel door, she entered the five-digit code into the keypad, the door opened, and the doctor walked in. Upon observation, the mouse was dead, not moving any limb. It wasn't reanimated.

She lowered herself into a chair and turned on the computer. After a minute, she located a time-coded video. She rewound the footage until she saw the time the mouse had a fit and died. According to the time displayed at the bottom of the video, death had occurred thirty-seven minutes, and fourteen seconds after she injected it. She tapped on the computer keys, rewound the video a few frames, and hit Play. Looking for clues, something she might have missed, she watched it again, but nothing stood out. She confirmed the timestamp of the experiment, logged the results, then shut down the computer.

The conclusion she drew was that animals die if infected and death was almost instantaneously. Animals were not brought back to life. And she was glad the mouse died. The last thing she needed was a zombie mouse in her laboratory.

Despite being separated from the other mice, in its own cage, she couldn't handle it without risking infection to herself. She would have had to ask Ken Langtry to destroy it. Knowing Ken, the way she did, he would have torched it, messing up the lab. This was something she wanted to avoid. Later in the day she would have to tell him to remove the dead mouse from its cage and dispose of it properly.

The results did not surprise her. Because she knew there were many diseases deadly to humans, which had no effect on animals, and vice versa. Such as a strain of salmonella found to be lethal in rats was harmless to humans. Looking at it on a global scale, she was relieved that the animals hadn't succumbed to the virus. She believed that the zombie plague only affected homosapiens. Therefore, there was a chance the spread of the virus could be contained.

She stood up and walked over to a stainless-steel tank. After opening the latch, she took the vial of infected blood used on the mouse and placed a timestamp on it, for when the mouse died. She sealed the tank, walked over to a refrigerator, and put the vial inside. Then she left the room.

After removing her hazmat suit, she walked through the lab. At that instant, James Stebbins came into the room carrying a case of vacutainers. From the look on her face, he could tell she was pleased as he handed it to her. She raised one eyebrow, and gave a look of curiosity.

"Hello, hello! Here they are. I brought them as fast as I could. And I printed out a summary of the results of the blood tests and placed it on your desk. I also logged the results into the computer," he said with a tone of satisfaction.

Placing the case on the table, she said, "Thank you. I've been looking forward to seeing this."

"By the way, how's your day going?"

"Oh, it's going along, I suppose. Thanks for asking. And you? Is everything all right, James?"

"As well as can be expected."

"Oh, James, I almost forgot to mention. I want to thank you for the Christmas present. It was very thoughtful of you giving me that crystal vase. It makes a very nice addition to my office decor."

"You're quite welcome."

"I didn't get you anything. I'm sorry. It's just that I've been so busy, you know."

"You don't have to apologize. I completely understand."

"James, you are too kind," she said, endearingly.

"Are you taking a lunch break today?" he asked in a quick change of subject.

"Yes. I was going to pick up something at the cafeteria and bring it to my desk."

"I was thinking of doing the same thing. After I leave here, I'm going straight there."

"It'll be another two hours for me. First, I'm going to look at these vials."

"Maybe someday, when we are not so busy, we can grab a bite to eat together."

"James, that would be really nice. Maybe soon."

"Hopefully sooner than later," he said with a grin.

"Sure," she said, her thoughts preoccupied now.

"Okay, well, after I grab some lunch, I'll be at my desk if you need anything," he said, turned around and left.

She wasn't in the right frame of mind for socializing. Most of all, she thought he was nice but hardly her type. He was a good assistant, but that was that. If only she had remembered to tell him about the dead mouse that needed disposing of.

Feeling tense, she took a breath to relax. She shouldn't read too much into it nor overreact. Maybe he was just being friendly. Anyhow, there wasn't time to think of it now.

She opened the clasp on the box and looked at the six vacutainers inside. Each tube was labeled by date and test type. She took a vacutainer from the case, twisted the top open, and put a swab inside. Afterward, she gently rolled the swab along the flat surface of a rectangular slide and placed a piece of glass over it. Peering into the microscope, she patiently adjusted the focus to examine the slide.

When after a long while her neck started to stiffen, she lifted her head from the microscope. She went to the refrigerator, took out four petri dishes, and placed them on the table, and closed the refrigerator door. After carefully looking at each petri dish, she placed them back on the table. Then she went back to the microscope.

Chapter 30

THE WEST WIND came just as the sun had broken through the remnant clouds. The cool breeze comforted Jenna, who had been walking for almost two miles. As she reached the corner of Sycamore Street, she heard gunshots coming from South 2nd Street.

She darted toward a nearby alleyway. When she heard the sound of growling zombies and shotguns pumping out lead, she placed herself against a wall of a building, too scared to move an inch.

When it was quiet again, she began walking slowly backwards. She edged slowly along the side of the building until she reached the rear. That was where she stole a quick look around the corner of the building. At first glance she saw police officers with their pistols and shotguns drawn, shooting at a ton of zombies. She had come to the wrong place at the wrong time. If the infected didn't get her, a stray bullet might.

She turned to look down the alley and saw there wasn't anywhere for her to hide. And she needed to find a way around the neighborhood before dark, which would be in less than two hours.

The idea to hide on a rooftop came to her when she saw a fire escape pull-down ladder in the alley. The wrought-iron ladder was a little more than four feet off the ground. Just as she ran to grab the ladder, she thought she heard a low moan. She shot a look in the direction of the noise. There were two zombies walking into the alley. She watched over her shoulder as they came closer to her.

Knowing there wasn't a second to lose, she got a firm grip on the ladder with both hands on the rungs, tugging it down to her level. She began climbing the ladder, one rung at a time, holding tightly, all the way to the stairs. As fast as she was able, she bolted up the stairs until she reached a ladder leading to the roof. Ascending the ladder, in her state of panic, she wasn't even worried about falling.

From the roof she looked down to check if the zombies were following her, but they didn't try to climb the ladder. Instead of looking up, the zombies were stumbling around, moving further down the alley. She took in a deep breath and let it out slowly.

After looking around, she crept to the other side of the roof and peeked over the ledge. There were bodies of dead zombies everywhere on the ground. But there were considerably more zombies walking from every direction, surrounding more than a handful of police officers. But the officers had plenty of firepower to fight them off. Seven young deputies were wearing armored vests and holding twelve-gauge shotguns, butts against their cheeks, pulling triggers and blowing holes in heads of zombies. Two other officers were cutting down every zombie moving toward them, with a barrage of bullets from their pistols. A dozen automatic rifles, along with many boxes of ammunition lay on the floor of the trunk that was opened of a Ford Interceptor police vehicle.

A burly officer tossed a stun grenade into a crowd of infected. The zombies scattered. At the same time, two officers, positioned behind a Dodge Charger opened fire.

Her eyes took in everything. She was worried when an officer's pistol ran out of bullets. In his late forties with salt-and-pepper hair and broad shoulders, he moved back, away from the incoming zombies. He was almost out of harm's way, when a greasy-haired zombie appeared and grabbed him from behind. He lifted his left hand to push her away and she bit into his fingers and held on like a bulldog. While he struggled to get his fingers out of her mouth, a deputy pointed his Mossberg 500 tactical shotgun at the zombie's head. With his right hand, the struggling officer pistol-whipped the side of her head. The zombie released its grip, and blood trickled from its mouth as it staggered back.

"I've got you covered. Go back," the deputy said to him as he pressed the barrel of his shotgun against the zombie's forehead, blasted her head off, and then pointed his shotgun at the zombies moving toward them.

The officer was in shock, staring at his wounds. The middle and pinkie fingers were severed above the knuckle and gushing blood. He tore off a piece of his shirt and bandaged up his hand.

"I can't believe this. I don't want to be one of those things. I can't turn into that," he cried bitterly.

His emotions were out of whack. He walked to the trunk of the Interceptor SUV and grabbed a box of bullets. He placed three bullets in the semiautomatic pistol's magazine and the box fell to the ground. Then he put the 9-millimeter Glock against his temple.

"God, please forgive me," he cried again.

The deputy saw what he was doing and yelled, "No, Mark don't do it."

Too late. Mark pulled the trigger launching a bullet into his skull. His body fell to the ground.

Jenna was brought to tears watching another life lost to the epidemic. Overwhelmed, she turned away trying to get the images out of her head. She walked over to the other side of the rooftop and peered down at the alley filled with only six zombies walking around. In the distance, about a mile away, she saw a large, old Catholic church next to a school with a playground surrounded by a chain link fence. She wanted to check it out before dusk fell.

The sound of gunshots and loud voices calling out continued on the other side. She walked to the door in the middle of the roof and hesitated there, wondering if it was locked or not. Shoulders trembling, she eased closer to the door and listened for any sounds, but heard nothing.

"Do it. Just do it," she spoke out softly.

She slowly twisted the knob, opened the door just a crack, looked down a stairwell, then shut the door. She couldn't risk going that way, to that side of the building. All she could do now was wait. To worsen the situation, it would be dark soon. Frustrated, she slid against the door to the ground as if to block the door if anyone tried to open it. She would be ready if they did.

In the time she was there, the gunshots went on and on, driving her crazy. It was so nerve-racking. She couldn't hear herself think. Hoping a cool drink would help, she uncapped a bottle of Sierra Mist and drank half of it down.

Close to an hour later, the gunfire slowed to scattered bursts and then stopped completely. She stood up, brushed herself off, wiping gravel and dust from her body. She looked over the side of the roof and saw that there was an array of dead zombies lying on the ground. There were two police officers loading their pistols and one officer sitting down sipping from a can of Pepsi. Three officers with shovels were digging a ditch. Two other officers were lifting the bodies of dead zombies and piling them for burial in the ditch. Looking at the corpses, she felt that it was an upside-down world she was living in.

Jenna walked to the edge of the roof where the fire escape was. She looked down into an empty alley. Carefully, she climbed down the ladder, quietly walked down the stairs, climbed down the other ladder, and dropped her feet to the ground.

Back in the alley, she looked out from behind a wall. Nothing moved. She snuck around the side of the building and set off toward the church.

Chapter 31

NEARING six o'clock, with daylight almost gone, Jenna held the metal handle of the gate around the St. Ambrose Catholic Church on Jeanette Street. She rotated the knob into her curled right palm until a dissonant click sounded. Then she opened the gate, stepped through, and closed it behind her.

Discovering the front doors of the church locked, she pranced around to the left side of the church wondering how she was going to get inside. She had just about given up trying to find a way in when she saw a side door that was ajar. Praying not to find zombies, she closed her eyes for a minute, then opened the door wider and poked her head inside, seeing that no one was there.

She took it as a sign that she was meant to enter the quiet candlelit church that was large enough to hold some two hundred worshippers. The sweet smell of incense drifted through the air as she strolled down the aisle of the church.

She gazed up at the stained-glass windows, the murals near the Italian marble altar, then down at the large gold-plated crucifix on the wall behind the altar.

Kneeling down beside an organ, before the flickering of the votive candles in front of the altar, she closed her eyes and for the first time in a long time, she prayed directly to Jesus. She said a few prayers for her sister, who she'd been thinking about lately. And she prayed that her father was now with Jesus and the angels in heaven. After shedding a few tears, she wiped her eyes and said a prayer for herself. Despite the strangeness of the situation and everything that had happened in the past three days, she believed that God had a plan for us all.

As she rose to stand, a white-haired man dressed in a black suit and a white clerical collar entered the vestibule, closing the door behind him. He spotted her and came toward her.

"Can I help you?" he asked.

Jenna hesitated, not sure what to say, then spoke frantically, "I was hoping I could sleep here for the night. I have nowhere else to go. During my stay I would be willing to help out in the church."

Seeing that she was serious, he waited about fifteen seconds before asking, "How did you get in here?"

She pointed to the side door. "Through that door."

He shook his head, looking displeased. "Our custodian Jesse sometimes forgets to lock the door when he returns from taking out the trash. Still, it could've been worse. I suppose I should be grateful you're not infected."

She was still waiting for him to answer her. Standing there solemnly staring at him, she was so afraid he might ask her to leave.

Another moment passed between them before he spoke again, "Being that it's Christmas Eve and all, I have to say yes. We have room for you for the night."

In a matter of seconds, her face went from worried to relaxed. She felt so much better.

"Monsignor Anthony Lucca. Welcome," he said with a smile, holding out his hand to her.

She smiled back, shook his hand with enthusiasm. "Jenna Winter. Thank you, Monsignor. It's so good to meet you."

"It must be God's will that you are here."

He told her that she was fortunate that the door was open. The church was open to the public every day in the week. Now with the epidemic, the church was locked up tight.

"Have you had anything to eat?" the Monsignor asked.

"Not really, if you want to know the truth."

"Come with me. Dinner is being served downstairs."

"Thanks. That's very kind of you."

He walked toward a hallway, ushered her through the door into the lobby, then down a flight of stairs to the basement level. At the bottom of the stairs, was a hallway leading to a dining room of a soup kitchen. When they reached the entrance door of the dining room, the Monsignor saw a man standing near the supply closet next to the women's bathroom at the end of the hallway. It was Jesse.

"Excuse me, Jenna, but I must have a word with Jesse. You

go on ahead to the dining room. Irene Polgar, our pastoral associate, will come and take you to your room later."

"Sure, Monsignor. Thank you again," she said.

"Jesse, the side door is unlocked," the Monsignor called out as he walked toward him.

Jenna stepped into the dining room. At one of the six long wooden tables, sat a young black couple and their eight-year-old son eating dinner. They didn't look poor at all, rather they looked like a typical suburban family, displaced, due to the circumstance.

As she drew close to the counter, the lady serving introduced herself, "Welcome, I am Sister Mary Ann. How are you this evening?"

"'I'm all right, and yourself?"

"'Well enough, I suppose. If you need anything, you come and find me," she said, passing her a plate.

"Thanks, Sister Mary Ann. It was nice meeting you. My name is Jenna."

Sister Mary Ann had a flat nose, small blue eyes, and a habit on her head. She gave her a plastic cup of apple juice to accompany her tuna salad sandwich, potato salad, and peaches.

She sat down at a table and ate quietly. Again, she was saved. She was grateful to God to have a place to sleep and food to eat. When she quickly finished her sandwich, Sister Mary Ann noticed and brought over a tuna salad sandwich on a paper plate.

"Would you like another?" the sister offered kindly.

"Yes, please."

Sister Mary Ann put the plate down on the table and walked back into the kitchen. She was gracious, looking after people, making sure that everyone was well fed. Her kindness made Jenna forget the horrors she'd survived.

She finished eating and stood up, taking her paper plate, plastic utensils, and used napkins to the trash can. When a conversation disturbed the quiet of the room, she stopped beside a table and looked at the African American family.

"Can I have some ice cream?" the little boy asked his mother.

"No, Patrick, you know there's no ice cream here. Now come, let's get you cleaned up," the mother said, and pulled him toward the hallway that led to the bathroom, while the father stayed seated at the table.

"Jenna, the Monsignor told me that you're spending the night. Welcome, my name is Irene Polgar," said the woman, startling Jenna.

She hadn't heard anyone walk over, but there Irene was, standing next to her. "Oh, hello. Happy to make your acquaintance."

Irene, an attractive, big-boned, middle-aged woman with cropped chestnut brown hair with a little curl in the end, continued, "If you're ready, come with me. I'll take you to your room."

"Yes, I am."

She followed Irene into the hallway, where she headed toward the staircase, talking as she went. "There are some things you should know. This is a holy place of worship that serves those in need. Our small rooms are being used to shelter us. There are three staff members, the Monsignor, and a family of three, staying here."

They climbed the flight of stairs to the top floor, where Irene stopped, turned down a hallway, still talking. "We have an eight-month supply of food, candles, and other goods. So, we're all praying this horrible nightmare will end soon."

As she made her way through a candlelit hallway, she turned her head to look at Jenna behind her. At last, she stopped by a small room and opened the wooden door. Inside the room there was a cot bed against the wall, a dresser with a lamp on top, and a wooden crucifix hanging on the wall above the bed's head, but no windows.

"There are fresh linens on the bed. You can take a shower in the bathroom down the hallway to the right. And you can stay here as long as you need to."

"Thanks. It's just for tonight."

"You let me know if there's anything you need. I am usually in the kitchen or in the Monsignor's office," Irene said lastly, as she left the room and closed the door behind her.

She emptied her backpack on the bed, grabbing one bottle of Sierra Mist and one bag of pretzels, which she placed on the dresser. Sitting on the edge of the bed, rummaging through her belongings, she became aware of the stillness of the building. A sense of peace fell over her, something she was lacking and longing for. She grabbed a towel, went to the bathroom, and took a long shower.

Chapter 32

TUESDAY, DECEMBER 25, Christmas day, I had woken up at ten, lying there thinking about how come I didn't get any presents. No one had wished me a Merry Christmas. I wasn't upset about it. Just analyzing it. It was half past eleven, when I finally climbed out of bed.

Despite what was going on, my mood was up-beat for the holiday. As soon as I stepped into the cafeteria, I saw Ken Langtry. He looked pretty worried, probably focused on his work. I thought to say something to him about Christmas. Not that it made a difference, but it never hurts to be nice.

As he passed me to leave the room, carrying coffee in a tall paper cup, he said, "Excuse me."

"Merry Christmas Ken," I said, trying to spread a little holiday cheer around.

"That's very thoughtful of you," he replied, with an expression that clearly displayed a lack of interest.

"Don't mention it."

"If you will excuse me, I really must go outside to check things."

In any case, I didn't speak to Ken much. Today was one of those rare occasions. And I couldn't blame him for feeling the way he did. Everyone in the company had someone they knew who might be dead already, assuming he wasn't any exception. It was something we all had in common.

After a quick meal, I went back to my apartment and did a little tidying up. I vacuumed and took out the garbage. At least that gave me time to think about what I was going to do today because I hadn't made any plans for anything. But I soon came up with something.

Since I couldn't go outside, I planned popcorn and a movie here. I rummaged through my DVD collection on the bookshelf next to the TV and selected *Rise of the Planet of the Apes*. Never mind that I had seen it twice before. The plot about a scientist that created a drug to cure Alzheimer's disease fascinated me. He used the experimental drug on his pet chimpanzee, which made it intelligent and humanlike.

With research and controlled experiments, the BDC attempted to develop drugs to combat Alzheimer's disease. Almost all of this data was exclusive to BDC personnel only, and classified. But all of that work was now on hold.

I set a bowl of popcorn on the end table next to the sofa. After putting the disc in the DVD player, I scooted over on the sofa to make room for the cat, who desperately needed a time-out. Awhile ago she started to get jumpy and wild-eyed because of the rattling noise of the vacuum cleaner. Since then, she'd been running between the living room and the bedroom.

I called to her and she galloped into the room. She looked a bit antsy, her eyes still a little wild. Then she meowed, looking at me as if to ask: "What is it?"

"Come here. You look like you could use a break," I said and reached for Mim.

I placed her in my lap and stroked a hand over her fur to calm her. She was still tense. Minutes later, she was purring. Before I pushed the Play button to start the movie, I laid her down beside me.

"Here we are. Just the two of us," I said to Mim.

For the rest of the afternoon, I ate popcorn and watched the movie. It wasn't long before Mim's head was bobbing and she was out, soundly napping for the duration of the movie. Not a peep out of her. No snoring, either.

After putting the DVD away, I was depressed and felt I shouldn't have watched it. The part about the virus spreading across the globe, upset me. All things considered, I needed something to take my mind off the situation.

It was so quiet all I could hear was the refrigerator humming. Mim was still sleeping, curled up mere inches from me.

The bag full of Christmas presents in the corner caught my eye. They were for my father and my sister. Maybe Jenna would come, and if she did, I kept them there, so that she would have something to open.

Where could she be? Being seven years older than her, in

many ways, we were different. Most people wouldn't be able to tell that we were sisters. Two inches taller than me, with lighter, longer hair, and a chest with a cup size smaller than me, Jenna could be glamorous while I tended to be plain and hardly wore makeup. On Friday nights, she often partied with the cool kids while I had my nose in a book describing code and algorithms. She could be funny too, when she wanted to be. As for myself, sometimes I acted pessimistic.

The details of that phone call came rushing back, the panic in her voice. I almost started crying.

"Merry Christmas Jenna. I miss you," I said to myself.

Trying not to wake her, I pet the cat a little as I thought about something I could do until dinner time. With the film still fresh in my mind, I couldn't stop worrying about the global pandemic. Best I put all the thoughts swirling in my head to video.

I carried the camcorder into the living room and put it down on the end table by the sofa. After tapping Record, I sat comfortably and spoke.

Today is Christmas and I'm sorry to report there have been no changes since yesterday. There's still no cure. The epidemic rages on.

I'm safe underground at the BDC, often worrying, while my sister Jenna, pray that she's still alive, I can only imagine is out there, somewhere, fighting for her life. From time to time, I can't help but let my thoughts wander back to her, wondering if she is dead. Still, every day, I hope for news from security that Jenna is at the gate and trying to get in. I have to believe that she's alive. At least, I can feel it in my gut.

In a period of four days, so many people have become infected. The TV news reported that in cities such as El Paso, the epidemic worsened. People evacuated by any means of transportation available to them, such as private jets, anyway, to survive.

Many of the scientists here are trying to develop a vaccine to prevent people from contracting the disease. I'm hoping for a solution soon, but there is no telling how long it may take. And there's no telling what will happen if a remedy isn't found soon.

The truth is, I don't know how much time I have. I'm creating this video diary because I want to leave behind something about the events that are taking place, some sort of explanation. In the event that I wind up infected and no one else is left in the facility, one day in the future, the footage will be found. Perhaps I'm being melodramatic, feeling lonely on Christmas, but I must get it all off my chest. Signing off.

I put away the camcorder and sat back down on the sofa. It wasn't a good feeling to be alone. Excluding the cat. I thought about the Christmas that might have been, celebrating with my father and sister in Albuquerque. The outbreak stopped that from happening. Not only did the virus take life, but it changed life too. Then I was missing my father, almost upset again. But it didn't last, because the cat woke up in time for dinner.

Chapter 33

LATE THAT MORNING, Jenna awoke feeling more relaxed than she had in days. She'd slept all night without waking in the early hours of the morning as she usually did. Slowly rising from the bed, she wasn't in any hurry to get up, today being Christmas and all.

After a visit to the bathroom, she proceeded to slip into the same old clothes, a red-and-black flannel shirt and black jeans, but left her jacket on the bed. She left the room and walked down the candlelit hallway to the church, where she knelt before the altar, whispering a brief prayer. Again, her prayers were for her sister Hannah and that her father rest in peace. Before the epidemic, she hadn't prayed much in her life since the days before her mother's death. But she was praying now.

Leaving the church, she entered the lobby and proceeded down the stairs for lunch, which was served daily at 12:00 p.m.

according to Irene who mentioned it the day before.

When she came into the dining room, the Monsignor, who, coincidentally, arrived at the same time as her, followed behind her.

He stood beside her at the kitchen counter and said, "Good morning Jenna and Merry Christmas."

"Merry Christmas to you too."

Sister Mary Ann gave Jenna and the Monsignor a Merry Christmas greeting before handing them plates. The Christmas menu was beef stew, baked beans, and corn.

Monsignor Lucca sat down at the same table with her. The table was covered in a red tablecloth and decorated with Santa Claus napkins and green plastic utensils. There was a tray of chocolate chip cookies on the table.

Immediately, the Monsignor brought his hands together in prayer and closed his eyes. "May the Lord have mercy on us. Please bless us, dear Lord and these thy gifts, which of thy goodness, we are about to partake of. For Jesus Christ's sake. Amen."

"Amen," said everyone in the room.

Then he said somewhat seriously, "There's something I've been meaning to ask you, Jenna. Are you of the Catholic faith?"

"Yes. I was raised Catholic by my parents. They thought it was important I learn about religion at a young age. I don't attend Mass every Sunday, but I attend occasionally," she replied somewhat enthusiastically.

"That's quite common at your age. I'm very impressed that you practice the faith at all."

He took a couple of bites of stew, then continued, "Is everything all right with your room?"

"Yes, it's very comfortable, thank you."

"I'm glad to know that. Well, I have to rush off now. And Jenna, you are welcome to stay just as long as you like," the Monsignor said, stood up, and left the dining room.

Quietly, she ate her meal, admiring all the Christmas decorations around her. And in the next moment, she spotted Irene, in a red sweater with a reindeer on it, walking into the room.

Irene walked up to her table and offered her a wide smile. "Merry Christmas."

"Merry Christmas to you as well."

"I trust that all is well with you?"

"Yes, it is. Thank you."

She noticed Jenna was wearing the same clothes from yesterday. Irene believed that she didn't have any additional clothing, and felt obliged to make a Christmas offering.

"We don't have any gifts, but if you would like a change of clothes, the church has a room with donated clothing ranging from like new to slightly worn. You can take your pick of the lot. And I can take you there now, if you like."

Pleased with the offer, Jenna scarfed down the rest of a cookie in one big bite. "Yes, I would like that. Thanks."

"Pardon me for a moment. Just you wait right there," Irene said, before turning and heading quickly to the kitchen.

She started writing on a clipboard while Jenna tossed her

paper plate and used plastic utensils in a garbage can at the end of one of the long tables. At about the same time, Irene put the clipboard away and stepped back into the dining room. Then she gestured for Jenna to follow her.

She opened the door, walked to the stairway and started to ascend with Jenna trailing close behind. When Irene reached the top of the stairs, she turned left into the hallway that led to a locked door.

Irene fished in her jeans pocket for the key, let herself inside the clothing donation room, and flicked on the light switch. Jenna stepped in after her and stood in the doorway, her face shocked by the disarray. There were nine black garbage bags overflowing with clothes shoved into a corner. There was a table piled with clothes and lots of clothes on the floor. In the center of the room were four free-standing clothing racks.

"You take as much time as necessary. I'll return in a little while to see how you're doing," Irene said as she walked out the door.

Jenna stepped over to the table stacked with blue jeans, selected a pair her size and took them. Rummaging through a bag, she found three pairs of clean panties, though she preferred thong underwear to full coverage. Digging through another bag, she took a thin gray sweater, blue flannel shirt, tiny flower-print T-shirt, dark blue sweatpants, linen pants, and two pairs of dark blue socks.

While waiting for Irene to return, she began tidying up the room. She set about folding the clothes on the table and smiled, thinking about how comfortable she felt, stress free, and most importantly, safe because the church was locked up tight. And the people were very nice to her. She wanted to stay another week or two, maybe even more.

Just seconds later, Irene came into the room, startling her from her pondering. "Did you find some things to wear?"

"Yes, I did. And there is something I want to ask you."

"Sure, Jenna. Go right ahead."

"It's just that I've been thinking a lot about what the Monsignor told me. Can I stay here for a few weeks?"

"You can be here for as long as you want. You seem like such a nice girl. It's not safe for you to be outside while those things are out there."

"Thanks so much. Maybe the zombies will be gone by the time I leave."

"Let's hope for all of our sake."

"And there's something else, too."

"Sure. What is it?"

"Irene, I'd like to help out by organizing the clothes in this room."

She looked at Jenna with surprise. "Well, bless your heart. I would be grateful if you did, although there is no obligation to do so. Between the four of us, there is so much to do each day, and only twenty-four hours in which to do it."

"I don't mind helping out during my stay. It's not like I have anything else to do. I'll start first thing tomorrow."

"Then I'll leave the door unlocked so you can come and go."

"Great."

"Are you ready to go?"

"Sure. Let me get my things."

Jenna grabbed the clothes and followed her out the door and toward the stairway. Irene headed down the stairs, and Jenna went up the stairs.

Chapter 34

AFTER BREAKFAST in the cafeteria, I had planned to go to the office, but there was plenty of time to swing by the security room. There would be no more procrastinating. I wanted to see them with my own eyes. How else could I prove to myself that this was all real?

Upon exiting the elevator, I saw that the door of the security room was open. I carefully stuck my head through the open doorway, trying not to disturb Lucas, who was manning the monitors.

He felt my presence immediately and looked over his shoulder at me. "What can I do for you Hannah?"

"Hello Lucas. Is Ken around?"

"No, he's not. Is there something I can help you with?"

"Yes. I came here so I could see the infected outside the gate on the monitors."

"Just make it quick because only security personnel are allowed in here."

I stepped into the room and stood next to Lucas, staring intently at the monitors. One camera was zoomed in on the never dead's awful faces. They behaved like rabid animals and looked like rotting corpses. Seeing them with my own eyes was the most gruesome sight I had ever witnessed — much more so than the bits of news footage I had seen earlier.

"They act on impulse. What do you think of them?" asked Lucas, pointing to a computer screen.

"I think they're terrifying."

"I forgot to mention. Did you have a nice Christmas?"

"Why thanks Lucas. It wasn't that eventful. I just watched a movie and cleaned up my place. And yourself?"

"I was working here with Ken."

"I saw Ken in the cafeteria and wished him a Merry Christmas but he wasn't in a holiday mood."

Lucas lowered his voice and added discreetly, "Perhaps I can explain. Ken may have lost his daughter. That's why he's been so distant. The day the news came about the viral outbreak, he was planning to get his daughter out of El Paso, Texas. He had everything set up to go. Then he was handed a memorandum requesting him to attend a meeting in the conference room. He tried his daughter's cell phone to tell her he would arrive later than expected, but she didn't pickup. She's now officially missing. And Ken still hasn't recovered from that."

"Well, that does explain it. I was at that meeting. Ken

showed up ten minutes late, looking very stressed out. But I didn't think anything of it because everyone in the conference room looked that way at the time."

"Hannah, I'd appreciate it if you could keep this under wraps, just between us. I learned all of this from Chris Nevins, one of our helicopter pilots. I don't want to get him in trouble."

"Don't worry, I will. Thanks for letting me watch. I've seen enough zombies than I cared too in my entire life."

"No problem."

"I appreciate all you're doing," I said, at the doorway.

"And remember: mum's the word," he said with a laugh.

"You can count on it," I said as I left.

I walked toward the elevator thinking about what just happened with Lucas. Something was there, a moment between us that had passed. Though it was the first time I had ever talked to him. Seeing him up close, Lucas was very good looking, but somehow I'd missed it before.

Riding in the elevator to my floor, I thought of my sister and the future looked dark again. Hearing about Ken's daughter missing, made me think of Jenna, still no word and sometimes feared dead. The thought made my heart beat a little faster. As the elevator's doors opened, I had to get her out of my head because I was on my way to work. Right now, I really wanted to be at work and put some space between myself and my thoughts about my sister.

I went into my office and sat down at my desk, glad to be back after two days off. I was determined to be productive. After booting up the computer, I updated all of the passwords, cleaned up the hard drive, and ran a system diagnostic check.

While the computer was being subject to diagnostic tests, I made a fresh pot of coffee in the break room and poured myself a mug. On the way back to my office, I took a detour passing Vivian's office, nodding to her as I went by. It was good to know she was here.

As I set the coffee mug on top of my desk, I wondered if there were any new developments, and if there was something I could do. It seemed like a good time for me to check on Julie and stretch my legs some more.

I peeked into her office and saw that she was sitting behind her desk, typing on her computer. The moment she sensed me by the door, she stopped typing.

"Hello, Hannah," she said, looking up briefly.

"I was just passing by and thought I would say hi."

"Okay," she said with a lack of interest.

Perhaps the timing wasn't right to ask her a bunch of questions. Saying nothing more, I headed to my office, but not before, almost bumping into James Stebbins as he came from the lab. I watched him rush in and out of Julie's office then head back to the lab. I could only pray to God that they would discover something soon.

Back at my desk again, I accessed the main computer system, trying to get some work done before lunch time. Just as I gulped down my coffee as quickly as I could before it had a chance to get cold, a male lab technician came into my office carrying an armful of files.

"These are the ones you were asking about," he said, put some files on my desk, and left.

It had been three weeks since I requested this. I looked down at the files, picked one up, flipped it open, removed papers from inside, and put the file back on my desk. After entering data into the computer grid, I reached to the right and scooped up another folder from the desk.

Before going to lunch, I took three of the folders and walked over to Vivian's office. When I stepped into her office, I found her there, laboring over the computer, working on some computer program.

"Sorry to interrupt. I'll just leave these here for your review," I said, placing the folders on her desk.

"Okay, Hannah," she said with barely a glance in my direction.

Some hours after lunch, I was engrossed in a database. Before I knew it, I found that five o'clock, quitting time, had crept up on me.

After shutting down the computer, I grabbed my handbag and left in a different direction, through Julie's department. Maybe I just needed a change of scenery. Walking past her office, I saw her sitting at her desk talking to James Stebbins.

"You still haven't shown me anything," she said to him wearily, then looked in my direction, "and the day is almost over. Will you excuse me for a minute?"

"Yes, go on," he said.

She turned toward me and called out, "Hannah, are you leaving for the day?"

"Well, yes, I am," I said, stopped outside of her office door.

"Can you come by my office tomorrow morning, say,

around ten? I could really use your help accessing a database. I have the permission to access the data from where the data is accessed regularly, but I'm denied access to it. It's semi-urgent," she said, waving me off, and not waiting for an answer.

She turned her face back to Stebbins. "You told me it would be ready this morning. I need to see what you have got so far."

"I'd be happy to. See you tomorrow," I said softly and walked to the elevator.

It was just one of those kinds of days. Maybe I should have taken another day off. Was it me or was I the only one who knew that it was the day after Christmas? Actually, I just remembered, Lucas knew. So maybe things weren't so dreary after all.

Chapter 35

ON THE FOLLOWING MONDAY MORNING, the last day of the year, I was performing the final software updates and configuring the firewall on Julie's computer. I spent much of last week doing everything else on her computer. Specifically, last Thursday when I checked her computer, the problems were obvious, especially for a tech-head like myself. The software used to access a database, otherwise known as a database management system, was an older version than the one currently used, and it wasn't working properly. Additionally, her computer did not have updated antivirus software. It was a wonder that she was able to get any work done. For all her intelligence, computers were not her strong point.

She wasn't inconvenienced by me sitting in her chair at all because she spent most of her workday in the lab. To make things convenient for me, she kept her password to access her computer written down on a sticky note stuck to her desk drawer. Something only she and I knew about.

Software updates needed to be done on a regular basis. It was something she had neglected to do and failed to bring it to my attention earlier. My only conclusion was that she didn't come to me sooner because she hadn't picked up on it before. With her latest research on this virus, she needed to access information from the database. A week ago, she noticed something was wrong when she couldn't access a particular piece of data.

I ran the diagnostic software installed on the hard drive. Lastly, I tapped a few keys to restart the computer. I clicked the mouse a few times, paused for a second, then the main screen came up.

"That should do it," I said, after seeing that Julie's computer was running smoothly.

I left her office heading for the laboratory to inform her that there was nothing more I needed to do. When I cracked the door of the lab wide enough to poke my head through, I didn't see her. Instead I saw James Stebbins sitting on a small stool at his bench with two labeled test tubes in front of him.

"Excuse me, James, I'm sorry to disturb you. I am looking for Julie. Is she around?"

"She stepped away to the restroom. Do you want me to give her a message?" he asked, not looking up, completely immersed in his work.

"Yes. I'd be grateful if you could tell her the computer is ready. I'm heading for lunch now."

"Sure will."

"Great. See you later."

An hour or so later, I returned from the cafeteria to sit at my desk and worked on modifications to a database. Then, it occurred to me that Julie might not be the only one in the company with a computer that needed maintenance, software installation and updates. Computers would have to be checked. This would be a job for Vivian.

I walked over to Vivian's office, and saw that she was generating reports. Standing in the doorway, I watched her working. She looked very concentrated. Sensing me there, her hands stopped on her keyboard but she didn't look up at me until I spoke.

"Knock knock."

"Yes, Hannah?" she asked.

"I would like you to run a check on all the computers operated by the employees. Find out exactly what software is installed on their systems. And document any technical issues you encounter," I told her.

"Be glad to. It will be just another minute," she said, tapping on the keyboard and generating a printout.

"You need to take the lead on this. I will need a report detailing the results, exactly what each computer needs."

"I got you," she said looking up from the printout.

I explained further that after I received the report, the maintenance would be started. And I understood that this would take time, maybe a month or weeks.

She grabbed a stack of folders, scribbled down some notes, and then looked toward me. "On it."

"There's no rush," I emphasized.

"I appreciate the assignment. And Hannah, let's do lunch this week."

I was pleased with my apprentice's enthusiasm and tossed her a smile. "Yeah, we can talk about our New Year's resolutions."

"That may take a long time," she said, leaving the room.

Back in my office, I glanced at the clock on the wall: 4:41 p.m. I was alone in the department. Vivian was performing the assignment I had doled out to her. But I wasn't complaining because I thought sometimes, it was better when I was alone. Or so I told myself.

But I spoke too soon. The loneliness crept in and I started to feel claustrophobic, utterly closed in and cut off from the world. Even I felt like walls were closing in on me.

So, I took a quick breath in and exhaled slowly, tilted my head back, and fixed my eyes to the ceiling, before forcing my thoughts elsewhere. For the first time, I noticed the low ceilings and dull fluorescent lighting.

For too long I had been underground, no windows and no natural light. I didn't know how long it would take until I would be able to go outside again. My mind was reeling, thinking I would never again smell flowers and fresh cut grass. I couldn't stand it anymore and had to escape the office for some fresh air.

I shut the computer off and clutched hold of my handbag. Then I discreetly departed, hoping no one would see me like this. Nobody needed to know about my anxiety.

I walked down the hall and locked myself in the bathroom next to the elevators. Looking at myself in the mirror, it was no surprise to find a worried face looking back at me. After a deep breath or two, I turned on the sink and splashed some warm water on my face which soothed my skin and nerves.

After such a busy day, I was trying not to stress about whether or not Jenna was alive. Right now, I couldn't bear to think that she could already be dead. Deep down inside me, I sensed, she might still be alive.

Feeling more relaxed, I went back out into the hallway. I stepped into the elevator and hit 4. Retiring to my apartment, I thought about going to bed early. No New Year's office party this year. And I was actually looking forward to spending the final hours of 2012 uneventfully.

Chapter 36

ABOUT TWO WEEKS LATER, Jenna had turned the room of donated clothing into what resembled a trendy clothing shop. After all, she was a fashion enthusiast. Besides modeling, she hoped to manage her own boutique, for which she would design the clothes. That was her long-term goal. But with the way things were going, her dreams were on hold.

For days, she had separated and neatly folded shirts and pants. Dresses, suit jackets, and coats hung on the racks. Areas were designated for men's, women's, boys' and girls' clothing. After finding three paintings in a closet, she hung them on the wall. She had even swept and mopped the floor, dusted the walls and felt a sense of pride in her work. Giving something back was really important to her. And she knew Irene would be pleased. It was the least she could do for all the kindness Irene,

Sister Mary Ann and Monsignor Lucca had shown her.

This morning she was taking out armfuls of clothes from the large, dark wood wardrobe a few feet from the wall. When the wardrobe was empty, she dusted it with a cloth. With some effort, she pushed it against the wall. For the next half hour, she put all of the clothes neatly back in the shallow drawers.

It was already the middle of January, and she was comfortable in her new environment. Maybe too comfortable. She was safe, but for how long? She knew it was only a matter of time when she would have to leave.

Putting aside her thoughts, she reminded herself that she was staying put for now. She needed all the strength she could get. So, the next time she encountered the walking dead she would be stronger and more courageous. Far from New Mexico, there was still a long road ahead of her, and there was no telling what to expect.

As she closed the doors of the wardrobe, she heard footsteps in the hallway. It was Irene.

"Oh, Jenna, it looks great in here. You've really turned this place around," she said as soon as she stepped through the door.

Jenna flashed a smile at her. "Tada! I'm actually finished."

"How are you doing today?"

"I'm very well, actually," Jenna said with a pleasant smile.

"How about I make you some coffee?" Irene asked, motioning for her to follow her.

"I'd love some. Lead the way."

"Sister Mary Ann left a plate of sugar cookies on the kitchen counter if you want some," she said, as she switched off the light and locked the door behind them.

"Yes, that will be great."

Irene chattered away as they walked down the hallway. "I've been meaning to ask you something, Jenna."

"Sure. What is it?"

"What's it like outside, if you don't mind me asking?" she asked, turned the corner, and started to walk down the stairs.

"What do you mean, you don't know?"

"I haven't been out of the building since the virus outbreak started. That day in December when it came on so suddenly, Monsignor Lucca told me not to go outside."

"It's awful, Irene. You don't know the half of it. I've seen many infected people die."

"For God's sake," Irene said, gasped, and shook her head.

"Have you watched the television news?"

"No, I haven't. There is no television on the premises."

"How did Monsignor Lucca find out what was going on?"

"The Monsignor listens to the morning news on the radio. A few days before Christmas, I was awoken by a knock at my door. I pulled on a bathrobe and rushed to the door. The Monsignor told me the shocking news. I immediately dialed my sister Lauren who told me it was true. She lives in the Baja area of California and was all right. She planned to stay at home, hiding from the infected, as the news reporters suggested."

"Thank God the Monsignor heard it on the radio and you didn't go outside," Jenna said, walking in the hallway toward the door that led to the dining room.

"The Monsignor is the heart and soul of St. Ambrose. He is one of the most selfless men I have ever known. We're all grateful to him for keeping this place running. He could have closed it down, but he wanted the church to be open to help those in need," Irene said respectfully.

Crossing through the dining room, Jenna followed her to the kitchen. Irene opened cabinets until she found a can of ground coffee, filters, two stoneware mugs and placed it all on the counter. She poured coffee grinds in the filter and put it in the coffee maker. Reaching for the water faucet, she filled the coffee pot with cold water, poured the water into the coffee maker, and pushed a button to start it up. Then she grabbed the plate of cookies and removed the plastic covering.

"Help yourself to as many as you want," she said, gesturing to the cookies.

"Why thank you, Irene," she said as she grabbed a cookie off the plate.

"I'm glad you are here with us," Irene said, and paused briefly, staring at the coffee maker.

"That's such a nice thing to say. I'm glad to be here with you all."

"You're very lucky to have survived out there on your own. If you don't mind me asking, do you have any family?"

Jenna shrugged. "My sister is safe. She works for Biogenetics & Disease Control in New Mexico. I talked to her just before the telephone lines went out. But my father died in a plane crash."

Irene thought about it a few moments as she poured

coffee into two mugs, before saying, "I'm sorry about your father. Tell me. How do you like your coffee?"

"Some of that powdered creamer and three spoonfuls of sugar, if you please," Jenna said, pointing to the bottle on the counter.

"I like my coffee the same way."

Irene added sugar and powdered coffee creamer into her own mug and into Jenna's mug. She handed Jenna the mug and they chatted a little while longer.

When Irene finished her coffee, she took a quick look at her watch. "Jenna, I've enjoyed our time together, but I must go now. I have to meet Sister Mary Ann for a quick inventory of the pantry. If you want another cup of coffee, please feel free to help yourself from the pot. I'll see you later."

Jenna thanked her as she left the kitchen. She took her empty mug and carried it to the coffee pot to refill it. Irene was carrying on about something while walking through the dining room. From what she could hear, she sounded frustrated about the lack of supplies.

Irene added, "We are conserving water and using toilet paper sparingly. But one must make sacrifices and take what precautions are necessary."

She helped herself to another sugar cookie, blissfully chomping on it, and sipped some of the coffee. The stillness of the room was interrupted by the sudden sound of keys jangling. Startled, she turned around and found Jesse, the handyman, approaching her with a smile.

"Good day, Miss."

"Hello."

"I'm looking for Irene. Have you seen her today?"

"She just left, actually. She went to help Sister Mary Ann with the pantry."

"Thanks for letting me know. You are the one, aren't you?" he mentioned, staring at Jenna a bit.

"I don't know what you mean."

"The one who came in through the side door, I had left unlocked some time ago."

"Oh, yes, right. Yes, that's me."

"I'm glad I left it open. Though I didn't mean to do it on purpose. In any case, if anything comes up where I can help, please let me know."

"That's so nice of you," she said, smiled, and took a sip of coffee.

The tall, skinny man with brown close-cropped hair fading at the temples and gray beady eyes turned around and left the kitchen. A set of keys hanging on his belt outside of his brown pants jangled as they bounced off his thigh as he walked down the hallway.

Jenna carried her coffee into the dining room. She sat down at a table and slowly drank the rest of her coffee.

Chapter 37

KEN LANGTRY stood by the gate where more than ninety-five zombies were gathered. It had gotten out of hand. There were too many for his taste.

"What a freaking nightmare," he said to himself, looking at the horde of them with disgust.

He had a plan, a course of action, to start 2013 off right. It was actually a New Year's resolution to eliminate all of them. Being late January, it was time to do something.

He gave a hand signal to Lucas, and he, along with three-armed security guards took a position at the gate, weapons ready. They lifted their rifles, pointing them at the zombies.

"Hold positions," Langtry said into his walkie-talkie.

Two tractors drove forward and stopped near the gate. Six men came forward and stood beside the idling tractors. They were all wearing white hazmat suits with masks covering their mouths and noses, rubber gloves, and protective shoes.

Langtry shouted the order. "Fire!"

The security guards pulled the triggers on their assault rifles simultaneously and watched their bullets tear holes in the heads of the zombies. For nearly ten minutes, they were firing their rifles, until every standing zombie was lying dead on the ground. Lucas was the first to lower his rifle. Stewart Cabrera and the other two men followed a few seconds later.

Lucas glanced down at the ground, saw that nothing moved, and yelled, "Clear."

Langtry lifted his radio and spoke, "Open the gate. Get those tractors moving. Ninety minutes is all you've got. The clock is ticking."

The lock clicked and the gate opened. One tractor drove up and pulled up next to the dead zombies on the ground. The tractor behind went forward about fifty feet and stopped to dig a hole of sufficient size and depth for burial. The operator used the front-end loader to scoop dirt from the ground. He raised the loader slightly, tilting it to drop the dirt load. During which time, Langtry watched him through his binoculars.

Twenty-five minutes later, a voice was heard on the radio, "Ken, we're done here. The grave is ready."

"Send in the cleanup crew," Langtry said into the walkie-talkie.

The men in the hazmat suits began lifting bodies and loading them onto the forklifts of the two tractors. Each tractor could carry eight corpses. The tractors hauled the bodies and dumped them into the hole. Each tractor would have to make six trips to completely rid the area of corpses.

With anticipation, Langtry watched every move. He looked at his watch and discovered more than thirty minutes had passed. Time was running out.

He keyed his radio. "Thirty minutes. That's all we've got left. There are twenty-four bodies on the ground. What's the hold up?"

Then Langtry waited and waited, but no answer came.

When the tractors pulled up alongside the corpses, he screamed into his radio, "Load twelve bodies on each. Do it right now!"

"Ken, the load on the forklifts attached to the rear of the tractors will force them to move slower," the voice on the other end said.

It was Lucas.

Langtry stiffened, and raised his voice a few notches. "Must I say 'That's an order'?"

"But sir…"

He stopped him from going on, then spoke again more calmly, but with just as much force. "One more thing. You're not in charge here. Lucas, you're a soldier, nothing more."

Lucas was staring at him, trying to get his mind around it. Why had he talked to him like that? He wasn't angry, just in a deep thought as he took off to inspect the grave. As soon as he was far enough from Langtry, he mimicked his voice and said to himself, "You are a soldier, nothing more."

Langtry watched the tractors loaded with dead zombies. A cloud of thin, black smoke from the exhaust pipes trailed the tractors as their engines roared under strain.

"Ken, nearly twenty infected are stumbling around and staggering toward you, about a half a mile away," the helicopter pilot said.

The gunshots and commotion had attracted a horde of zombies. Langtry could see the helicopter in the air, one mile west of the facility. Lifting his binoculars, he saw the tractors had just arrived at the grave.

He lowered his binoculars and called on his radio. "We've got to wrap this up. Unload those corpses and start filling that hole. I want everyone back inside. Only the tractor operators are allowed beyond the gate."

He signaled Stewart forward to join the two guards standing near the gate, ready for the zombies.

"Stand by with your weapons," Langtry demanded, then called out, "Lucas! Get over here fast!"

"Yes, Ken," Lucas said, running to him.

"Stay over there by the gate and keep the perimeter secure. That's an order."

"Understood. I'm already on it."

"Don't let them get through the gate!" Langtry cried out.

It just made sense that Langtry would try to avoid fatalities. In another fifteen minutes, there would be a swarm of zombies at the gate. And still the tractors were pouring dirt in the grave of the dead zombies.

Langtry turned his head away and spoke into his walkie-talkie, "How much longer is it going to take to fill the hole?"

"Ken, the tractors' operators need five minutes," the voice came back.

He lifted his radio and said, "Stand by to close the gate. The second the tractors drive through; I want the gate locked and barred. On my word."

"Heads up. Ken, you've got company. About twenty infected are now less than a quarter of a mile away," said the helicopter pilot.

"Is there anything else I should know?" he questioned, ironically.

After a long pause, a voice was heard on the radio, "Ken, the tractors are coming in."

Another pause. The tractors drove through.

With a sigh of relief. Langtry turned, grabbed his radio and said, "Lock it down."

The gate closed. No shots were fired. He was content with yet another successful mission because of everyone's hard work.

He picked up the walkie-talkie and said, "Well done. And best of all, no casualties."

Langtry dismissed everyone back to their duties. As he was leaving, he saw twenty or so zombies stagger themselves at the gate, already camping out, hissing and moaning. He dreaded the thought of having to carry out the same mission. But it was too early to worry about it, even if it was terrible. For now, his work was done.

Chapter 38

"YOU ACT AS IF you have no idea, how hard we've been working. Though I know you are aware that James and I are doing everything we can to discover a way to stop the virus. So, what, exactly, are you implying here, Dan?" Julie exclaimed, raising her brow as she crossed her arms.

"Spare me the details. I know quite well," Dan Saunders said.

She was seated in a chair across from Saunders' desk. This meeting had taken a turn she hadn't anticipated. It was a bitter feud. She was hanging in there, but it was hard to keep her temper, listening to his nitpicking criticism about all the time spent so far trying to develop a vaccine against the virus.

Sandra Ortiz was sitting at her desk catching up on her paperwork. She could hear every word of their conversation. For a brief couple of seconds, she squeezed her eyes shut, trying to block it out. She sympathized with Dr. Mehta, who she knew was doing her best. But she had come to expect it, having such a temperamental boss.

"You sound as if you have doubts about my ability to solve this. Do you have someone more qualified in mind, someone who is not a woman?" she asked him and released a long sigh of frustration.

He spoke again. "Don't you think you're being a bit dramatic? You misread my meaning. Julie, I believe you are quite capable. I am not bringing anyone else in, because there is no one else."

She unfolded her arms across her chest and spoke in a polite voice. "Your wife and daughter are both here. Safe and well. Did you ever stop to think about the rest of us? My family is in India. I'm completely in the dark about what is going on with them. Or even if they are alive or dead. I want to find a cure for this virus, a lot more than you do."

After a tense moment, he gave her a stern glare. For maybe a minute, the two of them were locked in a stare war.

"Come on, Sandra. Where's my coffee?" he shouted through the open door.

He still hadn't addressed what she had said to him. While thinking about it, he knotted his hands in his lap, not knowing what he was supposed to say. He was so deep in thought that he didn't see Sandra approach with his coffee, placing it on his desk.

"Dan, here's your coffee. Something else I can get you?" she asked, trying to keep her voice pleasant.

"Not at this time. Thank you, Sandra," he said in a more civilized tone.

"I'll be at my desk if you need anything," she said, then excused herself and left the room.

Saunders picked up his coffee and took a swallow. When he flashed a quick glance of assessment at Julie over the rim, he could feel a pulse pounding in his temple. He had considered what she said, and was going to speak again choosing his words carefully.

Julie could tell he was a little on edge. It was obvious that she had touched a raw nerve. She sat in silence, staring at the framed diploma from University of California, Berkeley on the wall and the two framed photographs of his wife and daughter on a shelf by the desk. Then she met his eyes, waiting for him to say something.

"Julie, come on, you know that's not fair. There is a lot of talk going around here that is not right. None of the company's resources were used for the retrieval of my wife and daughter. That day in December when this all started, my wife jumped into her car, with my daughter in the passenger seat, and drove here from our home in Chama. They got here in less than thirty minutes. If they had lived somewhere else, I would have probably lost them," Saunders said with much conviction in his voice.

"I understand, Dan. All of us are under a lot of pressure," she said, still speaking in a polite voice.

"February is just around the corner. The longer this drags on, the worse it is for us. I'm worried for all of us. Think about the supplies coming in. That is, until the supplies run out. I want you to see the whole picture, how we're in this together," he interrupted as if she had not spoken.

After all, he did have something of a point. And he could tell by the look on her face that she was thinking the same thing. How long would the supplies last? She was worried too but there was only so much she could do.

"I'm doing the best I can," she said.

"That's all anyone can ask or expect of you. I want to help you any way that I can. Let's not forget we're all on the same side here."

There was nothing more he could tell her. Now he folded his arms and just stared at her for a minute, hoping that her good sense would overcome her irritation with him. That she would see his point.

After another minute or so, he rose to his feet, a sign that the meeting was over.

He walked around his desk, rested his butt at the corner of it. "Let's talk later."

"Sure, Dan," she muttered before leaving the office, "let's do that."

Sandra was sitting at her desk, busy with something on the computer, but she caught a glimpse of Julie stepping out of Saunders' office. Noticing that Julie seemed almost worn out, Sandra didn't envy her. She thought that Julie had the toughest job in this global leading company in disease prevention.

Saunders stepped into the doorway of his office and watched Julie walk toward the door to leave. He glanced briefly at Sandra and then returned to sit in his chair.

Back in her office, Julie sat in a chair behind her desk, staring into space. She wasn't yet ready to return to work. Her meeting with Dan Saunders had unsettled her. Maybe he had gone a little overboard. Now she wanted to lay her head on her desk and wail. But she maintained control, despite the tears burning her brown eyes.

Her thoughts were scattered, struggling with doubts and fears. She wondered how 2013 would end and it had just begun. Then, she thought about the family she had in India, and how she missed them, especially on a day like this.

James Stebbins came out of the laboratory to confer with Julie, and gather more information about a blood culture specimen. Approaching her office, he found her in a funk. When he saw her wipe the tears from her eyes, he could see how upset she was.

He turned his head away, ran his fingers through his hair, thinking if he should say something or not. Then he turned to her and stepped into the doorway of her office.

"Bad day in the office?"

"You could say that," she said, looking up at him.

"Saunders again?"

"Uh-huh."

"Oy vey," he said in a Jewish accent, "sometimes he can put you on edge."

"Something like that."

"I know this probably isn't a good time, but there is something I need to discuss with you," he said, watching the play of emotions across her face.

"Sure, just a minute."

"If this is a bad time. I can always come back later."

Julie stared at him briefly and sighed in the process of pulling herself together. As the BDC's resident microbiologist, he was a big help to her for studying microscopic organisms such as bacteria and some types of parasites. She really did appreciate him.

She stood up, put on her lab coat and turned toward him. "All right, James. What do you have for me?"

Chapter 39

JANUARY 30, 2013, Jenna's birthday, I thought as I leaned back in my chair and stared blankly at the computer screen. I narrowed my eyes at the cursor that just clicked on a database and sadness hit me all at once. I was really missing my sister. Why was it taking her so long to get here?

A very busy week had passed without my having time to spare a thought about Jenna. Today being her birthday, I had to think of her. Now twenty years old, wherever she was I hoped she was okay, or rather alive. But I promised myself I wouldn't cry. That I would hold myself together.

It was half past four o'clock. The work day was almost over. And I was tired. Preoccupied with all of this, I took my mug from my desk and went to the break room to get some coffee.

Not too long later, I was coming from the break room with my mug of coffee when I saw Vivian near my desk, apparently waiting for me. She was holding a folder in her hand, gazing at the wall, possibly lost in thought.

"Hello, Vivian."

"Hello, Hannah. I have something for you," said Vivian as she handed me a folder.

Inside was a three-page report. It was the assignment she'd been working on.

"This is great. I wondered how it was going."

"Not many computers need servicing."

"I'll get right on it tomorrow morning," I said, placing the folder on my desk.

"I'm heading out of the office now. I thought you might like to know in case you wonder where I am."

"Okay. By the way, in case I didn't mention it before, I think you are doing a great job."

"That's really a nice thing to say. Oh look, I appreciate your concern for me. But you don't have to treat me with kid gloves. I'm managing pretty well under the circumstances."

"Yes, you're right. I have to admit that I've been a little worried about you."

"The pandemic has been hard on all of us. For me, not knowing about my husband and two sons has been devastating. I think the worst has already happened. Some days it's all I can do to get out of bed. Only my faith in Jesus Christ has kept me strong," she said with a degree of emotion that surprised me.

"You hang in there, Vivian, and have a nice evening."

"I'll see you tomorrow," she said and left.

It seemed fitting that she was leaving early. She'd been working really hard lately, probably to drown her sorrows. Earlier this afternoon, she had been super busy with work from what I could see when I passed her office. I wanted to wave hello to her, but she had her back turned to me, hunched over her computer.

As I sat down and started to take a sip of coffee, I saw Thomas Bauer walk into my department. He was dressed to the nines, quite well, I would say, in a Joseph Abboud light gray chalk stripe suit, white shirt, and patent-leather shoes on his feet. It wasn't typical for him to be around here checking things out, like inspecting the offices. Though it was hard to tell exactly what he was doing. I wondered what he was looking for. Rarely did he visit, practically never.

He straightened his dark gray tie at his neck then he cocked an eye at me. Nervous, waiting for him to say something. I rarely had direct contact with the president of the company. I could only hope nothing bad had happened.

When he didn't speak, I said, "Hello there."

His face broke into a smile. "Hannah, is it?"

"Yes."

"It is a pleasure to see you. Keep up the good work."

"Thanks."

He didn't say anything more to me. Rather he paced back and forth for a bit while he swept his hair back with his hand, as if he was trying to remember something.

I pondered the possibility that he was killing time, waiting to speak with Julie, but didn't want to say anything to me about it. What could he possibly want to discuss with her? But I shouldn't waste my time thinking about it, because I wasn't going to find out. It was hush-hush around here when it came to the subject of the virus.

Bauer stood there in the office hallway for a bit longer, then walked into the laboratory, and that was that.

My tiredness was creeping back into my bones, and my coffee mug was empty. Good thing it was five o'clock, and I was leaving the office. If there was anything going on — related to the virus or otherwise; I'd have to find out tomorrow.

Before I could stand up from my chair, Thomas Bauer came out of the lab. He rushed by me, didn't look up, and stepped out of the room. Whatever he came here for, it looks as if he didn't find it.

Just as I turned the corner, the elevator doors opened. I was about to step inside when Julie swept past me to get on the elevator. But in that instant, the elevator doors were closing. As luck would have it, I flung my arm out just in time and the doors rolled back open.

"There you go, Julie."

"Thanks Hannah," she said as she got into the elevator.

"Is everything okay?"

"Sorry, I'm in a hurry, can't talk," she said in her usual polite way.

"Never mind me. I'll get the next one," I whispered to myself as the elevator doors closed.

I wondered what was happening there, with her rushing around. If it had something to do with Bauer's visit to the laboratory. But that was something else I wasn't meant to know.

Chapter 40

MONSIGNOR LUCCA was in the hallway watching Jenna pray in the church. By her reddened and swollen eyes, he could see that she had been crying. It was painfully evident that her spirits were down in the dumps. When more tears rolled down her cheeks, he made the sign of the cross, and approached her.

Last night she had a nightmare, dreamed her father was at his house, waiting for her. Her current emotional state had been triggered by her memory of him. She really wished he was here to console her, especially today, her birthday.

The Monsignor came up alongside her. "Jenna, you okay?"

Her wandering thoughts came back to the present. She wiped her eyes, turned around to face him, and stood up from the altar.

"I was just thinking about my father."

"I see. And where is your father?"

"Oh, Monsignor," she said, raising her hands to cover her eyes.

Instinctively, he wrapped his arms around her. Embarrassed because she couldn't contain her emotions, she responded by burying her head in his shoulder.

"There, there, my dear. No matter how helpless or hopeless you are, look thou unto the Lord who is mighty to deliver."

A long moment later, he broke the embrace and stepped over and sat down in the third pew from the altar. "Come, sit and tell me about it."

Jenna walked over and sat beside him. It was then that she got a grip on her nerves and explained everything. That her father had died in a plane crash and she still had trouble accepting it.

"I truly am sorry for your loss. You've demonstrated a lot of courage for a young girl on her own. I'm sure your father would've been proud of you," he said, empathetically.

While he consoled her, she had been wondering about God, about what happened after death and more concerned with how the walking dead fit into the grand scheme of it all. Would Jesus Christ want these people raised from the dead? In her view, it was not a natural process of evolution. Perhaps the Monsignor could shed some light on the matter.

She changed the subject. "Monsignor, is it a sin to kill the infected, since they are already dead?"

"Jenna, I am bound to honor the Ten Commandments, the laws in Exodus, such as 'Thou shalt not kill,' a moral principle. And everyone should do what God has commanded. I believe that killing of any kind is wrong in the eyes of God."

"But they are mindless beasts, incapable of speech or reason, and without a soul."

"There is no way to know whether or not they have a soul. The infected were once like you and me. It's not their fault that the virus has changed them. They are dead but still functioning. If we can find a way to cure them, there will be no reason to kill them. I pray to God for a miracle that will prevent more people from perishing. And I also pray for the souls of the dead not at peace."

"There is no remedy at this time. Killing them is our only choice," she declared.

"This is a complicated issue and should be subject to more analysis. Let me consult the Bible for a passage that speaks to my heart. And we can liken the Scripture to ourselves and compare our lives to the lives of those spoken about."

The Monsignor reached over and grabbed a Bible out of the pocket on the back of the pew. He started turning the pages, while she sat quietly, watching him.

"This good book has the answers to many burning questions," he added.

Then he found the page he wanted and read from the Bible aloud. Isaiah 26:19 and 26:20.

"The dead men shall live, together with my dead body shall they arise. Awake and sing, ye that dwell in dust: for thy dew is as the dew of herbs, and the earth shall cast out the dead. Come, my people, enter thou into thy chambers, and shut thy doors about thee: hide thyself as it were for a little moment, until the indignation be overpast."

"What do you think of this Scripture?"

"I think what it means is that there will be a resurrection of the dead. And we have to hide until the wrath passes," she said.

"Certainly, it tells us that we shall rise again with our bodies. We have to repent and accept God's judgment of us all. I believe that our situation is only temporary, that we must wait for the plague to pass."

"My only birthday wish is that it will end soon."

"I can only pray. Anyway, I hope my words of wisdom have been helpful and will encourage you to keep the faith."

"Yes, I do feel a lot better."

"I'm glad. Wait. Let me backtrack a minute. Did you say birthday?"

"Yes, today is my birthday."

"You should have mentioned it before, Jenna. Happy birthday."

"Why, thank you ever so much," she said, and stood up.

She watched Sister Mary Ann walk into the church while the Monsignor put the Bible in the empty rack in front of him. As he was crossing himself, he felt a tap on his shoulder from behind.

"Please excuse the interruption, but Irene wanted me to tell you that she found the boxes of pancake mix," Sister Mary

Ann said.

"That's wonderful. Thanks for letting me know."

As Sister Mary Ann turned to leave, he said, "Wait a minute, Sister. Today is Jenna's birthday."

"Well, happy birthday Jenna," the Sister said as she turned back around.

"Do you have anything in the pantry for this special occasion?" he asked.

"Yes, actually, I do."

"You don't have to go through any trouble for me," Jenna said.

"It's no trouble at all," Sister Mary Ann said.

"Jenna, should we celebrate?" he asked, with uncertainty.

"Okay. That's very nice of you both," she said, caving in to the kindness.

"Let's go downstairs to the dining room and Sister Mary Ann will whip up a treat for you in the kitchen," he said.

He rotated toward the hallway, as Sister Mary Ann motioned them both to follow her down the stairs to the basement level. In the midst of Jenna's angst, that was the kindest thing they could do for her.

Chapter 41

THE HELICOPTER twisted around and then slowly began to descend until it touched down on the helipad in a cloud of dust. Something was troubling Ken Langtry, who stood several feet away, watching with an air of impatience. He huffed around on the sidelines anxiously waiting for Lucas and the others to arrive. Chris, the pilot of the other chopper, had just radioed him that a delivery was coming in.

Days had rolled into weeks with Langtry barely noticing the passage of time. Now in the middle of February, he felt uneasy. He was worried about supplies, even though the deliveries kept coming. Would they eventually run out? As the men left the helicopter, he tried not to show his feelings.

"Fine work!" Langtry said as Lucas and Stewart walked toward him.

With a queasy feeling, James Stebbins exited the helicopter, carrying a medical cooler. It contained the severed head of an infected female. He was rushing toward the elevator, when Langtry noticed him.

"Lucas, you know the drill. Go catch up with James, who is off in his own world. Tell him to keep the specimen secure and handle it with caution. Wait for him to give you the biohazard materials bag for incineration. Then come back here to help unload the helicopter carrying medical supplies," Langtry told him.

"I'm on it," Lucas said, and dashed off.

"Stewart, I need you here to unload the chopper."

"Sure, Ken," Stewart replied, taking a position next to him.

A tap came on Langtry's shoulder. He turned around to find himself face to face with a twenty-four-year-old Korean girl with long, jet black hair. She was wearing a black camisole under a black vest, black jeans, black combat boots, and holding a rifle. Suited up for battle, she looked more like a character from a video game you could play on a Sony PlayStation 3 console than a security guard.

"Ken Langtry?" she asked.

"Yes, and who might you be? And where did you get that company-issued rifle?"

"My name is Chloe Park. I'm the daughter of Linda Park, the manager of the Lotte Market store. Lucas Rawlett said I should report to you for a job in security. He gave me the rifle for protection from the infected near the gate. I recently graduated from Stanford University in California with a bachelor's degree in music. I am eager to work. You don't have to pay me. I just want to help."

"I'll have to talk to Lucas about that later," he said, thinking to himself, then asked, "Degree in music?"

"Exactly right!" she replied.

"So be it, you're hired. Do you know how to fire that weapon?"

"Yes, I got it under control. My dad taught me how to shoot a gun. He was a police officer in Korea," she reassured him.

"Chloe, you said your name was?"

"Yes, sir."

"Stewart, this is Chloe Park. She'll be working with you today," he said, turning to look at him.

"Hello, Chloe."

"Hello to you," she said, and went to stand next to Stewart.

"Right on time," Langtry said, looking out at the sky.

The rhythmic thumping of a low-flying helicopter approaching rapidly from the east pleased Langtry. But nearly forty of the infected at the gate were agitated by it. The sound grew and their moaning increased and was now punctuated with snarls. Some zombies were looking up toward the sound.

Langtry and Stewart looked at the infected in frustration and dull surprise. Chloe, who was smacking her gum loudly, was staring at them suspiciously.

One of the infected grabbed a hold of the gate, pulled on it firmly, and growled fiercely. The infected man attracted a lot of attention to himself. He held Langtry in a curious gaze, like he was trying to communicate with thoughts. Wearing torn bloody clothing and missing skin from his arms, his mouth was open wide, showing broken teeth. Langtry stared somewhat longer, then focused on the helicopter coming in his direction.

"That was weird," Stewart said, a bit confused.

"They're just full of surprises," Langtry said.

In one swift move, Chloe blew a bubble and popped it back into her mouth.

The helicopter landed on the other helipad. Stewart and Chloe began assisting Chris to unload some wooden cargo boxes from the chopper. Langtry watched Stewart and Chloe with an eagle eye until Chloe left for the elevator carrying two small boxes.

The load looked lighter than Langtry was expecting. His thoughts were disrupted when Lucas arrived on the scene to help in the unloading. Eight boxes were then lifted out by the men, but he was still concerned.

More than two weeks ago, Julie gave him a list of needed supplies which in turn he gave to Chris. Very early this morning Chris had found an abandoned medical center, practically untouched by the epidemic, in Springerville, Arizona. When the chopper was coming in but still at a little distance away, Chris radioed in that he had found the supplies on the list prepared by Julie, such as antiseptic swabs, gloves, syringes, cotton balls, and adhesive bandages.

Langtry had to know what was going on. He walked up to the cockpit. Not wanting to alarm Lucas or Stewart, he would keep it on the down-low.

"Let's step over here so we can talk. I have something important to ask you," he said to Chris.

"Yeah, just hang on," Chris said, and put a set of headphones down in the pilot's seat.

"No problem, I can wait."

After a couple of minutes or so, Chris exited the cockpit.

"Ken, how goes it there?" he said walking to him.

"Fine, thanks. Chris, there is something I need to ask you."

"Shoot away."

"Is there a shortage of supplies? Should I start worrying?"

"At the moment there is no need to worry. But ask me again in six months and I may tell a different story," Chris said, somewhat reassuringly.

Langtry quickly threw in, "Today's shipment looks light."

"The medical center in Springerville didn't have that much. I took everything that was there. There is no problem finding supplies and there are several well-stocked supermarkets in many towns accessible to us. The problem is that it takes time to get stuff. And I have to watch out for the infected."

"I want to know the minute anything changes. So, we'll be ready," Langtry said, prolonging the issue.

Chris read skepticism in his eyes. "I will notify you in advance."

"Thanks again for all your hard work."

"Well, at least you don't have to worry about paying for anything. Nowadays, everything is free," Chris said, and started walking, his eyes focused on his aircraft.

Chris began servicing the chopper, checking switches and the fuel level while Langtry went right back to watching Lucas and Stewart stacking boxes on a steel dolly. At one point Lucas caught his glance.

Langtry signaled him over with a snap of his fingers. "Get those boxes to the laboratory. Dr. Mehta has been waiting for them since an hour ago. Oh, and one more thing, Lucas, we need to talk about something later," he said to him.

"Will do," Lucas said, then called out, "Stewart, we got to get a move on and get..."

As Lucas walked and talked his voice disappeared into the distance. He caught up with Stewart, who was pushing the two-wheeled dolly stacked with boxes to the elevator.

It had been a long day and the pains of hunger had set in. Langtry was thinking about the lunch he hadn't had. There were still some doubts in his mind about his conversation with Chris, as he was still trying to sort it all out. But for the present moment, a quick meal and a cup of coffee might put his mind at ease. He took one last look at the chopper before he turned toward the elevator bank.

Chapter 42

A MOMENT AFTER Jenna sat down next to the African-American family at a table in the dining room, all the lights went out. They were in total darkness. Just a second earlier, she had smiled at the little boy who had smiled back at her. Now she was about to take off, fearing that the zombies had gotten inside the building. But she stopped herself, deciding to wait.

"Why is it dark in here?" Patrick asked his mother, tugging at her hand, while munching on a cookie.

"I don't know, sweetie," she said.

"Mommy, I can't see you," the little boy griped.

Annoyed, the father scolded him, saying, "Hush now, and eat your dinner."

"How am I supposed to eat in the dark?" Patrick asked.

"Hush up, I told you," the father said, and then asked, "Stephanie, what do you think about this?"

"Let's be patient. Monsignor Lucca or Irene will tell us if something is wrong," she said.

"They can't tell us if they are zombies," Patrick said, and giggled to himself.

"Boy, what did I tell you?" the father exclaimed.

Jenna was too scared to say anything. A door creaked open, sending light and shadow toward her. From what she could see, it was Irene. She sighed, the fear suppressed within her, knowing she was still safe.

Irene had entered the dining room with two lit kerosene lamps, and set them on a table. There was a long silence while she thought of the right words to say.

"Listen everyone, I have an announcement to make. There is no cause for alarm. There's a problem with the electricity, or a power outage, most likely a temporary situation," Irene informed them.

Jenna picked up that there was an edge of uncertainty in the normally confident voice of Irene. She knew that Irene put her faith in Jesus Christ above everything else. But Jenna's faith in the Almighty wasn't as strong as hers.

"Mommy, what's she saying? Are we in trouble?" Patrick asked.

"No, baby. Miss Irene says everything is fine," Stephanie said.

"Hush! She's not finished talking," the father said.

"But mommy!" the little boy insisted.

"Be quiet now, sweetheart. Listen to your father."

"Jesse couldn't get the electricity to work. He tried the fuse box, but it didn't make a difference. This was to be expected due to the epidemic. It's just a little setback. That's all," Irene said to everyone in the room.

In an easy manner, she explained that there would be changes to their day-to-day lives. She did her best to reassure everyone that all was well and things would get better. And she tried to sound confident and optimistic because she wanted to prevent panic.

Irene continued, "There is no way to heat or cook food. However, our food supply is abundant. We can live off canned foods and powdered food mixes."

Lost in her thoughts, Jenna wanted to believe that things were fine. But something inside her felt otherwise. The place didn't feel the same. She longed to be in New Mexico. It was her sister she missed — now more than ever.

"We'll keep the curtains pulled back on some windows for natural daylight. All other areas in the church will be candlelit. Thank goodness we have a good stock of candles. And we have a few kerosene lamps for the bedrooms. The water supply hasn't been interrupted. Trips to the bathroom, and showering can continue," Irene chattered on.

There was nothing for Jenna to do but worry. She picked at her food without appetite. The kerosene lamps cast shadows in every direction, so no one noticed the doubt in her eyes. In fact, nobody was even paying any attention to her. So, she got up and left without saying anything.

She walked up the flight of stairs, turned left into a candlelit hallway. Now that she was alone, she thought about everything Irene had said. The time had come for her to consider leaving. But not at this instant because she needed a few days to sort things out.

She turned right, passing a room next to the Monsignor's office. Fading sunlight poured through the two small, curved windows into the cluttered room. A particular streak of light caught her eye. It cast a shadow over a Bible on a bookshelf.

With curiosity, she walked into the room to check it out. Just as she picked up the book, a shadow passed by the windows. That was all she could see from that angle. It took her by complete surprise and left her momentarily flustered. For all she knew it could have been a bird, or a flock of birds.

On second thought, she doubted it. Someone was definitely walking around outside the church, very likely a zombie. She knew it wasn't Jesse because he went outside in the mornings, usually on Mondays.

Suddenly aware she could be seen, she ducked into the corner. Now, from where she was standing, she was sure no one could see her. She waited, staring at the windows, wanting to know what was out there.

Five minutes went by. Then it happened again. A shadow fell across the room. She spotted a head moving by the windows. Judging by the way it moved, it had to be a zombie. It was only one, but there were probably more in the vicinity. This made her scared.

Before leaving the room, she took one last look at the windows. There was nothing out there that she could see.

She stepped into the hallway and headed toward her room. Depressed by it all, her pace was slower than before. The moment she entered her room, she fell into bed. She flipped her pillow over and lay on her back. Trying to relax, she closed her eyes and put aside her thoughts about leaving. Taking deep breaths, she tried to clear her head and fell asleep in minutes.

Chapter 43

THREE DAYS LATER, on Monday, March 4, Jenna had made up her mind. She would go, and that morning, after her shower, she dressed and found herself packing up her backpack. Then she left the room heading toward Monsignor Lucca's office.

Knocking lightly on the Monsignor's office door that was partly open, she waited. When there was no reply, she pushed the door all the way open, only to find the room empty.

She was about to leave when she heard footsteps coming up to the door on the other side of the room. It was the Monsignor. He stepped into the office and found her standing in front of his desk.

"Jenna, how may I assist you?"

"I actually have to leave here."

"And where will you be going?" he asked with concern.

"Dulce, New Mexico. I promised my sister that I would

meet her there. She works for Biogenetics & Disease Control, at their underground facility.”

“It sounds like you’ve planned it all out and thought it through,” he said with an uncertain look.

“I sure have,” she said, and nodded at him.

“I’m sorry to see you go, but I understand that you have your own life to live. It’s been a pleasure having you here. We’ll all miss you, especially Irene,” he said endearingly.

“I’ll miss all of you too.”

“Make sure you eat something before you go.”

“Thanks. I’ll have a quick breakfast.”

“Oh, Jenna, before you go, I want to give you something,” he said, opened his desk drawer and pulled out black rosary beads with a wooden cross hanging from it.

“Thank you so kindly,” she said, placing it in her jacket pocket.

“If you need to pray, use them and ask the angels to keep you safe,” he said, stepping away from his desk.

“What’s the phone number here?”

“What for?” he asked.

“When the telephones work again, I'll call you to let you know where I am, and that I’m okay.”

“Here’s my card, with the number,” he told her, coming back to the desk, retrieving and handing her his card, “and may God be with you.”

She put the card in her backpack and glanced at the battery-operated clock on his desk. “I appreciate all our time together, but I need to get going.”

On the way to the kitchen, she passed Irene, who was sitting at a table in the dining room. Sister Mary Ann handed her a glass of iced tea and a breakfast plate with a bagel, yams, and four shortbread cookies on it. She brought her plate over to sit beside Irene.

While Jenna ate, she explained that she was leaving and going to New Mexico, to be reunited with her sister. It didn't go over well with Irene, who raised an eyebrow at her. She looked at Jenna the same way Monsignor Lucca had looked at her, with skepticism.

"Are you certain you want to do this? You still have a long way to travel, and the situation could quickly get worse."

"Yes, I'm certain. I can do it," Jenna said, standing up.

"You've been so helpful. I'm going to miss you dearly," Irene said, rising to stand beside her.

"I told Monsignor Lucca as soon as the telephones come back on line, I will call here."

"I'll look forward to hearing from you then. Please stay safe," Irene said, and gave her a hug.

It was an emotional moment for both of them. Irene had come to think of her as a daughter. Somewhere in the back of her mind, Irene hoped she'd stay longer. But she understood it was time for Jenna to leave.

"Don't forget to call," Irene said as she pulled away and looked her in the eyes.

"I won't forget."

She gave Jenna another hug, then headed out of the dining room. Irene's heart was in the right place. She was the most generous person she had ever met, a teary-eyed Jenna thought as she watched her walk away.

Next she went to the kitchen to say goodbye to Sister Mary Ann.

"It's been wonderful knowing you, Jenna. You take care out there," the Sister said, with emotion in her voice.

"I'm glad to have known you, too."

"Hang on, there," she said, opening the refrigerator.

"You don't have to do that."

"Here's a little something for your trip. Take a bottle of water and two wrapped peanut butter and jelly sandwiches. Don't worry none about it. They are extra."

"You are too kind."

They hugged briefly, and Jenna thanked her for everything. Sister Mary Ann broke their embrace and began wiping tears from her eyes. Jenna reassured her, telling her not to worry and that she'd call her later when the phone lines were working.

After she put the sandwiches and bottle of water into her backpack, she crossed through the dining room. Entering the stairway, she hurried up the stairs, only to be caught by Monsignor Lucca, who, surprisingly, appeared at the top.

"There's another thing before you go, Jenna," he called out to her.

"Yes, is everything okay?" she asked, approaching him.

"Here are the keys to my two-door silver Toyota Prius. You'll enjoy driving it. It's great for the environment. Not that it makes a difference now. It's in the parking lot outside."

"I don't feel right taking it, Monsignor," she said.

"I insist. I'm not going anywhere. My place is here, serving the people in the community of Abilene," he said, and handed her the keys.

She choked up, almost crying. "Thanks for the wheels."

"Whatever I can do to help."

She gave him a quick hug. "I'm so grateful to all of you."

"I will keep you in my prayers," he said, as she entered the lobby heading toward the church.

Inside the church, she was quietly going out the side door, the same door she came in through about ten weeks earlier. *What would happen to them?* she thought. She had to wonder if they'd made the right decision by staying? For just a moment, she prayed to God that the zombies would never penetrate the walls of the church.

As she walked outside to the Prius, she heard a gunshot not too far off. The sound of it sent her heart leaping in frantic panic. She didn't see anything and couldn't even be sure which direction the shot came from.

Car keys in hand, she raced to the driver's door. She opened the door, slid behind the wheel, and started the car. After buckling up, she inhaled and exhaled, bracing herself for whatever would happen next.

Without hesitation, she sped out of the driveway onto the street, heading south. When she turned left onto another street, she soon discovered that she had taken a wrong turn. She almost drove off the road as she watched a teenage boy running across the street from zombies, who were everywhere on the street and sidewalk. A man grabbed the boy by the arms before a zombie almost bit him. The man was having a hard time restraining the boy, who was desperate to escape.

Jenna reversed her direction and headed back toward the west. On her way out of there, she drove into a zombie knocking it to the ground. Half a block later, she hit another zombie. Nothing had changed on the outside. Getting back to speed, she was taking it all in, right in the middle of the mayhem again.

Chapter 44

SEVERAL MINUTES LATER, Jenna was traveling west on Interstate 20. Someone behind her leaned on their horn and then sped up to pass her, almost causing her to collide into one of the multi-car smash-ups on the road ahead of her. After switching lanes, she pulled alongside the car, maneuvering so they were side by side. She could clearly see the driver.

The Hispanic male driver looked at her, rolled down the window, pointed to the Nissan Frontier truck directly in front of her, and yelled, "Watch out."

In that space of an instant, she saw a zombie hanging out of the passenger window of the truck. Rather than slow down, the driver of the truck revved the engine, while at the same time he was trying to push the zombie out of the window.

Jenna peered into the rearview mirror, checking how close the car behind her was. Too close. Driving faster, she tried to change lanes several times, but other cars were not letting her. What amazed her was the fact that a half a dozen vehicles were on the interstate. She could only assume that they were fleeing from zombie-infested areas.

The driver of the Frontier turned the wheel hard to the right causing the truck to slide and then straighten. She slammed the brakes, sending the car into a one hundred-eighty-degree spin. The driver of the vehicle behind her gunned their engine and rammed the back of the car. The impact pushed the Prius into the truck in front of her and sent the zombie tumbling in her direction, missing her by centimeters. Thinking she was going to die, she tried to scream. But before she could make a sound, the airbag ballooned into her, saving her from crashing through the windshield.

The second the car had stopped; from her position, she could see the driver of the Frontier was still strapped to his seat, a deflated airbag in his lap. His legs were pinned under the steering wheel. Blood oozed from a wound on his head that was face down on the steering wheel. From the looks of it, Jenna had the impression that he was either unconscious or dead.

By a miracle she had suffered no injuries. But the Prius wouldn't turn on and she smelled gasoline fumes. She whipped her head around and saw four zombies whirl around and start walking toward her. In one move she released the seat belt, opened the door and swung her legs out. Bolting from the car, she ran out onto the highway, not caring where she was going.

By surprising good luck, the driver of the car that hit the

Prius was still alive. She passed the young man, as he was pulling himself out of the driver's side window. As far as she could tell, he was going to be all right. Or, so, she thought until a group of zombies encompassed and trapped him, pushing him down to the ground.

All she could think about was getting away. She kept running on the shoulder of the road, and wouldn't stop until she was a long way off.

Twenty-five or so yards later she reached the exit ramp. She stopped to rest, breathing hard, almost hyperventilating. Above her the sky was swirling with clouds.

It began to rain as she left the expressway, walking into the city of Roscoe in Nolan County, Texas. The cool rain felt good on her face. When she turned right on Broadway Street, she glanced over her shoulder and saw three zombies staggering in front of a smokehouse restaurant. She ducked out of their view just as an SUV roared up behind her.

"Quick, get in!" a voice yelled, startling her out of her thoughts.

She turned around and saw a woman leaning out of the driver's side window of a red Toyota RAV4. The Hispanic woman in her early forties drove the sport utility vehicle forward, stopped beside Jenna, leaned across the seat, and opened the passenger-side door. In one long moment, Jenna was glad that the woman offered to help her. She didn't have to say it twice. Jenna got into the car.

The woman angled herself to better face Jenna. "You're out here alone?"

"I sure am."

"Where are you going?" the woman asked, shifting into drive and pulling away.

"Dulce, New Mexico," Jenna answered.

The woman turned the car to the left, then made a U-turn. "That's a long way from here. What's in Dulce, New Mexico?"

"My sister is there, working at Biogenetics & Disease Control's underground facility. It's secure and safe."

Glancing in the rearview mirror, Jenna saw the crashed Prius in the distance. Before they reached the corner, she leaned back, breathed a sigh, then moved her light-brown hair away from her face, hooking it around her ear.

"I'm going to my mother's house in Lubbock to pick her up. It's nearly two hours away. We don't have anywhere to go."

"You are welcome to join me."

"Buckle up. We're going to New Mexico!" the woman said without any hesitation.

"How did you know I wasn't infected?" Jenna asked.

"I didn't," she said, rather whimsically.

"I almost forgot to tell you. My name is Jenna."

"I'm Elena Zambrana."

"Thank you for picking me up."

"Say no more. I'm glad I did," Elena said and turned onto U.S. Route 84 heading west.

Heavy rain beat down on the windshield blurring Elena's vision. She turned on the wipers, and concentrated on her driving while Jenna stared out the window watching the raindrops trickle down the glass. They were both surprised that despite the pouring rain, the zombies roamed the streets.

When a zombie stepped in front of the RAV4, Jenna pointed. "Look out! Drive faster."

Elena accelerated the SUV and ran right into the zombie, knocking it out of the way. Only a minute or so after, when she reduced her speed because of the pouring rain, a sedan came up behind them and honked their horn. For some odd reason, it was tailgating them practically bumper to bumper. Jenna looked dumbfounded, while at the same time, Elena wondered if it was some strange act of road rage she'd provoked when she had slowed down. So, Elena veered sharply into the other lane. Then, just as suddenly, the sedan sped up and dropped out of sight.

It wasn't long after that the storm had passed, leaving a clear sky. The bright sun was radiating warmth. For the miles ahead, they rode along in silence.

Chapter 45

A LITTLE DAYLIGHT was still left, but Elena was looking for a place to hide out. Though they were less than an hour from Lubbock, with the coming darkness, she thought it was best to pick her mother up and drive away with her in the morning.

"So, now what?" Jenna asked her.

"We have to find somewhere to stay for tonight. Keep your eyes out for something."

As Elena passed through Post, Texas, driving along U.S. 380, she saw the hangars of the Post-Garza County Municipal Airport. The door to one of the hangars was open and there was no one around. Jenna noticed, and thought it would be the perfect place to hide overnight.

"What about over there?" Jenna asked, pointing to the hangars.

"Yeah, I saw it. Let's check it out," suggested Elena.

"But you just missed the turn off."

Elena hit the brakes, threw the RAV4 in reverse, backed up halfway down the street, hit the brakes again, and turned to the right. She circled around the parking lot a few times until she was satisfied the place was empty. As she drove into the open hangar, streaks of orange and pink shot across the sky as the sun was starting to set. She parked out of sight behind a small, silver Cessna aircraft. They were going to sleep in the vehicle.

Elena turned the SUV off leaving the keys in the ignition on purpose, prepared to take off at a second's notice. She leaned back in the driver's seat and became very quiet. Tears formed at the corners of her eyes, and her shoulders hunched up.

"My husband was killed trying to save me from those things," Elena spoke heatedly, staring out the window.

"I'm sorry. It must have been terrible."

"I don't know if I can say anymore."

"Go on, tell me what happened," Jenna said, wanting to hear more.

To calm herself, Elena loosened up her shoulders. For one long second, she closed her eyes, trying to make sense of things.

"We had been hiding in our house until this morning when we were completely out of supplies. Our plan was to stop at a store on the way to Lubbock, where we would then hole up in safe cover at my mother's house. We found a convenience store not far from Roscoe. It was eerily quiet, and we didn't see anyone around."

After another beat, Elena sighed and related the story with tears in her eyes. "My husband, Bill, and I were thankful that the store had only been partially looted. I sat in the driver's seat of the Toyota looking out for any zombies, as he put groceries in the trunk. Out of nowhere, I heard a deep moan. I didn't know where it came from. And then, just like that, the sound was gone. Sometime later, I saw a zombie appear around the back of the Toyota, grab my husband and bite him on the arm. It happened so fast, Jenna, that it seemed like seconds later another zombie came. Bill hollered at me to drive away because he was infected and didn't have a chance. He kept the zombies distracted as I frantically drove off."

Trying to control her emotions, Elena stopped talking for a moment. The grisly events from earlier that day were still fresh in her mind.

But she had more to say. "We had been married for almost three years. We planned to have kids, and now we won't be able to."

"I'm sorry you went through that," Jenna said, feeling bad for her.

"Thanks for listening and being a shoulder to cry on."

"I'm glad to be of service."

"If you're hungry, there's plenty of groceries in the back," Elena said, bouncing back to life with renewed energy, suppressing her emotions, trying to pretend she was all right.

"Yeah, actually I am."

"Then, let's dig in."

"Great, thanks, Elena."

Elena unbuckled her seat belt and crawled between the seats into the back, too scared to leave the SUV. She pulled a latch and put the seat down to access the trunk, which was loaded with brown paper bags filled with groceries.

Quickly, she reached into a bag and pulled out a big bag of Doritos. Elena ripped the package open, took a handful of chips and stuffed them in her mouth. Then she handed the bag over to Jenna and reached into another paper bag. She grabbed two cans of 7UP, tossing one to Jenna. Elena popped open the lid and gulped down half the can. Then she searched the bag again, feeling around for something.

"Ah, ha! Look, I found it. These have lots of protein," Elena said, holding up two power bars.

Tearing off the wrapper, Elena bit off a piece of the chocolate-flavored bar, thoroughly enjoying it. She gave one to Jenna, who passed the bag of Doritos back to her. Elena drank the rest of her 7UP and finished off the bag of nacho cheese flavored tortilla chips.

Feeling satisfied, Elena put the seat up and crawled into the driver's seat. Then Jenna crawled into the backseat and huddled by the window. They were both very sleepy.

"See you in the morning, Jenna."

"Have a good rest."

Elena passed out almost immediately and didn't wake up until a little after eight a.m. It was the most uncomfortable place she'd ever slept. Glancing in the backseat, she saw Jenna was still sleeping. Anxiously, she wanted to get on the road. So, she took it upon herself to wake her.

"Rise and shine, Jenna," she said loudly.

It was too early, and Jenna was too tired. Curled up under her jacket in the backseat, she looked around hazily. At first, she didn't recognize any of it, however, bit by bit she was able to remember Elena.

"I would like some coffee," Jenna said, looking like she could use some.

Elena laughed. Jenna glanced over at her, and the two of them laughed. Ever so briefly, it was as if they forgot where they were and why they were there.

"We'll be at my mother's house in forty-five minutes, tops. Jenna, you still in?"

"Yes, let's roll."

"Just a second," Elena said, shuffling in her seat.

"What is it?"

"My butt is still asleep."

Jenna made a face at her.

"Well, you asked," said Elena, who threw the RAV4 into drive and pulled away from the hangar.

Chapter 46

ELENA ZAMBRANA was driving fast as Jenna crawled into the passenger seat. She hit the gas pedal, flashed her lights, and blew her horn at the pickup truck in front. The truck refused to move over, so she swerved around it to speed down the lane.

A quick glance in the rearview mirror showed there were no cars behind her. At a perfectly moderate speed, she drove the rest of the way into Lubbock.

At nearly nine o'clock in the morning, the feeling of familiarity hit Elena, as she drove into the neighborhood of Skyview, devoid of the sounds of birds and largely absent of people. She turned onto North Ivory Avenue, pulled into the driveway of her mother's house, came to a halt, and grabbed the keys out of the ignition.

She turned to Jenna. "This won't take too long."

"I'm going with you."

"No. Stay here. I'll go get my mother and be out of there faster than a flash of lightning."

"Fine. I'll be right here," Jenna said, not wanting to argue with her.

Elena got out of the SUV and approached the white colonial house, noticing blood on the front door frame. Feeling slightly panicked, she glanced around. Nothing. She reached forward and rang the doorbell. There was no response. Several more moments passed until she pressed it again, and still nothing happened.

To her surprise, the door wasn't locked. Her mother would have locked it. Slowly, she turned the knob, opened the door ever so slightly and peaked into the hall. It was unusually quiet.

She stepped inside, keeping her eyes on the hallway floor, which was smeared with blood. That didn't sit well with her as she walked on the other side of the hallway, to avoid stepping in it. The blood trail ended at the door of a small bathroom.

"Mother, I'm here," Elena called out.

She stood there in the hallway for a few moments in the expectation of a reply. There was none.

Turning a corner, she walked through the living room, stepping over the remains of a glass vase and dried flowers scattered across the hardwood floor. Her heart was sinking as she walked the short distance to the master bedroom.

She called out again, louder this time, "Mom, it's Elena."

In the bedroom, she listened for movement. Nobody there. Just an empty silence. And it brought tears to her eyes. All her worst fears were coming true. First her husband. Now her mother was gone. It almost looked as though someone had it in for her.

"What's happened to her?" she asked herself out loud.

Slouched in her seat, Jenna was bored to death. Already twice she had studied the map for the way to New Mexico from Lubbock. She had waited and waited for Elena to come out of the house. What could be taking her so long? A sufficient amount of time had passed and she was starting to get a really bad feeling. Leaning forward in her seat, she swiveled her neck, and looked in the direction of the house.

Another minute or so passed before Elena appeared in the doorway of the house. She was alone and she looked like she'd been crying.

"She's not here, Jenna. I don't know where she could be," she said fairly loud.

Jenna shook her head in disbelief and started fumbling inside her backpack, putting away the map. Elena started walking toward the vehicle.

It was none too soon that a zombie charged across the driveway. Following a few steps behind her, the short, bald, black-eyed, pasty white-faced zombie, wore a bloodstained flannel shirt and torn black trousers. Yet, she hadn't heard him approaching.

The zombie practically got in her face, taking her completely by surprise. She stopped right where she was and screamed when the zombie grabbed her arm. No way! Emotionally, she couldn't grasp it. She wasn't ready to die.

She screamed, "Go away, let me be."

Jenna barreled out of the RAV4, but stopped in front of the hood. She was too stunned to move as the zombie bit deeply into Elena's neck. She tried to keep the shock off her face. Tense moments passed, while her eyes looked back and forth, trying to come up with something to do — and all the while thinking, 'Is this really happening?'

Elena looked at her and screamed at the intense pain and lashed out at him with her nails. She felt her skin begin to tear as the zombie released its bite on her neck. Blood poured from the wound in her neck, soaking into her blouse and oozing into her pants.

"I'm so sorry," Jenna said, her voice breaking with emotion.

"Just get going!" Elena said with urgency in her voice.

Realizing she had the keys to the RAV4 in her pocket, Elena started to reach for them. She failed. Her legs went out from under her and she fell to the ground. She lay there trembling helplessly, with tears of terror streaming down her face.

Jenna sprinted to the passenger side of the SUV and pulled her backpack from the seat. Mesmerized, she hesitated to leave and stopped to look at Elena, knowing there was nothing she could do.

"I'm so sorry," Jenna got out again.

The zombie started walking toward her. In that very moment she fled, running up the street to the corner of East Purdue Street.

Stopping to survey her surroundings, she looked back toward the house. The zombie was trailing far behind her. And Elena had pulled herself off the ground, hobbled into the house, but didn't close the door behind her. Jenna watched in horror as three zombies arrived on the scene and followed in pursuit of her.

The zombies cornered her in the living room. She pushed hard against them. The least she could do was put up a fight. But she lost her footing and toppled to the floor. They swarmed her. A look of horror crossed Elena's face as she fully understood what was about to happen. There was no strength left in her to rise. She lay on the floor, dying as they bit into her flesh.

Jenna Winter was out there alone. The zombie was closing in on her. After a few minutes of running again, she stopped at the stop sign at the corner of North Cedar Avenue and East Purdue Street. There she spotted a white Toyota Sequoia SUV with the driver's door open in the driveway of the house ahead. There wasn't any movement inside.

She moved in toward the Sequoia, circling around, checking it out. It had a smashed headlight and a few scratches in its white paint. Not that it mattered to her. And keys were on the driver's seat. That was when she pulled herself into the SUV, put the key in the ignition, and turned on the engine. She locked the doors, and snapped the seat belt into place.

But she wasn't ready to pull out of the driveway. She sat behind the wheel, feeling that what had happened to Elena, was her fault. That she should have paid more attention. She didn't do anything. But there was absolutely nothing she could have done to prevent it.

"I'm so tired of all of this," she said, slapping the palm of her hand on the steering wheel.

Jenna felt so distraught. She wore a deadpan look on her exhausted face. She tried to shake it out of her head, taking several deep breaths, trying to keep her thoughts from racing.

After another moment, she flicked her eyes to the mirror. All clear. She was sniffling as she backed the Sequoia out of the driveway and then stepped on the accelerator. After making a U-turn, she drove down the road and turned right onto East Purdue Street heading west toward Interstate 27.

Chapter 47

A MAN dressed in an orange jumpsuit was running toward Jenna on the shoulder of the interstate. Right after seeing her, the tall man with close-cropped hair stopped and leaned over, hands on his knees, catching his breath. She didn't like the sight of it.

As she drove closer, he looked up, mouthed something she couldn't read, and stuck his thumb in the air. It was just as she thought. He was trying to hitch a ride.

"Hey, stop," he yelled, and waved his arm back and forth.

"Not happening," she said to herself as she passed him.

She decided not to play the good Samaritan. There was no way she was going to pick up an absolute stranger, especially because he was wearing the common prison uniform in the United States. Her lips twitched at the thought.

"Won't you help a fellow out?" he shouted from the distance.

Looking in the rearview mirror, she saw that the man had turned and began running. Stamped onto the back of his jumpsuit in block font was the word "CLEMENTS," the name of a prison. She felt more certain than ever that she'd made the right decision not to pick him up, not that she'd even considered it.

Half an hour later, she turned right onto Canyon Drive and, shortly after, she cruised into Amarillo. The sun was slowly going down in the western sky, and she began looking for a place to hide, a place to sleep. She turned left on West McCormick Road and kept going till she reached South Coulter Street and made a right. Still, she didn't know where to go.

A handful of minutes went by, before she found something, or thought she did, as she made a left turn on Hollywood Road. Pulling to the side of the road, she stopped the SUV, and raised herself up in the seat for a better view out the window. She gave the Sunrise Motel on Soncy Road a hard look. The place was isolated and spooky, reminiscent of the Bates Motel from the movie *Psycho*. All the rooms were on the ground floor, minus the house on the hill. It seemed as desolate a spot you could disappear into. And that she liked.

Turning into the lot, she pulled the Sequoia around the back of the building, parked in a space in front of the rooms, and switched the engine off. She put the keys in her jacket pocket and grabbed her backpack. After locking up the Sequoia, she crossed the parking lot to the motel office.

Outside the office, she didn't see a single person. The glass door entrance was shattered and ajar. The room looked like a hurricane had gone through it. She decided to go inside, but she was ready to run at the first sign of trouble.

Carefully, she looked around as she walked into the office. She went behind the counter and took a look at the key rack on the wall. At her feet, on the floor, was four twenty-dollar bills. After a thought or two about it, she helped herself to the cash and to room key number nine. What difference would it make if she stayed for a while?

On the way to the room, she saw vending machines full of snacks and drinks. The tempered glass panel of the snack machine was shattered, but still in place. She pushed the glass and a large chunk broke off.

A plan quickly took shape in her mind. She had to move fast because the light was fading.

Moving as silently as she could, she ran to the SUV, rummaged through the trunk and found herself a tire iron. After quietly closing the trunk, she returned to the vending machines. Using the tire iron, she broke what was left of the glass panel of the snack machine. Then she filled her backpack to the top with candy bars, bags of potato chips, and everything else from the machine. Carrying it wasn't easy, but she managed to open the door of the room. She emptied the contents of her backpack onto the king-size bed and went back for more.

She slipped the flat end of the tire iron into the side groove of the drink machine and broke off the lock. It took twenty-five minutes to pry open the machine. By that time it was dark.

She hustled as if her life depended on it, filling her backpack with weeks' worth of bottles of Coke, Diet Coke, Sprite and Dasani water.

Mission accomplished. She dragged her overloaded backpack into the room, tired. After locking the door, she snatched a chair from the room, and quickly stuck it under the doorknob. She wouldn't be going outside again, at least for the next three weeks depending on her food supply. Bottles were loaded into the small refrigerator and placed on the desk beside the snacks.

The dull room wasn't much to look at, however, it was clean, and the electricity was working. She put the tire iron in her backpack and set it on the table by the TV. Then she went over to the bathroom, flipped on the light switch, and washed her hands and face. After undressing, she stepped into the shower.

She came out of the bathroom with a towel wrapped around her body. The only light in the room was from the cracked-open door of the bathroom. As she dressed, she was surprised by the quiet. A peek around the edge of the skimpy curtain showed her that there was no one outside.

After the emotional roller coaster, she'd been on for the past eleven hours, rest was the thing she needed most. She crawled wearily into bed, the events of the day flashing through her mind. She released a sigh of frustration, broke down with tears, and put her hands to her face.

Even as she trembled, she kept asking herself 'Why couldn't she save Elena?' Guilt built up in her for staying in the SUV. She should have insisted on going with her. There was nothing she could do now. Elena was gone. But today, she, too, could have died.

Sensing she was close to a meltdown, she breathed deeply a couple of times to relax. When she was calm, she stared around in the darkness with no thoughts. Not too soon after, she placed her head on the pillow, did she allow herself to drift into a deep sleep.

Chapter 48

AFTER A QUIET dinner, I stood up from the table and saw Dan Saunders, his wife whose name I thought was Meaghan, and daughter Georgia enter the cafeteria. Their occasional presence around the facility over these past months had taken some getting used to. Saunders couldn't have been more down-to-earth and relaxed around his family. I liked seeing that side of him, the side most people didn't see.

A week back, the day after St. Patrick's Day, he introduced me to his daughter Georgia. She had told me that she wanted to be at college and hanging out with her friends, rather than stay here. If her friends were alive? That was the sixty-four-thousand-dollar question. She was still naïve in many ways. And she didn't realize how lucky she was that her father worked at Biogenetics & Disease Control. Not everyone had access to an underground safe haven.

As I was walking out the door of the cafeteria, and while Saunders chatted with the cashier, swiping his credit card at the register, I waved to Georgia in a friendly manner. She smiled and waved back to me. Seeing her reminded me of Jenna. They were coincidentally the same age, and had been attending university, different schools, of course. I thought she would get along well with Georgia, should she arrive.

I took the elevator to Lotte Market, the store on the eighth floor. I wanted to get the shopping out of the way so I could stay at home this weekend. On the ride there, I wondered if the reason I look for things to remind me of Jenna, was, as a way of keeping her alive in my mind. I didn't want her to be dead and I didn't want to forget her. And I refused to give up on her. The reason she wasn't here yet was because the never dead were constantly interfering, preventing her from getting here. That had to be why.

This horrible epidemic made you appreciate the smallest things in life, such as the salmon-flavored canned cat food that Mim loved so much. During these uncertain times, I was glad to see it on the shelf, given that we had to ration our food supplies. Lately, Linda Park, the manager of the store, had kept a watchful eye on the inventory, making me feel guilty for buying anything. I didn't buy too many items because I took most of my meals in the cafeteria. Come to think of it, the cafeteria meal portions had been smaller and extra helpings of food were not offered as of late. I quickly checked out, before anyone asked me to put everything back.

I was barely able to open the door to my apartment carrying two full shopping bags. At first, I didn't see Mim anywhere, but then I heard a meow when I dropped the bags on the kitchen counter. Just as I started putting away the groceries, she came running in from the living room to rub up against my legs and purr loudly.

"Meow!"

"I have your favorite," I said, holding up a can of cat food in one hand.

"Meow!" said the cat again with more intensity.

After feeding the cat, I went and sat on the sofa and thought about all the things I could do, rather than the things I could not. Should I squeeze in time for my video diary? Or shouldn't I? It was time for an update, though, I didn't have any notes prepared. So, I would just have to ad lib it. Jenna would get a kick out of the videos, if she ever saw them. I had even thought about uploading these videos on YouTube or another social media site such as Facebook or Twitter.

With all that in my mind, and eager to get this over with, I set up my camcorder on a tripod on the coffee table, pushed the Record button, and spoke to the camera.

Hannah Winter here. Yes! I'm still alive. I find it hard to believe myself now that it's the end of March. That's the only good news to report because the virus continues to spread. It's Friday evening and I'm speaking to you from the Biogenetics & Disease Control facility in Dulce, New Mexico. Research in the laboratory for the development of an antidote for the virus also continues.

Things are bad outside. I've seen the so-called never dead, zombies, hanging around outside on the video feed from the cameras at the entrance gate. They are rather scary and look crazy. It's hard to believe they were once regular people. The virus changes them. Now they are walking dead cannibals.

Why can't things be like they were before? I keep asking myself that question. Will it get better soon? Another question I want answered, but with no answer in sight.

I'm going to get real. Not that I haven't already been real, but I really worry about the supply of groceries and similar goods. There are slightly over one hundred people here. Everyone is rationing, because it's a concern for us all.

I'm safe down here underground, but I don't know for how long. And, of course, my other concern is that I have no information about my sister Jenna. But I'm not going to get depressed. I'm getting through it, one day at a time. All I can hope is for better news next time. Signing off.

When I finished recording, I turned to see Mim come running out of the kitchen. She was all playful. As for me, I just wanted to wind down in bed with a good book before going to sleep.

After washing up in the bathroom, I got dressed in my pajamas, and got into bed. I grabbed the book "Insurgent" from the nightstand where I had left it after last night's reading. With all my procrastinating, I had only read halfway through it. It was my mission to finish reading it over the weekend. I flipped the book open, thumbed to the page I had dog-eared and started reading.

"Meow!" said Mim the cat, running into the room.

"Well, look who's here!" I said, not caring that she had no grasp of the English language.

I patted the bed and called her name. Mim jumped up and dropped down beside me. I cuddled her in close, and she fell asleep happy.

After reading a few more pages, I closed the book and placed it on the nightstand. I fell asleep instantly, cozily tucked in with Mim curled up beside me.

Chapter 49

ON TUESDAY, April 2, the day after April Fools' Day, Jenna climbed out of bed after a long night's sleep. There was nothing else to do but sleep. She thought about how the weeks had gone by. One day blended into another, the waiting for this pandemic to be over, occupying her thoughts every waking minute of the day.

It was about twelve o'clock, lunchtime, when she came out of the bathroom after showering and dressing. She had little left to eat and had rationed the food carefully. Famished, she gobbled down potato chips and a Snickers candy bar. Instead of coffee, she had to settle for the last bottle of Coke.

In the middle of cleaning up, she heard a clanking noise outside. In truth, she wasn't too worried, because she had a tire iron and was willing to use it on the infected. If it was a zombie and not somebody else altogether. But either way, she needed to know what it was.

Peering out from between the curtain flaps, she had a bird's eye view of the whole thing. There was a scruffy-looking man lurking around the parking lot near the Sequoia. He was five-nine, in his early thirties, and carrying a denim jacket on his left arm. There was no doubt to her that he wasn't a zombie. She waited and watched, hoping he would leave.

The man was peering through the windows looking for keys dangling in the ignition. Every so often, he checked over his shoulder, probably watching out for zombies. After searching the ground, he knelt to look under the SUV, then circled around the vehicle.

Frustratingly, she was wondering if he was ever going to leave. When he began trying the doors of the Sequoia, she had had enough of him. She thought it would be a good idea if she walked right to the door of the SUV, get in and take off as fast as possible. And if he said anything to her, she would simply ignore him. So was her plan.

She put her things into her backpack. After touring the room, checking that she'd left nothing behind, she slung the backpack over her shoulder and hurried toward the door.

No sooner had she stepped outside, this became one of the few times she was inspired to say something. "Is there something you're looking for?"

His right hand fumbled with his denim jacket as he kept his back to her. Almost a minute had passed before he turned around, looked at her, his blue eyes glimmering with amusement.

He simply smiled. "Ma'am, by chance is this your vehicle?"

"Yes. And if you'll excuse me, I'm in a hurry."

He smiled again. "You're not infected, are you?"

"I most certainly am not. Are you?" she replied, walking toward the SUV.

He flashed her an exaggerated smile, but then changed his tone abruptly. "No, I'm definitely not. Now that we got that out of the way, hand me the keys, now!"

He pulled a gun from under his jacket and pointed it at her chest. "Now means now."

Her heart was pounding in her chest, her eyes fixed on the barrel of the gun. Yet she had to say something.

"You have no right to do this. I can give you a ride. I'm driving to New…," she pleaded, her body quivering.

"Shut your mouth," he barked, stopping her from finishing the sentence.

Jenna held her tongue.

He racked the slide of his 9mm Beretta, chambering a round from the magazine, ready to pull the trigger. "You're going to give me the keys or I'll shoot you."

She knew he wouldn't hesitate to use it. The look in his eyes said it all. Digging her hand into her pocket, she fished out the keys, and tossed them to him. It wasn't like she had a choice. She couldn't wrestle the gun away from him. It might work for Jet Li in the movies, but it would not work for Jenna Winter in real life.

With an arrogant look on his face, he held the keys. Sensing her discomfort, he knew there was nothing she could do aside from stand there and take it.

Realistically, all she could do was look at him with disgust. Yes, she wanted to hit him with the tire iron. But if she tried to use it against him, he would shoot her dead.

A satisfied smile crossed his face as he put the key in the lock, opened the door, and climbed in. "That's just how the cookie crumbles. If you were in my place, you'd do the same."

He laughed in her face, as he shut the door. She wanted nothing more than to wipe that smirk off his face. The desperate man in desperate times, forced to use desperate measures, was all an act, and it didn't work on her. Not for one minute did she pity him. All she felt was disdain, giving him a dirty look as he started up the Sequoia and drove fast out of the parking lot.

"Jerk," she yelled, as she kicked up gravel with the toes of her sneakers.

She looked helplessly as the SUV turned the corner and disappeared. Her eyes watered up, and she turned away, not allowing the tears to fall. Folding her arms across her chest, she held it all back. She wasn't going to let him get the better of her.

And that was when something suddenly struck her. She was lucky he didn't shoot her. It could have been a lot worse. She could have been killed. Placing her hand in her jacket pocket, she grabbed the rosary that Monsignor Lucca had given her a while back. Eyes squeezed shut, she breathed in.

Half a minute later, she exhaled and opened her eyes. Now she was ready to move on. She walked around the motel passing the vending machines that she had emptied some weeks before. Making a quick turn, she headed west as if she knew where she was going. Pulling out a bottle of Dasani water she drained a quarter of it in one long swallow.

Still upset, she was thinking about the man who had carjacked her. She was filled with anger both at the man and at herself for going against her better judgment. Confronting him was dumb. Really dumb. It was a bad move on her part. If she had not encountered him, she wouldn't be walking. Once again, she was without a car. But at least she had the tire iron, good for clobbering zombies.

Chapter 50

THE SUN had been glaring down from a clear sky above Jenna. A mile and a half later, she blotted sweat from the back of her neck with the sleeve of her jacket all the while she kept moving forward. Though she was tired, she struggled with fears, unable to stop, as her eyes darted everywhere as if she anticipated a zombie attack at any moment, from anywhere.

She was crossing Hillside Road when she saw a Sonic Drive-In on her right and walked over to check it out. Just looking at the place made her think of the food served there. But all she smelled was rotting flesh. That smell that seemed to follow her everywhere she went.

The restaurant was in disarray, trays and broken glass all over the floor. There was some kind of spill on the floor — dry now — next to the overflowing garbage bins.

Then she found her thoughts were wandering. In her mind,

she pictured the way it used to be: serving burgers and French fries, and loaded with customers. Would life ever be like that again? All she desired was to return to the simple pleasures of life such as shopping at the mall with friends and talking and texting on the phone. Social media had become a big part of her social life. So, she greatly missed surfing the Internet for news, sending e-mails, and scrolling through her Facebook account.

As she thought back on it, sadness fell on her with each passing second. It got to the point where she couldn't bear the sight of the restaurant anymore. She turned her head away, her eyes pointed in the direction of the back parking lot. And lo and behold there was an empty black Nissan Rogue SUV with the driver's door slightly open.

She headed over to it, praying that she would find the keys, so she could drive it away. Up close, she saw a stain of blood on the driver-side door, near the handle. The keys were not in the ignition, or on the seats, neither the floor. But there was a handbag on the driver's seat next to a Sonic Drive-In name badge that read EMILY LAMB, MANAGER.

She opened the door of the Rogue. It had a new-car smell, as if it hadn't been driven. Grabbing the handbag, she rummaged through it until she located the keys. She tossed the handbag in the passenger seat, pulled herself into the driver's seat, shut the door, and started the SUV. The gas gauge read full.

While the Rogue was idling, she took the tire iron out of her backpack. She placed it on the floor of the passenger seat while her mind was preoccupied by something else. After careful consideration, she took thirty-five dollars and some loose change from the wallet in the handbag and asked for God's forgiveness. Quick as a blink she tossed the handbag over her shoulder and onto the floor of the backseat. She placed the money in her wallet, which she tucked hurriedly into her backpack, then buckled her seat belt.

Not bothering to look in the mirror, she moved a damp strand from her forehead. She was feeling a little tired from all the walking she had done earlier. None the less, she was glad to be in the SUV and ready to go.

Just as she was about to back out of the lot, there was a whack on the window. She almost jumped out of her seat. A growling zombie's face appeared in the driver's-side window. *That was some timing*, she thought. The zombie had wild red eyes, bruises on her forehead, and chunks missing from her arms, where skin had been pulled off. Because she was dressed in a Sonic Drive-In employee uniform, Jenna believed that the zombie was Emily Lamb, the owner of the SUV.

"Forgive me. Is this your SUV?" she asked with a devilish grin, holding up the plastic name badge in the zombie's direction.

She couldn't resist the opportunity to poke fun at the zombie. After all that she'd been through, she could use a few laughs. Even she was giggling when the zombie hit the window harder than before, desperately wanting to get her. And now it was hissing and growling louder.

At this moment, Jenna wasn't feeling afraid. No matter the zombie's ferocious behavior, she wasn't going anywhere...yet. Smiling wickedly, she wasn't finished venting.

"Not anymore," she said, carrying on the joke.

Once she started indulging in her newfound courage, there was no stopping her. This time, she was the carjacker, and it felt good to be bad. Relishing in the moment, she couldn't stop herself from laughing.

But the moment ended all too soon. She had settled down, put the car in reverse, the tires spinning on loose gravel kicking up dust in the zombie's face as she drove out of the parking lot. The zombie certainly couldn't be any angrier, additionally to the fact that Jenna had escaped.

Jenna was laughing as she drove onto the road. She kept one eye on the road and the other on the rearview mirror, watching the zombie stagger and drag its feet, waving its arms and growling through clenched teeth. And she wanted to provoke it again. In the spur of the moment, she seized her chance. She stomped on the brakes and rolled down the window on the passenger side.

She tossed the name badge out of the window, and yelled, "I think this is yours."

With her confidence boosted, she laughed again. After rolling up the window, she punched the pedal and the Rogue darted forward. She drove up Hillside Road and made a right onto Soncy Road. There were no cars on the road as far as she could see.

Not too long driving, and still no one was behind her, not a single car. She thought she shouldn't have any trouble if she drove the Rogue on the smaller roads. None the wiser, she was about to find out how wrong she was.

Chapter 51

IF THERE was one thing that Jenna had learned about the situation during these past months, it was to not be surprised at anything that happened. She had turned left on W. Country Road 34 where the dead were walking, and men were shooting at them. As soon as she heard gunshots, she stopped the SUV, otherwise she would have run straight into it.

Her eyes darted left, and with a glance to the right, she saw a man close his hand around the rubberized grip of his nine-millimeter Glock pistol. The tall and stocky brown-haired, fortyish man aimed his pistol at a zombie and fired twice. That was all she needed to see.

She was putting her car in reverse to back out of the street when a zombie came closing in on the man. She couldn't help but stare at the zombie dressed in a Grateful Dead T-shirt and slightly tattered blue jeans. He had buggy eyes and stringy hair hanging down over the lacerations on his face. The man stretched out his arm, aimed his pistol at point-blank range into the ear of the zombie and fired. It fell to the ground with a loud thud that muted the sounds coming from the bloodless zombies on both sides of the street.

"Now, I'm so grateful you're dead," the man said amusingly.

He erupted in wild, uncontrollable laughter. But it was short lived, and soon forgotten. He scanned the crowd of zombies approaching from several directions, but his view was obstructed by Jenna's SUV.

"Get out of the way!" the man yelled at her, raising his pistol.

Jenna had a split second to decide whether to drive away or stay put. She was about to back the SUV up, until she saw a young man with a submachine gun, blocking her from behind. He had neatly cropped blond hair, ice-blue eyes, and an eagle tattoo on his bicep just below the sleeve of the dusty blue T-shirt he wore with a pair of khakis. He motioned with his hand for her to get down.

She did that very thing. Without any further hesitation, she hunched down into the seat, shifted into drive, and slammed her foot down on the gas pedal. The Rogue lunged forward. The tires screeched, and the smell of burnt rubber filled the air. In the process, she drove over one of the dead zombies on the ground.

Saying to herself, with her foot pressed to the floor, "Can't this vehicle move any faster?"

The young man sprayed bullets back and forth, knocking several zombies to the ground. Jenna kept her head down, trying not to get caught in the crossfire. Bullets smashed through the rear window and exited out the windshield, narrowly missing her. Everything seemed to be moving in slow motion. Luckily, she hadn't been hit. But the Nissan Rogue wasn't so lucky, as it was built to handle bumps and jumps, but not bullets. She heard a pop as the hissing sound of air escaping from a tire upset her.

"Aw, for Christ's sake!" she exclaimed to herself.

She couldn't stop the SUV because she was still in the line of fire. What made it worse was she had to reduce her speed to a crawl. Her fear grew as the Rogue inched its way forward. When she finally made it to the next street, she stopped abruptly.

Wouldn't you know it, she had never changed a tire before. She couldn't ask anyone for help, at the risk of being carjacked. And with many zombies around, there wouldn't be enough time to do it anyway, or so she convinced herself. Realizing what must be done, she hated to abandon the Rogue. It was the first time in her life that she was bitter at the hand she had been dealt. Now she wanted a cigarette.

She moved the rearview mirror, needing to see what was behind her. About twelve feet away there was a man holding a bottle of beer in one hand and an assault-rifle in the other hand. At least it wasn't pointed at her. He looked to be in his mid-fifties, of average height, with his blond hair in a ponytail, sharp blue eyes, and wearing a white T-shirt under a black leather vest, blue jeans and polished snakeskin boots. She didn't like the looks of him.

When the man turned to the right, his back facing her, she swiped up her backpack, and practically jumped out of the SUV. Keeping her head down, she nervously passed him as he dropped the empty beer bottle on the ground and started loading his weapon. When he suddenly turned around, she briefly glanced up and noticed an amused look on his face, as if he enjoyed killing the infected.

"Is there a problem?" he asked looking at her out of the corner of his eye.

With a slow shake of her head, she got the message. "No problem. It's all good."

"The zombies only kill what they intend to eat. They're not doing anything illegal. Cannibalism is not against the law!" he joked, slurring his words slightly, and winked at her.

Tossing his head back, he laughed, showing his nicotine-stained teeth. He almost doubled over laughing at his own joke.

Jenna wasn't amused by his drunken stupor. As he moved, she moved, trying to distance herself from him. She didn't want to be around an intoxicated man carrying a loaded rifle.

"Oh, hardy har har," she whispered to herself.

He called out to her saying, "You ever shot a gun? I can teach you how."

When she heard him talk, she could not help thinking that it was utter nonsense. She didn't say a word, didn't look up, and began walking a little faster. She knew how Texas men practiced their second amendment rights, to keep and bear arms. And there were more guns around than there were zombies. It was then that she remembered reading articles in the San Antonio Express-News about a bill in the Senate to be incorporated into the crime bill to ban assault weapons. Due to the current situation, she could only assume that the proposed gun control legislation was on hold.

All the same, she would feel better when she was far from this area. Alone and unguided, uncertain of her destination, she wasn't sure exactly where to go, sure only that it was somewhere else.

Chapter 52

NEARLY AN HOUR had gone by. Jenna shuffled along, but could not keep herself from twisting back to see if any zombies were following her. As she turned the corner onto Arnot Road, her heart skipped a beat at the sound of a gunshot. She stopped walking, the breath catching in her throat as she felt like the wind was just knocked out of her. A dead zombie was lying on the ground only a few feet away from a man holding a smoking gun in his hand. But there was no need to fret. Turning her head in another direction, she continued on her merry way. Maybe she had become desensitized to death, but she didn't want to analyze it.

It was not many minutes later, when she heard grunts, biting and chewing sounds. Looking in the direction of the noise, she saw something she wished she hadn't seen. In a field about twenty feet from the road, there sat a zombie with both hands inside the stomach of a woman. From where she stood, she couldn't tell whether the woman was unconscious or dead. But she had a much better view of the zombie's face. He had a receding hairline, black and broken teeth, and eyes red from broken blood vessels.

Moving on tiptoes, she passed the zombie, who was moaning with excitement, consuming the woman. She thought she'd seen it all — until the zombie pulled out an organ, probably the liver, and bit into it with relish. She shook her head, turning away from the gore.

Barely making a sound, she made her way to the end of the street. She passed a parking lot filled with trucks. Unfortunately, she could tell they were all locked up tight. Up ahead, she could see a gated trailer park. With a wary glance around, she hurried to investigate it.

Near the RV's park office was a swimming pool and a convenience store. An overpowering smell of rotting flesh filled the air, sending shock waves of nausea through her. A swarm of flies were buzzing around the five dead bodies near the swimming pool. They had probably been infected because she noticed the bodies had bullet holes in their heads. Oblivious to the fly crawling on her face, she zigzagged around the corpses.

Desperately thirsty, she went into the little store and found it was stocked with lots of food. She grabbed a bottle of water from the cooler, took a couple of large gulps, paused, and then took another gulp. Then she poured a little water into her hand and splashed it on her face.

When she swept the area, there wasn't a living soul as far as her eyes could see. On second glance, an RV, with its door open, was directly ahead. Cautiously, she walked toward it.

When she got close to the door, she got a whiff of that horrible death smell. Suddenly, she didn't want to explore anymore. Before she could turn away, her eyes caught a glimpse of something shiny. From the angle she was standing, she could see, lying on a table in full view, the steel frame of a revolver. It was as if it had been placed there precisely so that she would see it.

Staring at it for a moment, she wanted it bad, and for justifiable reasons. She had nothing to defend herself from a zombie attack because she had left the tire iron in the Nissan Rogue.

Curiosity got the better of her and she moved closer to the motorhome. Standing to the side of the door, she tried to see what was causing the smell. But she really couldn't see anything.

She thought about the gun again. Knowing nothing about guns, she really didn't want it, because she had survived all this time without it. And just because it was there didn't mean she had to take it. Why was she wasting her time on it? That was a question she needed to answer for herself. Then she, thought about the jerk, the man who had carjacked her.

She stepped up into the RV and found the body of a dead woman, face down on the floor. There was a pool of blood around her head. Covering her nose and mouth with her sleeve, with her right hand, she grabbed the revolver and the box of bullets off the table.

"Oh, the stench! For the love of God," she said plainly, and safely exited the RV.

After inspecting it, she put the thirty-eight revolver in her jacket pocket. She shoved the box of bullets inside her backpack. It wasn't like she stole it, she reassured herself. Still, she could have kicked herself for taking it.

It was late afternoon, and she was starting to wear down. At length, the thought came to her that a motorhome was a good hiding place for the next weeks. She had hid out before in the motel, and she was eager to do it again. Though she didn't care fore the smell in the air, it was pleasantly deserted.

Without wasting another minute thinking about it, she started checking the doors on RVs. After seven locked doors, she finally found one that was unlocked. Her right hand gripped the revolver inside her jacket pocket, turned the doorknob with her left hand. Looking right and left, she didn't see a single soul. Certain it was empty, she let out a breath she hadn't realized she was holding.

Soundlessly, she slipped inside and shut the door. Her first thought was that she needed groceries. So, she stripped a pillowcase off one of the pillows on the bed.

Stepping out of the RV, she walked a complete circle around the Georgie Boy motorhome. There were no signs of life, other than hers. Time was a-wasting as the light was starting to fade. As she hurried toward the convenience store, she hoped she wouldn't encounter anyone along the way.

When she reached the pool, her body shook as she crept by the dead bodies lying on the ground, unable to tolerate the smell. Still, she was glad they weren't moving.

Once inside the store, she began loading her backpack and filling the pillowcase with everything she liked to eat: chips, candy bars, crackers, bottles of water, and sodas. Once loaded to the hilt, she rushed back to the motorhome and dumped it all on the bed. And then she did it again — four times. That was when she knew she had enough food to last a month or so.

She locked the door and closed all of the curtains on the windows. After putting away the groceries, she went to the bathroom, washed her hands, then undressed and showered. The water was cold, but she got used to it. After drying off with a towel, she got dressed again.

Feeling hungry, she went into the kitchen and ate to her heart's content. Then she checked the bedroom closet for clothes. She found a blue hoodie, blue sweatpants, and put them on.

Glancing at her jacket on the bed, she thought about the gun inside the pocket. She pulled it out and laid it on the bed. She stared at it for a while, her mind racing. Was it a wise thing to do? She sure didn't feel ladylike around it. And yet, there it was. Now, she was scared that she would shoot herself in the foot.

If she was going to keep it, she had to learn how to use it. Picking up the revolver, she studied it. She pointed the gun toward the floor, checked the cylinder, and found five bullets inside. Then she took a single bullet from the box, inserted it into the cylinder, made sure it was fully loaded, and locked the cylinder back in place.

Jenna practiced holding the revolver with both hands on the black rubber grip and aiming at the wall, even though it felt a little awkward. Turning, she pointed the revolver at the kitchen chair as if she was about to pull the trigger.

Only a short while later, she discovered that she was very tired and decided to practice again later. She put the gun into her jacket pocket, then put the jacket and backpack on a shelf by the bed. She laid out on the bed in the darkness, her shoulders propped up on a pillow. Her eyes slowly closed, and she fell asleep almost immediately.

Chapter 53

THE STENCH of the dead bodies was fouling the air. At night, when the wind blew from the east, all Jenna could smell was death, even though the windows were closed. The smell of the site and the number of the dead lying around didn't appeal to her. All she could do was grin and bear it, somehow, forcing herself to get used to it. Where else could she go? The motorhome served as a place of refuge, giving her a break from the zombies and the gunfire.

Looking out the window, she was restless, adjusting to the confinement of the RV. Nothing moved outside. And it was too quiet. She hadn't heard any gunshots, hadn't seen nor heard a peep from a bird or rustling of a wing. You could blame that on the stinky corpses, like scarecrows, scaring everything away.

She had wanted to dig a hole and pile the dead bodies into it, the way she had seen the police officers do it in Abilene when she was on the roof of a building. All this time thinking about it, she had managed to put the idea aside. She had arrived at the conclusion that the smell might work to her advantage. It seemed wise to camouflage one's smell from the zombies. If left undisturbed, the place gave the impression that no one lived there. That she preferred.

Over a week had gone by since she had begun squatting in the RV community. She was the community now. But she'd vowed to herself she wouldn't be there for very long. Once her supply of food ran out, she would be back on the road heading to New Mexico. Seeing it in her mind's eye, she longed to be there with her sister. But after all this time, she doubted it was possible she could get there. It was hard enough trying to stay alive by avoiding the zombies at every turn. Still, it didn't stop her from hoping.

What could she do now? Jenna asked herself turning away from the window. She looked at the end table beside the bed. There was always the book of sudoku puzzles. Just lying there, she couldn't help but look at it. It was the first thing she looked at when she woke up, and the last thing she looked at before going to sleep. But she couldn't stand it anymore. It had served its purpose in taking her mind off the gun inside her jacket pocket, whiling away the time. Now she needed something to take her mind off sudoku puzzles. Was she addicted to it?

As soon as she had found it, she started filling in the boxes like a madwoman. She worked through the puzzles in the book as if there was no tomorrow. Binge-playing for hours, she'd been an obsessive gamer — and she excelled at it. Never did she expect that a 9 x 9-square grid subdivided into nine 3 x 3 boxes containing each of the numbers from 1 to 9 exactly once, would excite her so much. Was she turning into a geek? Maybe she was a geek and just didn't know it, or had been one, and could easily be one again.

Lying there on the table, it was so weird — as if it was saying, "Pick me up. Please."

"No. I won't pick you up," she answered.

Tired of the same routine, there had to be something else she could do. She was thinking along the lines that reading a good book would be a better way of spending one's leisure time. It wouldn't hurt to fantasize a little bit. After putting the book of sudoku puzzles on the shelf, saving it for a rainy day, but she didn't have to worry because she knew it wasn't going to rain, because it hadn't rained in a while, she began searching through the books.

After some deliberation, she took "The Shining" by Stephen King. Skimming through it quickly, she worried about reading it. Would it terrify her? She could have another nightmare. She thought that the horror novel about a writer who took a winter job as a caretaker of a hotel and went insane from seeing ghosts, might scare her. But then again, if she could handle living among the walking dead, she might as well go ahead and read it. At the very least it would take her mind off numbers.

She plopped on the bed and flipped the book open. One page into reading it, she unwrapped a stick of Trident gum and shoved it in her mouth. To stretch the time, she read each page slowly. After a few chapters, she took a wrapper out of her flannel shirt pocket, spit her gum into it, and tossed it into the trash can beside the end table.

At one point in her reading, she was so comfortable that she almost fell asleep. Perhaps she needed more coffee. She brewed one pot a day to prevent the odor from penetrating the walls. Even if she believed the scent of decomposing human flesh outside overpowered the smell of coffee, there was no way she was going to put on another pot. Considering her situation, she could only take so many risks. She poured three mugs full of the steaming brew from a full pot, a lot more than she needed. She was lucky enough to have a coffee maker, the only perk to being holed up in an RV. It also helped that the recreational vehicle had a can of ground coffee, sugar bowl, and a quart jar of powdered creamer.

When she had been at the Sunrise Motel, she had followed a routine. And here she was, doing the same thing. She went to sleep almost as soon as it was dark and woke up at the first light of day. Ordinarily she used little electricity. Once it was dark out, she didn't risk turning on the lights. There was a flashlight in the bathroom and another one on the end table by the bed. Every time she turned on the flashlight, she aimed the beam downward, away from the windows.

Hours passed and she had read enough of "The Shining" to get the gist of the story. And so far, she wasn't scared. She would read more later, because right now she needed to make dinner. As she stood up from the bed, she felt lightheaded, a feeling that came from eating small portions of food, three times per day.

Chapter 54

KNOWING THAT THE VIRUS might be one of the deadliest pathogens known to humankind, now at the end of April, with no cure in sight, Julie Mehta worried that the situation was spinning out of control. Thinking about this last week, which had been nothing short of miserable for her, she pulled out her desk chair and sat down. Lifting her mug, she gratefully took a sip of her favorite Darjeeling tea, which was a pleasant distraction from her jumbled thoughts. The taste reminded her a little too much of home, as in India. In quiet moments, especially in her office with the door closed, how she missed her native land.

Her meditative thoughts were interrupted by a flash of light coming from a sparkling jewel in a glass specimen jar on the shelf next to "Gray's Anatomy." The platinum wedding ring with a four carat round diamond stone, surrounded by smaller diamonds, glinted in the fluorescent light from the ceiling. The ring was all that was left to remind her of her almost three-year relationship with Sam Walters. To her it was merely something to be studied and examined.

While she stared at the ring in the jar, she thought back to the lavish engagement party she and Sam had enjoyed. Happily, in love, she felt like the luckiest girl in the world. Clearly, now that the marriage was dissolved, she didn't feel much of anything. Those days were gone and would never return.

Now, she was remembering something she regretted. It seemed like it had just happened yesterday. And she wanted to kick herself for being so stupid. Over the telephone Sam had told her he would be attending a medical conference. And in Las Vegas of all places. She should have known something wasn't right. When he showed up at the house, he had behaved coldly to her as he began to fill his suitcase with clothes. Then he left without any explanation. Two weeks later, he returned for the rest of his things, during the day when she was working.

The next thing that happened was that she was contacted by an attorney for Sam, who was in a hurry to marry the new woman in his life. She'd been grateful that she and Sam hadn't had any children to fight over during the divorce, making it quick and easy. She got to keep the house. But he didn't care because he had a six-figure income as a physician and could afford to purchase another house.

Her family never did like him. They felt Sam, who was an American of Irish descent, wasn't right for her. Her parents had hoped that she would accept a proposal of marriage from a well-to-do Indian man of their choosing and social standing. Arranged marriages were common in India, and had been successful. Now she wondered if her parents had been right.

Upon divorcing, she returned to her maiden name of Mehta. Since Sam didn't love her anymore, there was no reason to carry his last name. Simply swell, she had never got used to being called Julie Walters. It sounded so generic to her.

For some crazy reason, here she was thinking about it all over again. Maybe she was feeling lonely. After her divorce the year before last, she'd been absorbed in work. Then a couple of weeks before the epidemic started, she met someone, a handsome accountant two years younger than her. She still had his business card in the top drawer of her desk.

His name was Rick, another American of Irish descent. That was the type of men she attracted. And she could just imagine what her family would say. She was on a plane returning from a business trip to Atlanta, Georgia for the 28th World Vaccines & Immunization Congress. He was sitting in the aisle seat, she sat by the window, and the seat between them was empty. They became acquainted and got along well. Four days later, he called her at work. They talked about meeting for dinner sometime soon. But she had said she would get back to him about it.

It didn't happen. She didn't remember to call him. As simple as that. Now there was no way of knowing if Rick was even still alive. Maybe it was for the best. That was what she kept telling herself.

It might be a long time before she met a man she wanted to go out with. And it didn't help that she worked insane hours, underground, closed off from the outside world. But it was something to worry about later.

Just when she wanted to stop dwelling on the past, her eyes wandered over to the ring in the glass jar again. Even after all this time, she felt a resentment toward her ex-husband for leaving her for another woman. Ridiculous that she could feel envy for a woman she'd never met. Not even in the slightest way. Rather she prayed to the god Shiva that Sam and his new bride were zombies. She didn't care to find out either.

The best thing to do would be to send her mind somewhere else for the rest of her break. She took a long sip of her tea and then decided to do some reading. Glancing at the shelf, she picked up "Gray's Anatomy," and reclined in her chair and thumbed through it. Then she started to read it.

Looking at the illustrations began to make her sleepy. She kept her head tilted toward the book, but her eyes were closed. If James Stebbins hadn't knocked on the door panel before opening the door of her office, she would have fallen asleep. From the angle at which he stood, he didn't notice that she was nodding off, and went right into it.

"Knock. Knock. Are you busy, Julie?"

Julie looked up to see Stebbins standing there holding up a couple of loose sheets of paper. "No, I'm not, what's up?"

"Did you get a chance to look at the report?" he asked, as he stepped into the office, stopping in front of her desk.

"I did."

"I have something I want to show you in the laboratory concerning it."

Julie glanced into her mug and frowned. Her mug was half full of tea. It hadn't even been fifteen minutes. So much for a break.

"Okay, lead the way, James," she said, placing the book on her desk and standing up.

"There is one thing bothering me," he added.

"First, why don't we go over what we know so far?" she asked as they walked out of the room.

Chapter 55

THIS LAST MONTH flew by. The day was Tuesday, May 7, 2013. As sunlight slanted through the curtains onto Jenna Winter's face, she awoke to the sound of a door slamming and turned to the bedside clock. Squinting against the glare of the sunlight, she tried to make out the time as her body sprang to life. It was nine o'clock.

The chaos in her mind grew. Staring at the wall, she stayed under the blanket while waiting for another sound, waiting for it to come again. Nothing happened. Her pulse beat faster and faster. For several minutes, there was just the sound of her breathing. She was almost certain she had heard something. Or had it been a dream within a dream, the kind of dream which seemed so real when you woke?

Needing to know for sure, she sat up and swung her legs over the side of the bed. Standing up, she went to the window.

Before too long, she heard something again, and a hint of fear appeared in her eyes. She listened to the shuffling echo of footsteps from inside a blue RV directly across from her. Someone, or some zombie was out there. But she couldn't see them. It was real. It was clear there was no dream about it.

The little voice inside her head reminded her that she had little food left. Tired of sitting around, tired of living like a hermit, she wanted to leave yesterday. But something in the back of her mind had told her to stay. Now the voice in her head was saying, *Leave immediately!*

With that in mind, she eased away from the window and went to the bathroom. After dressing, she swung her backpack over her shoulder and stepped over to the window. There was nothing in her view. Then she hurried over to the door and listened to make sure no one was there. When she didn't hear anyone, she unlocked the door, and slipped out of the motorhome without making a stir that would attract the attention of any zombie.

Her nerves were on edge. She hoped she might be able to avoid any confrontation as she headed toward Arnot Road. After what had happened with the man who stole the Toyota Sequoia — unable to forget how she was carjacked in the parking lot of the Sunrise Motel, she didn't want to run into someone.

Just to be on the safe side, she kept her hand near the gun in her jacket pocket. It was all she had to protect herself. If any person or zombie tried anything, she felt capable of pulling out the revolver and shooting anything that moved.

Jenna had reached the road, then looked back at the recreational vehicle park. It was a relief to her that nothing looked back at her. Whoever it was that had been over there hadn't seen her. But she couldn't bet her life on it. And she wasn't going to stick around and find out. For now, she figured she was in the clear.

The last of her agitation dissipated as she turned her attention back to the road ahead. As far down Arnot Road as she could see, there was no sign of life. As she started walking, she pulled out a bottle of 7UP from her backpack and took a few sips. Once again, she hadn't a clue where she was going.

It took no more than half an hour to reach a Park-N-Shop in front of a Motel 6 at the corner of Interstate 40 and S. Bolton Street. No one was around that she could see, only four big rigs in the parking lot. She felt she needed to make a pit stop to eat something.

One more quick glance around confirmed that the coast was clear. Ridiculous wishful thinking on her part. When she opened the door of the Park-N-Shop, she heard a sound like a foot scraping on the ground behind her, and smelled that terrible smell, she knew all too well. The stench of a rotting corpse.

Her eyes went wide, and her mouth fell open at the sight of a zombie walking toward her. Bloodshot eyes fixed on her with a menacing glare. The female zombie with long, dark, matted hair, wore a blood-soaked shirt and torn-up jeans. Beyond the greenish coloration, the skin was peeling from her hands.

As she removed her hand from the door so it would close, a growl came from behind a truck. Jenna swung her head to the left as another zombie walked slowly forward. This female zombie had curly blonde, blood-splattered hair with a stump for a right arm, and was dressed in a Motel 6 housekeeping uniform.

Should she stay, or should she go? She considered backing up, running for her life, but decided to hold her ground. There was no choice other than to reach inside her jacket pocket and grab the handle of the thirty-eight caliber. She had never thought of killing anyone before, never shot a gun before. It was all she could do not to scream from the agony of it. She didn't like guns, and she didn't like to have to shoot them.

What if she missed?

Then again as she thought about it, how hard could it be? She had seen it done in the movies. And she had even practiced in the motorhome.

Her instincts kicked in. She pulled out the pistol and put both hands on the grip. Her heart was pounding so wildly, she could barely hear over it. Holding the gun steady, she aimed it at the face of the zombie closest to her and fired off a round. The shot jolted her, causing her to take a step backwards. Knees wobbling, she almost dropped the gun. And it took a moment to get her bearings.

Lucky first shot! It was a direct hit to the head. She watched the zombie collapse to the ground, maybe four feet from her. One down, and one more to go.

Her ears were ringing from the blast of the pistol, drowning out the growls of the other zombie approaching her. She was shocked to see the zombie seven feet away from her and closing the distance between them. As it grunted and raised its arms up to grab her, she didn't hesitate to lift the gun with both hands. She pointed it at its head, and pressed the trigger. A tiny hole opened in the zombie's forehead as the bullet cut through bone, brain tissue, and blew out the back of its skull. After falling to the ground, the zombie lay there motionlessly.

The gun was still in her hand, but she couldn't pull the trigger again, even if her life depended on it. She couldn't move a muscle. All she could do was stare at the zombies lying on the ground, gunshot wounds to their heads. Her head hurt and her ears were buzzing. As she exhaled heavily, she choked back the tears.

After calming herself, she turned her eyes away from the zombies. She scanned the surroundings and didn't see any movement. So, she put the gun into her jacket pocket, then walked into the Park-N-Shop. Right away, she grabbed a lighter from a display and three packs of Marlboro Lights from the shelf behind the counter. The stress of having to shoot the zombies, even if they were already dead, had taken a toll on her. Not surprisingly, she wanted a smoke to help her think and to relieve the built-up tension.

Before she lit up a cigarette, she took two bottles of Sprite from a cooler and an armful of snacks and packed them in her backpack. Next, she grabbed a bottle of water, popped the top, took a long swallow, and then exhaled slowly. A few minutes after, she was all ready to tear into a bag of potato chips, but her body was shaking — from thoughts of what had just happened. Unconsciously, she slipped her hand in her jacket pocket and grabbed the rosary that Monsignor Lucca had given her, in what seemed so long ago now.

Chapter 56

JENNA left the store in a hurry, but stopped for a last look at the dead zombies lying on the ground. The reality of the situation hit her again with full force. Ever since firing the gun, she was so confused and her emotions were all over the place.

She didn't know what she was thinking when she first took the gun. Only that she never expected to have to use it. Funny, but now that she'd fired the gun, rather than pull the trigger again, she preferred to just run from the zombies.

Now she was having second thoughts. Maybe having a gun made her feel less safe. But she decided not to get rid of it just yet. Flustered and totally confused by it all, she needed to think about it some more first.

The stench was so strong that she couldn't stand close to the dead bodies anymore. She had to get going.

As she walked past the parking lot of Motel 6, she saw a black Mercedes-Benz sedan with the driver's-side window rolled halfway down. Just as she was wondering if the keys might be in it, she heard a familiar sound behind her. Her heart dropped, knowing that it was the snarls of a zombie. She turned to see a nasty looking zombie sneaking up on her.

She started to run toward the car. Moving as if in a dream, where she willed herself to move faster. There was no way she could possibly know if the keys were inside. But something in her gut told her to get in the car. She so desperately wanted them to be there.

Arriving at the driver's door, she peered inside. The keys were not in the ignition. She stuck her arm through the open window, unlocked the door, yanked it open, and got behind the wheel. As she eased the door shut, she tried to calm her frantic heart, as she spared half a second to glance over her shoulder and saw the zombie coming after her, approaching at a slow pace. With no time to lose, she had to find the keys.

After locking the door, she started searching. The first place she looked was on the floor under the driver's seat. They weren't there. Strike one!

Frustrated already, she glanced out the window to see the zombie, closer now, dragging a twisted foot. He was short with curly gray hair and deep scars on his face and neck. Making gurgling sounds ... he stared ahead with glassy eyes, holding his mouth wide open. She averted her eyes to avoid eye contact.

Cursing under her breath, she rummaged in the glove compartment for the keys. Still nothing. She blew out a frustrated breath. Strike two!

"Where can they be?" she asked herself.

She raised her head and looked at the zombie in the rearview mirror. Only fifteen feet away from her now, he was even more intimidating. She wanted to scream. Without the engine on, she couldn't roll up the window. In the next two minutes, if she didn't find the keys, she would have to pull out the gun, point it at him, and pull the trigger — something she didn't want to do.

Refusing to give up, she closed her eyes and thought hard. There was only one place left to check — the sun visor. Sure enough, they were there, shoved under the sun visor. She flipped down the visor and the keys fell on the passenger seat. She scored!

Without losing another second, she snatched the keys from the seat and put them in the ignition. She breathed in, let it out, and started the car. In the seconds that she was rolling up the window, simultaneously, she stomped on the gas, and the zombie tried to put his arm through the car window, missing her by inches. He swung out his arms, lifted his chin, and growled as she drove away.

After driving for about one mile, she failed to see a black Honda Accord coming fast behind. But her mind was in a different place. The two right tires lifted off the ground as the Accord swerved to avoid hitting her. The driver hit the horn. As the car passed her, the driver stuck up his middle finger, shot her the bird. She wasn't surprised as the zombie situation could bring out the worst in people.

The tires screeched as she guided the car toward the shoulder, stopped, and killed the engine. Closing her eyes, she put her head down on the steering wheel. Unable to contain her feelings any longer, she broke down, burst into tears. She felt a kind of dread take hold of her stomach as she remembered what she had done. Even if the situation demanded it, she regretted firing the gun. It was as if her innocence had been torn from her life. And it was enough to send her over the edge.

"But, that's not me. Why does it have to be this way?" she demanded with quiet emotion.

She lifted her head, wiped her eyes dry. "Okay, Jenna, pull yourself together."

"Not a living, breathing human being," she whispered, checking the rearview mirror.

Rolling down the driver's side window, she wanted to smoke a cigarette, possibly two. In these recent months she had become too dependent on tobacco. It was the only way she knew how to cope with the trials she was facing and the fear she was feeling.

Time and time again, she had wanted to quit smoking. The thought had crossed her mind on more than one occasion. When all this madness was over she would — she hoped — be able to stop. Putting the matter aside for now, it wasn't the right time to remind herself.

Searching through her backpack, she found a pack of Marlboro Lights. She flicked the box open, took out a cigarette, and lit it. Taking a deep puff, she slowly released a cloud of smoke into the air before she leaned back in her seat. Staring out the window at the road ahead, she enjoyed a quiet moment until the cigarette was finished. There was ample time for another, she told herself. She lit it with the butt of the first one. Lifting the cigarette to her lips, she took a pull, and then exhaled a puff of smoke.

Shortly thereafter, she tossed the cigarette butt out the window, checked herself in the mirror, and pushed the button to roll up the window. She turned the key in the ignition, starting the car and eased out into the street. Now she was heading to New Mexico, as long as she had a car.

Chapter 57

FOR THE NEXT forty minutes, Jenna drove east along Interstate 40 without stopping until she noticed the gas gauge was almost on empty. By some coincidence, within five minutes, a Pilot service station in Vega appeared on her left. She thought this would be the opportune time to fill the car with gas — as long as no zombies were around.

She turned left onto U.S. Route 385 and pulled up to a pump at the station. Not a sound came from the store, and she didn't see anything moving. She turned off the car and checked her rearview again. There was no sign of anyone around.

As a precaution, she wanted the gun fully loaded. Still, she hoped to God that she wouldn't have to fire it. She took the box of bullets from her backpack. With the revolver in her hands, she opened the cylinder and slid two bullets into the empty chambers.

Jenna stepped out of the car and scanned the area. Luckily for her, the lights for the pumps were on. She couldn't see that anyone was manning the store. So, she wouldn't have to pay. She unlocked the gas tank, flipped up the cap, grabbed the nozzle from the machine and began pumping gas. Every half a minute or so, she looked over her shoulder for any sign of pursuit, any sound.

As soon as the tank was full, she put the pump back in its cradle. Then she decided to check out the store and found a trail of blood that led to the door. Upon seeing it, she gripped the handle of the gun in her jacket pocket. Dropping low, she peered in through the glass door and saw nothing.

Upon opening the door, the smell hit her immediately. It was the smell of decay. Nothing like rotting flesh on a cool spring afternoon. She cleared her throat to prevent from gagging and placed her hand over her nose. It was even worse when she saw a rat scurry by with a piece of flesh in its mouth.

And there, behind the counter, where the blood trailed off, she could see the legs of a man who was sprawled face down on the floor. He was unquestionably dead. The back of his head had been blown away. She stepped away and made her way to the bathroom.

Seven or so minutes later, she left the bathroom and began walking the aisles. As quickly as she could, she loaded her backpack with sodas, candy bars, and chips, all that she could find. Passing the counter, she covered her nose with the sleeve of her jacket, overwhelmed by the smell of rotting flesh again.

When she walked out the door, she heard what sounded like a moan. Without any conscious deliberation, her focus shifted, and she ducked back into the store. Behind the door, she stood at an angle where she couldn't be seen, watching the zombie stumbling alongside the Mercedes-Benz, on the other side of the gas pump. Patiently, she waited, watching him walk toward the road.

Once the zombie's back was turned and he was walking further away, not turning back, she quietly eased the door open and crept out. On her way to the Mercedes-Benz, she stepped on a candy wrapper lying on the ground hard enough to make a cracking sound that echoed all around. The second she heard the sound; she ran in a frenzy to the car, hoping the zombie wouldn't catch it.

Crouched behind the Mercedes-Benz, perfectly still, she peeked at the zombie. It stopped, growled, and whipped around, facing the direction from which the sound had come. As she reached inside her jacket pocket for her thirty-eight revolver, she watched the rising and falling feet of the zombie walking toward her and thought, for the tenth time, of how she didn't want to do it. She dreaded having to do it.

She stood up and took a stance where she could face the zombie. It stopped three yards away, stared at her as if she were food, and gave a loud shriek. She didn't back down, both hands on the revolver in front of her, straight and locked. The zombie, with spiky blond hair, a bloody gash on his thigh, wearing bloodstained khaki shorts and a bloodstained T-shirt, wasn't intimidated by her at all.

When he started to move toward her, she stared hard into the dead man's eyes as she fired a shot directly at him. The shot went wide and ricocheted off a wall. And the zombie was furious. It shrieked loudly again and moved faster toward her. Firing off another shot, she got him in the right shoulder. The hit caused him to lose his balance, stopping him for a minute. That gave her some time to figure out why she kept missing, though she was aiming for his head.

It only took a moment to realize her aim was off because of the awkward weight of the backpack. And just as the zombie started moving toward her again, she slipped off her backpack, letting it drop to the ground with a thud. Breaking out in a sweat, she knew this might be her last chance. Forcing her shaking hands to be steady, she took a step back, pointed the gun directly at his head, and fired a shot. The bullet went through, sending little bits of coagulated blood to splatter on her nose and cheeks. There was a perfectly centered bullet hole between his eyebrows. She used the sleeve of her jacket to wipe the zombie's blood off her face. Shooting zombies was a really messy business. Then she walked slowly to the body, and looked down, confirming to herself that he wasn't coming back from the dead another time.

"I know I look good enough to eat, if I say so myself. Well, too bad for you. I am not on the menu," she said, rubbing it in.

Walking over to her backpack, she heard a noise behind her. She wheeled around and saw three zombies a dozen feet away.

"You've got to be kidding me," she whispered with frustration.

With quiet resolve, she didn't move a muscle and just stared at the gun in her hand. She was in the habit of weighing her options. And not a moment too soon — a small smile crept across her face. That was it. She was just sick of it.

"Ah!" she yelled and charged toward them, gun in both hands.

When she was about two yards away, she stopped, lifted the thirty-eight revolver and shot one of the zombies in the head. Two more quick shots, each to the head. A smile of gratification crossed her face, almost satisfied with what she had done. What looked like bravery was in fact a form of rashness. She was driven by danger and all the anger she had been suppressing.

Something was different about her. Once upon a time she was scared to death of firearms. Now, she had no idea exactly what she was capable of with a gun in her hands. The sight of zombies usually frightened her off. But not anymore. That was, until she caught a glimpse of four zombies no more than ten feet away. She aimed, pulled the trigger, and nothing happened. Now she was frightened, beads of sweat forming on her forehead as she tried to steady her hands still holding the gun in front of her face.

She was done. Just when she thought she knew everything there was to know about guns. She was out of bullets. Who knew? Hastily, she put the gun in her jacket pocket, and did the only thing she could do: she ran.

After grabbing her backpack, she scrambled to the car. She hopped into the driver's side and fumbled until she got the key in the ignition and started the engine. Driving in reverse, she slammed on the brakes, turned the steering wheel hard to the right, and hit the gas, skidding onto the road. She couldn't get out of there fast enough. As she headed away from the zombies, she was flooded with emotions, her face flushing red, but she kept the vehicle under control.

Chapter 58

SOMEWHERE AROUND twenty-five minutes had elapsed since Jenna left Vega, Texas. Approaching the Texas-New Mexico state line, her consciousness was suddenly overwhelmed by an incredible rush of chaotic emotions she could barely control. The fact that she had made it this far considering where she had started from, was a miracle in itself. With the car idling, she focused for a moment on the sign that read,

WELCOME TO NEW MEXICO
LAND OF ENCHANTMENT

She drove the car slowly across the state line into Quay County, New Mexico and pulled into the Glenrio Visitor Center parking lot. After turning off the engine, she leaned back in the driver's seat and reflected on her situation. If only the telephones worked, she thought with a sigh. Then she would call her sister. She wanted to tell Hannah that she was only five hours away.

She could only say it to herself. "I'm here in New Mexico, Hannah."

Wiping away the tears that were flowing down her face, she left the car and walked to the entrance to the building. When she stepped inside, she saw a fiftyish Hispanic man in gray pants and a white T-shirt talking to a young Hispanic boy of about ten, dressed in a red T-shirt under denim overalls. They were standing outside the door to the men's bathroom.

"Manuel go to the car. I'll meet you there in five minutes," he told the boy.

"Okay, dad," the boy said and sped past Jenna as she put her hand on the bathroom handle and turned it.

On her way to the car, she saw the Hispanic man walking across the parking lot. Once inside the car, she reached down to one side of the seat, tugged at the lever and moved the seat back. Maybe a catnap would do her good. She rested her head sideways on the driver's side window. And she planned to stay like that, for a chunk of time, until she heard shouts.

She sighed and looked out the windshield to see what all the fuss was about. But she couldn't see anything. Glancing in her rearview mirror, she saw the Hispanic man running to the other side of the parking lot. She moved her head to get a better look. There were two zombies on top of the Hispanic boy on the ground.

"Stop! Get off him. Please, anyone! Help!" yelled the Hispanic man.

Just after that, three Hispanic men drove up in a blue Nissan Armada SUV. One of the men rolled down the window, stuck out a rifle, and shot the zombies in the head. The man reloaded the rifle and pointed it at the boy's head.

"Wait! Don't shoot! That's my son," the Hispanic man yelled, waving his arms in the air and putting himself in harm's way.

"Step aside. You can't do anything for him now. He's infected," the man holding the rifle said.

"That's my business, not yours. Stay away from him," the Hispanic man said.

"Aw, come on, man. He's going to turn into one of those things. Let me take care of it for you."

"No, I'll handle it. Just leave."

"Suit yourself," the man said, then pulled the rifle back inside the SUV.

The window rolled up and the Armada sped off while the Hispanic man stood looking at the unconscious boy, who had bite marks on his arms and neck. Shaking his head, he had this faraway look in his eyes. As tears began to form in his eyes, he fell onto his knees.

"Mi hijo," he said, grabbing the boy's arm in a tight grip, begging him to wake up.

Watching it all take place, seeing the Hispanic man in his personal anguish, was something that would stay with her the rest of her life. That marked a realization for Jenna; that could've been her lying on the ground. She realized how close she came to being killed that day. If the infected had attacked her there would be no one to mourn her death, she told herself. Even worse, later on, she would become a zombie. Hypothetically, of course.

The fear of that happening wrenched her thoughts to the here and now and focused on the boy, who would soon rise from the dead. She didn't want to be here when it happened. After clicking her seat belt in place, she turned the ignition key and drove out of the parking lot in a hurry to get back on the road.

After driving about three miles, she saw Tyrell's Truck & Travel Center. Perhaps she could get the break she needed. So, she pulled into the parking lot and killed the motor. Then she looked from left to right, checking that there were no zombies around. There wasn't a soul in sight. With a sigh, she tilted her head back, closed her eyes, inhaled then slowly released her breath.

Only a few seconds had gone by when she remembered the gun inside her jacket pocket. Her eyes flew open. It was still unloaded. It appeared her nap would have to wait. She looked around for a second time. Since nobody was around, she took the gun out. Working fast, she inserted six bullets and spun the chamber. Lastly, she put the gun back into its rightful place.

After rolling down the window halfway, she stuck the box of bullets into her backpack and pulled out a pack of Marlboro Lights and a lighter. Grabbing a cigarette, she lit it and enjoyed it for a long, quiet moment, smoking to her heart's content.

The break was short-lived.

It was late afternoon, meaning she had only a couple hours of sunlight left before darkness surrounded her. It was almost a three-hour drive to Santa Fe. That was as far as she could drive. The trip to Dulce was going to have to wait for another day. She turned the car back on and drove out of the lot.

As she faced the long drive ahead, she couldn't help feel disappointed. So badly, she wanted to be in Dulce. She spent the entire three hours thinking about how much time it would take to drive to Dulce and the many routes she could take to get there from Santa Fe.

When she reached Santa Fe, the last rays from the setting sun slanted through the windshield almost blinding her. She blinked the spots out of her eyes, and just as they cleared, she saw half a dozen police officers on motorcycles appear on the road. As the motorcycles rode off in a cloud of dust, she spotted the overhead sign:

SANTA FE

As to be expected there was little gas left in the tank. The Mercedes-Benz needed a break. She was even more tired. If she wasn't careful, she would fall asleep behind the wheel. She was going to have to stop somewhere for the night, relax and recharge her batteries, so to speak. If only she knew where she was going.

She slowed the car down and looked at one side of the road. In the near distance, she spotted what looked like a rest stop. Hoping it wasn't a mirage, she began driving toward it.

Chapter 59

THE PRAYERS, Jenna hadn't said, were answered. After driving a little further in the outskirts of Santa Fe, she rolled to a stop on what seemed like the most deserted highway in the middle of nowhere. On the corner of Old Las Vegas Highway and Bobcat Trail was a secluded rest stop. There were two big rigs, two motorhomes, and five cars parked in the crushed-stone parking lot of the Blackstone Diner. Moreover, there was a gas station next door. It was quiet, looking like the place had been passed over, relatively unscathed by the epidemic. She marveled at the strangeness of it. Something about it felt like time had stopped for them while, everywhere else, the world was perishing.

She looked at the fuel gauge. The needle hovered near Empty. On a whim, she said a prayer to God that she could get a night's sleep, a bite to eat and some gas. Then she slowly cruised into the parking lot of the diner. Her attention was instantly caught by the figure of a man, shadowed by the rays of the fading sun, coming toward her. She stopped the car.

"You can park over there," he yelled, pointing to the south end of the parking lot.

After parking the car, she sat back for a minute or so watching the sun disappear, and darkness creep up. She turned her head toward the passenger window. There was an old woman, watching her from the driver's seat, sitting very still in one of the motorhomes. She smiled at the old woman, who in turn smiled back.

She reached over to the passenger seat and made sure she had everything she needed in her backpack. Her chief concern wasn't the couple of bags of chips, bottles of soda and candy bars she had stored inside, but rather that she had plenty of cash. Just because the epidemic had been going on for about five months didn't mean it was the end of the world. She had to expect that currency was still exchanged. She counted out close to three hundred dollars, including the fifty-dollar bill folded behind her driver's license. After she brushed aside a strand of hair that had fallen over her cheek, she put the car keys in her jacket pocket. Then she unbuckled her seat belt, opened the car door, and hoped for the best.

When she was crossing the parking lot, she noticed an intense looking, muscle-bound guy also walking toward the door of the diner. The same man who had told her where to park her car. He was thin lipped, with a tight haircut, strutting in his black cowboy hat, tight white T-shirt, belted on blue jeans and alligator boots. He carried himself like a man who had spent time in jail. Reaching the door first, he picked up a rifle propped up against the wall.

While she had stopped a few feet from the entrance, he stood there like a security guard. From the corner of his eye, he saw her gaze dart to the 9mm pistol strapped to his belt. It didn't faze her at all. Neither did it worry her as it once had. She, too, had a gun but she didn't advertise it. Nor would she admit she had it.

Jenna stood there idly for a little time, rehearsing in her mind what she would say — something she thought was important. The Mercedes-Benz was hers if anyone should ask her. Technically, it was her car because possession was nine-tenths of the law. And she planned to keep it until she reached her final destination.

Shrugging off her unease, she proceeded forward, and said to the man, "Hello."

He smiled, and nodded at her. "I'm much obliged to meet you. My name's Ron Pagano. So, you know for next time. Step right inside."

She tuned out what he'd said and pushed through the door to enter. The first thing she noticed about the Blackstone Diner was how wonderful it smelled. She paused, taking a moment to look around. There were six people seated at the tables and two at the counter. It all looked so normal. No doubt an attempt to retain a sense of normalcy to their lives.

For a few split seconds, it felt like every eye was on her as she walked toward the end of the counter. She felt like the new girl in town. Which in a way, she was. Soon after she sat down on a stool, from time to time they stole a glance at her, which she ignored. But her mind was only half there. The other half was wanting to eat, then sleep in the car, all the while wondering: was that a safe thing to do?

A waitress put down the rag she had been using to clean the counter, picked up a pot of coffee, and came to her. "Welcome to Blackstone Diner. My name is Lynn Martz. Grab a menu and I'll pour you some coffee."

"It's very nice to meet you. I'm Jenna."

Lynn was a petite woman, with a thick head of curly red hair, and a heavy smoker's gravelly voice. She was welcoming and friendly and resembled a young Lucille Ball of the *I Love Lucy* TV sitcom of the 1950s.

"Milk?" she asked Jenna, pouring coffee into a white mug and putting it in front of her.

"Yes, please."

After setting the pot down, Lynn poured milk into her coffee then stepped away. Like pizza, Jenna thought coffee was one of life's treasures. She savored the smell of it. One by one, she reached for the sugar packets — four in total, tore them open, and poured them into her coffee. She stirred the coffee with a spoon, while she glanced over the menu.

Lynn came from the kitchen and asked, "What will you be having?"

"A grilled cheese on Texas toast, potato chips, and a Sprite," Jenna answered, setting the spoon down on the counter.

"Will that be all?"

Jenna shook her head for yes.

"I'll be right back with your order."

Jenna glanced around the diner then swallowed a mouthful of coffee. She set the mug down on the counter. And Lynn appeared and topped it off.

"Would it be safe to sleep outside in my car?" Jenna asked nonchalantly.

"You should be okay. There is an elderly couple camping out in an RV parked in the lot. And we have twenty-four-hour security with Ron and Roy. They have rifles and shotguns, ready to shoot any zombies that come this direction," she said putting the coffee pot down.

"Yes, I met Ron," Jenna said.

"Ron and Roy are truck drivers. When this whole zombie thing started, they got stranded here. They had to find something to do besides truck driving. So, they offered themselves to work as security for the diner in exchange for half-priced meals. They sleep in their trucks out there and shower in the Phillips 66 station bathroom. It's not glamorous, but it's a living."

"I can understand that."

"We're so cut off from everything here — off a desolate highway. We don't get too many customers. We don't get many zombies either. We've kept the zombies away for a couple of months now. Which reminds me, I'll be closing up in fifteen minutes. I do that as soon as it gets dark. We don't want the infected to see lights on. We're trying to keep them away. We're all doing our best to hold it together here," Lynn informed her.

"Okay. I'll give it a try," Jenna said, and yawned, her voice drowsy.

"If you have any problems, come and find me. I stay in the tan colored RV parked closest to the diner."

Lynn left briefly and came back with her order. Jenna ate quickly, paid for her meal, then made a quick stop in the bathroom. From there, she hurried out the door of the restaurant. As she headed for the Mercedes-Benz in the parking lot, the darkness spooked her. So much so that she increased her pace and glanced over her shoulder from time to time all the way to the car.

Once she got inside the car, she slid down into the backseat. Using her jacket as a cover, she kept her hand close to the gun. She knew it was a false sense of security. But for some reason, doing that made her feel safer. Though she was too tired to think much about it. And, seconds later, she was asleep.

Chapter 60

LYNN MARTZ knocked on the window of the Mercedes-Benz startling Jenna awake. She was still slumped in the far corner of the backseat, her eyes partly open. Very slowly, she raised herself up. Seeing who it was, she put her ear close to the window.

All she could get out was, "Yeah, yeah. I'm up."

"Hi, good morning, I hope I didn't disturb you. The diner is open for breakfast, just in case you're hungry," Lynn said, a bit too enthusiastically.

"Sure, thanks. I'll be there in a minute."

"See you inside," Lynn said, and left.

Jenna climbed out of the car with her backpack slung over her shoulder. She looked at Ron, who was in his usual spot by the door, holding a double-barreled shotgun. He greeted her, and she gave him a friendly smile as she pushed through the door to enter the diner. She first went to the bathroom to clean up.

When she came out of the bathroom she headed to the counter. She took pleasure in the smell of eggs, pancakes and coffee in the air. Her stomach began to rumble with hunger, but not loud enough for anyone to hear.

Lynn had just come from the kitchen to attend to a customer. She set a plate down in front of the old woman Jenna had seen the day before, sitting in the driver's seat in a motorhome. There was an old man sitting across from her at the table. Before Jenna could sit down, she was already back behind the counter, beaming from ear to ear at her.

"Please have a seat," Lynn told her, and pointed to a stool at the far end of the counter beside the swinging door to the kitchen.

"Don't mind if I do," Jenna said graciously.

"I hope you like scrambled eggs, buttered wheat toast, and pancakes," Lynn said in a sweet voice, and set a plate in front of her.

"Yes, it looks great. Thank you, Lynn."

"Let me get you some coffee."

Lynn set a steaming cup of coffee in front of her, poured milk, and went away again. Jenna was going to tell her that she was leaving but decided not to say anything. *Best to keep things to herself*, thought Jenna. She really didn't know Lynn well.

Her face was all lit up with delight as she devoured her pancakes. Lately the stress had begun to stick. She had a larger appetite. She drank nonstop until she had managed to drain the mug of its very last drop. There was no time to wait for Lynn. She left cash on the counter to pay for the meal. Then she left.

Jenna hurried out the door of the diner, heading for the car. She was dead set on reaching Dulce today. She got behind the wheel, fired up the car, and drove out of the lot toward the Phillips 66 station next to the diner. The car coasted up to the pump and stopped on its own. It desperately needed gas.

A man came out of the convenience store and walked swiftly toward her as soon as she stepped out of the car. He was short, with bright green eyes, a tall nose, gray hair and a mustache. Probably around sixty years old, he had on a light blue dress shirt, suspenders, and dark blue trousers.

"There is no gasoline here," the man said in a reserved tone.

"You can't be serious?" Jenna asked thinking she might faint.

"I kid you not."

"I only need a couple of gallons. So, can you make an exception?" Jenna asked in a desperate tone.

"No, I'm sorry. I can't help you out."

"Is there another station nearby?"

"Nope, sorry. This is the only gas station for miles."

"Oh God, I never expected this to happen," she said, starting to cry.

"No need to worry yourself, miss. Perhaps I should've

explained it better. Gas is being delivered later than usually on account of the present situation, often falling four weeks behind schedule," the man told her.

"When will there be gas?" she asked, still shaken up.

"Most definitely the end of the first week of June."

"That's a long time," she said as a tear slipped out of the corner of her eye.

Seeing her like that, the man said, "It's all right, dear. You come back in about that time. I promise you. There will be gas. I guarantee it. Otherwise, I will do something drastic, such as siphon gas out of somebody's car and give it to you. I mean it."

"Okay, I'll wait here. What other choice do I have?"

"My name is Larry Simmons. It's very nice to know you."

"Jenna Winter. Thanks. I'll come back."

Half blinded by tears, she got back inside the car, turned the ignition switch and coasted into the parking lot of the Blackstone Diner. After stopping the car, she sat behind the wheel for a little while. Inside she was exploding with rage, feeling her plans had come to nothing. Here she was, stranded all over again. Except this time, she didn't care to smoke.

What she needed was another plan. She didn't want to make any hasty decisions and then regret them, such as abandon the car and walk the rest of the way to Dulce. Not after coming all this way.

Maybe she would think about it over coffee. She got out of the car and headed toward the door of the diner. Without so much as a word she passed Ron, bolted into the restaurant, and slipped onto a stool. She put her elbows on the countertop and buried her face in her hands as she released a sigh of frustration. She didn't care if anyone saw her. Unhappy.

When Lynn came out of the kitchen, she could tell something was not right with Jenna.

"Honey, you all right?" Lynn asked.

"Oh, Lynn, it's just terrible. There's no gas. I can't leave here," she said, with tears in her eyes.

"It's not safe with those zombies out there. Where do you need to go in such a hurry?"

"My sister is waiting for me in Dulce, but I don't have enough gas to drive there. I just have enough gas to get to the gas station."

"Maybe, you saw the vehicles parked in the lot. Their gas tanks are on E. We're all pretty much in the same boat."

"I would have never guessed."

"Did you meet Larry?"

"Yes, I met him."

"Well, what did he say to you?"

"He told me to wait 'til June and come in again."

"There, there, young lady, don't you worry no more about it. You wait here like he said. He will help you. Because he's a good man."

"Okay, I guess I will wait," Jenna said, with strength in her voice this time.

"The days will go by fast. You'll have gasoline and you'll be back with your sister before you know it."

"I hope so."

"You were going to leave? Without saying goodbye?"

Knowing she was caught, Jenna looked up at her, cracked a smile. "I was coming back after I filled the tank."

"It's okay, I get it. You don't have to explain."

"I really was going to come back."

Jenna was fibbing her way into her good graces. It was all right with Lynn, because she was just trying to lighten up the conversation and help make her feel better.

Chapter 61

AFTER THEIR emotionally charged conversation, Lynn poured Jenna a mug of coffee, adding milk, and set it in front of her on the counter. Afterward Lynn went into the kitchen and returned with a small plate of peanut butter cookies. Jenna truly appreciated her hospitality.

"I don't mean to pry, but since you're going to be here a while. There's a cot bed in the stockroom. If you want it, it's yours. It's not much, but it's a whole lot more comfortable than the backseat of a car," Lynn said.

Jenna worried that it would cost more money than she had with her. When she hesitated in answering, Lynn suspected as much.

"Since you're already paying for your own meals, I won't be charging you," Lynn added.

Jenna was quiet for another moment, then said, "That will

be great. I'm grateful for your help."

"If you want, I'll take you to the stockroom now."

"Sure. I'm ready as I'll ever be," Jenna said and stood up to go.

Lynn led her through the swinging door to the adjacent kitchen. A medium-sized man in his sixties, with thick salt-and-pepper hair, clad in a chef's apron, white T-shirt, and plaid pants, was preparing a sandwich.

Lynn stopped to introduce him. "Jenna, I want you to meet my uncle Eduard."

"Hello, it's nice to meet you."

"I'm glad to make your acquaintance, Jenna," he said, then returned to his work.

They continued on and down two steps into an attached stockroom. There was a walk-in refrigerator, a laundry area to wash the restaurant linens, bathroom, and a cot-size bed against a wall near boxes of what appeared to be supplies.

"I run this diner with my uncle. It used to be open twenty-four hours a day. Despite our isolated location, we used to get lots of customers. Waitresses took breaks between shifts sleeping in this bed. That's why it's here," Lynn said and then pointed at a door, "Through that door over there is a bathroom with a shower stall."

Lynn tossed sheets and a blanket on the bed. She began preparing the bed, even though Jenna told her not to go to any trouble.

"It's no trouble at all."

"Well, thank you again," said Jenna.

"Once it gets dark, we all hide until first light. Ron and Roy take turns patrolling the area. They've picked off a few zombies and buried them too. You'll be in here by yourself. I'm sure I can trust you to keep the lights off and stay quiet," Lynn said, as she tidied the bed.

"I'll be quieter than a mouse."

"I'm going back up front. If there's anything you need, give me a holler."

"I'm so grateful for this," Jenna said.

Lynn left while Jenna sat down on the bed, lost in her own thoughts. She didn't want to tell her she had a gun. It might change the way Lynn saw her. She didn't think anyone would ask her if she had a gun, but still she worried about someone finding out. After carefully thinking about her options, she planned to hide it in the trunk of the car.

Her eyes wandered to a shelf full of supplies, a Panasonic TV, and a DVD player. Then her eyes shifted to the bathroom door. Deciding to take a shower, she went into the bathroom, locking the door behind her. Pulling her backpack off her shoulder, she let it drop to the floor. Then she undressed and showered.

About twenty minutes later, she came out of the bathroom dressed, her backpack hanging on one shoulder. With a mission on her mind, she walked through the diner. As soon as she stepped outside, her hand raised in automatic response, trying to protect herself from the harsh glare of the sun shining directly into her eyes. Then she glanced around to find a man standing next to her beside the door holding a shotgun.

It must be Roy, she thought. Because she'd already met Ron. Roy was a burly man in his late twenties with light brown hair, brown eyes, a diamond stud in his left ear, and dressed in a long sleeve shirt and jeans. Despite that he had an Arizona Diamondbacks baseball cap pulled down over his eyes, she could feel his stare on her.

The sunlight on her face, made her look beautiful, he thought. Roy was smitten with her at first sight. He tried not to stare, but he couldn't help it.

"Nice afternoon isn't it?" he asked.

"Sure is," she said.

Before he could speak again, she walked over to the Mercedes-Benz, and opened the trunk. Turning her back to Roy, he couldn't see what she was doing. She grabbed a rag, wrapped it around the revolver, and placed it along with the box of bullets in-between the spare tire. It was a good hiding spot. She closed the trunk and then headed back toward the diner.

"Please forgive my manners. I forgot to introduce myself. My name is Roy Goecke. And you are?"

"Jenna."

"Well, it's nice to meet you, Jenna."

She found she had nothing else to say and so, she smiled, walking past him and through the door into the diner. At the same time, Lynn came from the kitchen and stepped into the dining area juggling water glasses. She saw Jenna walking into the diner just as she set the glasses on the table where the old woman from the RV was seated.

"Peggy, what will you be having for lunch?" Lynn asked her.

Before going to the kitchen, Lynn set a glass of water on the counter in front of her.

Jenna was thinking how comfortable she felt, sitting on the stool. Sipping her glass of water, she gave the place a long look over the rim of her glass. Swallowing another sip, she set the glass down. Now she was feeling something she hadn't felt in a long time ... safe. The next few weeks might not be so bad after all.

Chapter 62

ON THURSDAY, June 6, 2013, shortly before ten o'clock, Dr. Julie Mehta had developed a vaccine to prevent infection by the virus. Over the course of the past three weeks, all of the testing in the lab was proof positive of the vaccine's safety. It wasn't a cure, but it would be an effective treatment, awakening the body's B-lymphocytes to produce antibodies against the virus, preventing people from contracting it. The vaccine, however, couldn't eliminate the virus from the body of an infected person. It was during the latter part of the three weeks that she had come to accept the grim fact that there was no way to reverse the effects of the virus.

Earlier that morning, in the lab, she had performed one last test to determine the ability of the vaccine to induce an immune response. The vaccine was injected into a mouse. Afterward, the infected blood was injected. It didn't die.

Julie left the lab heading for her office. When she arrived at her desk, she clicked the mouse to open a file on the computer. Before leaving the room, she quickly pulled off her lab coat and hung it on her chair.

When she exited the elevator, she headed down the hallway in the direction of Dan Saunders' office. With a bounce in her step, she rounded a corner, anxious to share the good news. As she came close, she saw his assistant, Sandra Ortiz, seated at her desk, typing away at her computer keyboard.

Julie stopped in front of her desk. "Is he in?"

"Yes, but he's with…," Sandra answered without finishing the sentence, letting the words hang in the air, because Julie had ignored her.

The door to Saunders' office was open, and Julie walked in. She found him engaged in a conversation with Thomas Bauer, seated in the guest chair across from his desk. Saunders looked up as she came through the doorway. And Bauer stood up when he saw her enter the room.

"Dan. Thomas. Forgive me for interrupting your meeting," she said.

"Think nothing of it. To what do we owe the honor of your visit?" Saunders asked with a smile.

Bauer threw in his two cents. "I'm certain you wouldn't be here unless it was important. What have you got for us?"

She got right to the point. "I have a vaccine."

"Please tell us more," Saunders said bolting from his chair.

"And you guarantee it will work?" Bauer interrupted.

"It will work. I'm convinced of it."

What she'd said took Saunders' aback. There was an expression of relief on his face, and it looked for a moment as though he was searching for something else to say.

"That's terrific news. I knew you could do it all along," Saunders said thoughtfully to her, then he looked at Bauer. "We need to have a meeting about this. Everyone here has to know. Sandra will type up a memorandum."

Bauer, who was calmer, nodded his head agreeing. "Slow down, Dan. This kind of thing takes time. We haven't even started production of the vaccine in the mass quantities for distribution."

"I agree. Let's think it through," Julie said.

"I like what I've heard so far. I'll leave you to work out the details. I must deliver the message to the board of directors," Bauer said to them.

"We'll talk about this some more later," Saunders said.

Bauer reached out to shake her hand. "Very good work, Dr. Mehta. If there are any other developments, I would like to be notified. You report directly to Dan, and he'll relay it to me."

Thomas Bauer released his grip on her hand and left.

"I have to summon the heads of the departments into conference with medical teams on standby. Everything must be in place when we blow the lid on this," Saunders said, clearly overwhelmed.

"Take it easy. Remember what Thomas told you. You can't do it all in one day."

"You're so right. I need a minute to think."

"Take a deep breath and relax," she said.

He sat down in his chair, but he couldn't stay still. A few moments later, he got up and began pacing around his desk. Then he stopped his pacing. He had more to say.

"I wish to have a written report from you covering the components of the vaccine. We have to get the vaccine patented pronto."

"Sure, Dan. I will prepare it immediately. I'm familiar with the procedures."

"I know I've been rambling on a little. I don't want to forget something important."

Julie could feel her patience starting to run out. "I understand that you've got a lot on your plate — a lot to take care of."

"Come to my office tomorrow at twelve with that report. We'll discuss this situation further."

"Is there anything more before I go?"

"Thank you from the bottom of my heart. At any time during these past months, if it sounded like I doubted you, I apologize. You've saved us. Saved us all," he said, with utmost sincerity.

"I'm just doing my job."

"And a great job you're doing."

"I appreciate your gratitude, Dan."

"At least I could say that much, considering everything you've been through."

"I'm going back to my office," she told him.

"Bravo. Julie, my hat is off to you."

He came around from his desk and ushered her toward the door. Then he sat in his chair. She stepped out of the room, and slowly started to close the door behind her.

"Leave it open. I need some air in here," he said, before she could close the door.

Sandra didn't even look in her direction. Not having heard what he had said, she couldn't help noticing that Julie had left his door open.

"Sandra, get in here!" Saunders roared.

Mere seconds later, Sandra stepped into his office.

Chapter 63

IT was closing time, the sun setting outside the Blackstone Diner in Santa Fe. Jenna sat at the counter, drinking her third cup of coffee, savoring every sip. For a brief spell, she closed her eyes, and couldn't help but think that the weeks had passed by much more quickly than she would have expected. It was the second Saturday in June, and just yesterday, Larry Simmons, the manager of the Phillips 66 station, told her that the fuel tanker would be coming any day now. That thought made a small smile flicker at the corners of her mouth as she reopened her eyes.

She wasn't the only one in the dining area. Roy Goecke sat at a table nursing a beer, presently staring at the tabletop, deep in thought. The whole time he'd been sitting there, he had not said a word to her. Yet he had barely been able to take his eyes off her.

After setting the mug down, Jenna looked at herself in the mirror on the wall behind the counter. It wasn't but a few seconds later that she caught him staring at her. But she didn't let on that she noticed and kept on playing it like this. That was, until, looking up, she busted him staring at her, again. Unconsciously, unintentionally, she smiled at him while he took a gulp of his Corona Light. He blushed, and immediately looked away, doing a terrible job of trying to hide the fact that he was checking her out.

At first glance, he knew that she was out of his league. He wasn't her type for one thing, and for another, his jokes wouldn't be enough to gain her interest. Still, he thought, she was the prettiest girl he had seen in a long time.

His interest in her, was obvious, but she wasn't attracted to him. There were times when her good looks had worked to her advantage. This wasn't one of those times.

Lynn emerged from the kitchen to clear the tables. Roy gulped down the last of his beer when he saw her walk in the room. He took the bottle and upended it. Not a single drop fell out.

"It's all gone," he said to himself.

Lynn paused, a stack of dirty plates in one hand, and looked down at Roy. "Would you care for something else, Roy?"

"Honestly, I would love another Corona Light. But I can't risk it. I'm on the night watch. I won't be having anything else."

She looked at Jenna and said, "Roy watches out for us. Looks mean, doesn't he? He only acts that way to the zombies. Otherwise he's a sweetheart of a guy."

He looked slightly embarrassed. A brief minute later, he stood up, dug into his pocket for money, dropped it on the table and excused himself to the bathroom. He moved the chair against which his double-barreled shotgun had been propped, taking it with him as he crossed the room. A little bit later, he came through the dining area.

Lynn saw him leaving. "Bye, Roy. Have a good night."

"Thanks, Lynn. You do the same."

"All right, Jenna. I'll be gone in a jiffy. Then you'll have the place all to yourself."

"What about Eduard?"

"He left a short time ago."

"Okay, Lynn," she said getting up from the stool.

Lynn carried a tray with dirty dishes on it, shouldering her way through the swinging door into the kitchen. She set the tray on the counter and began to load the dishwasher.

"Jenna, if you get hungry or thirsty, there's plenty of food in the refrigerator. You're welcome to help yourself," she announced as she came through the swinging door, took off her white apron and hung it on the wooden rack near the register.

"Yes, Lynn, I know. Thanks for reminding me."

"I'm going to lock up and go. My RV is parked close by, but I still worry about those zombies creeping up on me in the dark. If any of them come after me, I want to see them. So, I can try out my latest karate moves on them," she said, demonstrating a kick, a chop, and a block.

They were both laughing, while Lynn walked toward the front door. "Good night. I'll see you in the morning, Jenna."

"Look forward to it."

She watched Lynn until she closed the door. A few moments later, she heard the deadbolt lock slide into place. After that, it was quiet. She stood by the swinging door, staring at the empty dining room, and thought about how she had settled into a routine that found her retreating into the stockroom each evening after the place had closed.

A while later, she walked toward the back door. Usually at this time, she made sure it was locked up tight. It was.

She went into the kitchen and opened the refrigerator, which was well stocked with beer. She took a bottle of ginger ale. Beer wasn't her thing.

When she entered the stockroom, she perused the collection of DVD movies on the shelf. She picked up *Pirates of the Caribbean On Stranger Tides* and looked at it for a short bit. A memory jolted through her, sending her thoughts back to the day she'd first seen the movie. She remembered that day so well. It was the month before she graduated from high school. She went with her friends Camille, Rachel and Tara, to the movie theater at the Cottonwood Mall in Albuquerque. Right there and then she vowed that one day she would reconnect with her old friends, hoping that they were still alive.

Feeling close to tears, she put the disc in the DVD player and sat down on the bed. She picked up the remote control, turned the volume down, and hit play. Then she shifted into a more comfortable position and tried to enjoy the movie.

Chapter 64

TODAY was Tuesday, June 11, 2013, and something great had happened. Everyone was assembled in the conference room. All we knew was that there had been a significant development, and it was good news. I was standing in the back of the crowded room. People spilled out into the hallway and Ken Langtry propped the door open against the rubber doorstop.

At 10:00 a.m. Dan Saunders walked to the front of the room, turned around and faced everyone to address them. All eyes were on him. We were eager to hear what he would have to say. His small brown eyes went from row to row, and he looked more intense than usual.

At the same moment Julie Mehta walked over and stood next to Saunders, Thomas Bauer swept into the room. He was dressed to the hilt in a navy pinstripe suit and a navy tie with silver stripes, as though he'd just come from court. He made eye contact with Saunders as he adjusted the shiny gold cuff links that secured the sleeves of his white dress shirt. Bauer then moved to the rear of the room near me. When he saw me, he nodded. I smiled a hello to him, meant to show that I wasn't intimidated by him in the least.

Saunders gave the room a quick glance, cleared his throat, and then the room fell silent. You could hear a pin drop.

"Ladies and gentlemen, may I have your attention, please. There has been a significant break. It's taken us several months, and now I have the pleasure to report that we have a vaccine to prevent this dreadful disease."

A smile surfaced on the Chief Executive Officer's face, and everyone in the room clapped their hands. It was a moment of celebration for us. I looked at Saunders, dry-eyed with an overwhelming sense of closure, like the ending of a movie. Vivian, who was standing next to me, was crying pitifully. She was the most relieved person in the room. The poor woman had been an emotional wreck since the day of the outbreak.

Saunders had paused, waiting for the room to quiet down. It didn't take long because we were all very anxious to hear what else he had to say.

Before continuing he looked at Bauer, who gave him a tight smile of reassurance. "I regret to inform you that there is no cure for those already infected. Eliminating the virus from the body is virtually impossible. There is no way to reverse the process. The infected will be eliminated and disposed of by burial or cremation."

My stomach turned at the thought of more people dying. It made Vivian cry some more. We had a hard time swallowing that cold bit of news.

"In the development of a vaccine to prevent the infection, for those of you who don't know her, I want to introduce you Dr. Julie Mehta. Without her it wouldn't be possible," he said, gesturing to Julie.

Saunders continued talking. "Born in India, undergraduate at University of Mumbai, and Harvard Medical School graduate. Hardly more than a year ago, she was appointed to be a resident virologist. In the laboratory she spent countless hours testing, researching, and analyzing data. Please give a warm hand to Dr. Julie Mehta."

The crowd clapped, and Julie smiled graciously, appreciating the warm reception by her coworkers and bosses. A warmer, more tender emotion flowed through her.

"Thank you," she said, nodding to the others, "but I couldn't have done it without all your support. The development of the Never-DEAD vaccine was not easy by any means. Thank you all so kindly."

Julie looked at me with a gleam in her eye, as if she wanted to see if I'd caught the emphasis of what she'd said. And I did get it. It was like an inside joke between her and me. "Never dead," she had said. I knew how she had come up with that name.

After all these months, Julie had returned to her old self, looking sharper than I remembered. Her clothes were neatly pressed, and her hair was fastened in a bun behind her head.

The Never-DEAD vaccine couldn't have come at a better time, a time when we had almost lost all hope. With this vaccination people wouldn't die from a bite wound or scratch from those infected. I couldn't say it in my mind enough times. It was the proudest I'd ever been to work for Biogenetics & Disease Control.

"When are the telephones going to work?" Langtry hollered behind me.

I looked over and saw him standing beside Lucas and Stewart. He wasn't celebrating. Instead, he seemed sullen, as if he wasn't affected by the news.

Saunders shrugged and answered him, "As we speak, engineers are working to restore the telecommunication lines and switching, more specifically, restoring power for these essential services, such as cellular phones, land-line telephones, and utilities. Nothing else. If there are no further questions, then everyone may leave. Thanks again for your time."

Bauer approached Saunders, who was standing in the far-left corner of the room. Julie remained where she was, standing fairly close to them, regarding Bauer with a cocked brow. Though she didn't participate in their conversation. Langtry left with Lucas and Stewart following behind. Then James Stebbins walked out the door with everyone else.

Mind spinning with the news, I wasn't in any hurry to leave. Neither was Vivian, who was still standing next to me, not sure what to do next.

"That's great. What a relief," I said to her.

"It sure is Hannah."

We talked for a few more minutes. Then we got the momentum to leave. I waved goodbye to Julie and turned to follow Vivian out the door.

Standing by the elevators, I decided that I wanted some time off. Whatever was piled up on my desk could wait till the next day. Surely, she would not mind my absence for one day. I was grateful she agreed to do it. The moment we got on the elevator, I pushed the button for the floor of my apartment.

Chapter 65

EARLY THE FOLLOWING MORNING, I sat at a table in the cafeteria staring at my plateful of scrambled eggs, crispy home fries, and two pieces of wheat toast liberally buttered and found that the portions were larger.

The sound of the television news brought me out of my thoughts. A special bulletin interrupted the regular broadcasting. The noise in the cafeteria dulled as a correspondent appeared on-screen and said there would be an announcement from the White House. CNN flashed a text crawling along the bottom of the screen announcing that: "Press Secretary Neil Crellin will address the nation shortly."

I knew Vivian wouldn't want to miss this. Maybe she was waiting in line to pay at the register, but I just couldn't see her anywhere. Knowing her the way I did, I was certain she would show up sooner or later.

Fascinated by it all, I looked at the television, taking a sip of coffee and watching over the rim of the mug. Neil Crellin stepped to the podium in the James S. Brady Press Briefing Room. He was an average height man in his early forties, slightly overweight with short blond hair and glasses. The black suit with a light gray shirt and black tie he was wearing made him look like he was going to a funeral. He greeted the press with a smile. He had the confident look on his face of someone about to deliver good news.

It was as if the whole world was holding its breath, waiting for him to speak. I was sure everybody in the cafeteria was tuned in.

The camera zoomed in closer, and I saw Crellin scanning the audience. After a short pause, he adjusted the microphone and leaned toward it.

Crellin launched into his speech, reading from a script. "My fellow Americans, in the grip of a viral epidemic that has killed hundreds of thousands of people over the past year, the primary goal has been to develop a vaccine, our only hope of halting further transmission. The people have long suffered. Many of you have lost someone close to you. I sympathize for your loss. Yet I stand before you to tell you that there is hope for us now."

I turned my focus to Vivian who came and sat at my table. Still rushing, she took a quick sip of her coffee and a quick bite of her bagel before turning her eyes toward the television. We both stayed silent, watching, not sure what would come next.

"What did I miss?" she asked.

"Nothing significant yet," I replied.

The president's press secretary paused, took a sip of water, and peered at the camera over the rim of the glass. He set the glass down and stood motionless for a few seconds before taking a quick glance at his audience.

"Now, a major breakthrough has been made with the Never-DEAD vaccine developed at Biogenetics & Disease Control by Dr. Julie Mehta. It was prepared from infected tissue cultures. This viral disease can be brought under control," he said directly to the camera.

Half the people in the cafeteria clapped their hands and cheered after they'd heard the BDC mentioned. They settled down almost at once because they wouldn't want to miss something important.

The press secretary continued. "The vaccine is being delivered free of cost by ambulance or other alternative vehicles to tens of thousands of health care institutions, public clinics and private practice providers. The vaccine will be injected at separate body sites using separate syringes and the safety precautions that apply to each. Not a cure but a prevention. Please be patient. This is the beginning of a long process."

He looked down at his notes, then raised his eyes and spoke. "In other news, a range of federal activities are underway, including efforts to clear roads of debris and dead bodies. Needless to say, all communication systems including telephone service, Internet, and Wi-Fi are being restored. Once recovery progresses, evacuees will return to their homes, damaged buildings will be repaired immediately, and new buildings will be constructed. While we can rebuild our communities, unfortunately, nothing can replace the lives that have been lost. In time, we will heal. Thank you. That's all I have for you now."

Neil Crellin was ready for questions from the press. The press photographers' cameras were flashing and popping. Several hands shot up at once. He pointed to a reporter in the back of the room.

The reporter introduced himself and asked, "Is it true the infected can't be cured?"

Vivian and I stopped watching the television because most of what he had said, we already knew. For a brief moment, I hoped my sister had seen the broadcast. Was I fooling myself to think she could still be alive? After all this time, a small part of me, was holding onto hope that I would see her again. Deep inside my heart, I wasn't quite ready to accept she might be dead.

"God, everything is happening so fast. It makes me feel nervous," Vivian said in a low voice.

I swallowed back the emotions, fighting back the tears in my eyes and answered her. "I know, right?"

"Do you think it's really over?" she asked, failing to notice my emotional state.

"Rest assured, if the vaccination works, it will all be over soon. But, like you, I'm skeptical about it. All I'm saying, is to be patient and not to jump to any conclusions."

"I'm with you on that," she said.

Returning to a normal life, was too hard to grasp immediately. For the duration of our meal, we ate quietly thinking to ourselves, and during the long silence I got my emotions under control.

On arriving at my desk, I found a curt memo notifying me that all employees of the company were required to get the vaccine. The memo additionally stated that "Members of Security had eliminated the infected that had been gathered around the gated entrance. A medical tent has been erected off to the side of the entrance. Hours of operation are from 9:30 AM until 6:00 PM daily. The vaccine will be administered at no cost. Visitors will undergo and examination from a physician to check for signs of infection."

There was no reason to question the authority of the BDC. If the management believed people would come, maybe they would come here. Maybe Jenna would come too.

Suddenly, I felt overwhelmed by all the sudden changes and from thoughts of Jenna creeping in upon my mind. As I returned to my duties, I had an empty feeling inside of me, not being able to share this with my sister. Still, I was anxious to get inoculated. And not because it was mandatory.

Chapter 66

ON A SUNNY FRIDAY MORNING Jenna was asleep in the stockroom. Slowly waking up, she could smell the breakfast that Eduard, the chef, was fixing in the kitchen. It was enough to get her out of bed. She showered and dressed before she exited the kitchen through the swinging door leading into the dining area and took her usual seat in front of the counter. Lynn came and took her order of pancakes, eggs, toast, and coffee.

Breakfast came and went, and she climbed off the stool. After leaving some money on the counter to cover the tab, she headed to the door to the outside. The instant she stepped out of the diner, she saw it. The tanker driver was directing gasoline down a long hose into a large tank in the ground outside the Phillips 66 station. She stepped forward, but in her haste, she bumped into Ron.

"Excuse me, Ma'am," he said.

"Sorry. It's a glorious morning, isn't it?" she asked ecstatically.

"It is a fine morning," he echoed mockingly.

Without wasting another moment, she ran to the car, scrambled inside and drove to the station. Just as she parked next to a pump, the fuel tanker pulled out and drove away. As she filled the tank, she saw Larry Simmons watching her from the window. After returning the nozzle to the pump, she loped into the small store to pay for the gas.

"Welcome. Good to see that you got gas in your car," Larry Simmons said from behind the counter.

"Yes. Thanks so much."

"I was going to tell you after the tanker left. When I saw you pumping gas, I figured there was no need. I told you it was coming."

She grabbed a can of Sprite from the cooler. "How much for this and the gas?"

"That'll be seventeen dollars," he replied.

She opened the zipper of her backpack and took out her wallet. The only money she had was the fifty-dollar bill folded behind her driver's license. She gave it to him. He gave her change and put the can of Sprite into a plastic bag. After thanking him again, she put the bag and her wallet inside her backpack and left.

Outside, everything was sharp and bright. She felt exhilarated because she was leaving Santa Fe. Then, instead of driving, she walked the short distance to the Blackstone Diner. She had to say her goodbyes.

After a quick farewell to Ron, she breezed past him, pushing through the door into the diner. Her mind raced with things she wanted to say until Lynn entered the room. She suddenly found herself at a loss for words.

"You got a spare cigarette, sweetie?" Lynn asked her.

"Sure, I got plenty. On second thought, why don't you take my whole pack of Marlboro Lights," she said, reaching into her backpack and pulling out the pack.

"Why, that's mighty kind of you, Jenna. Wait a sec. Are you going somewhere?"

"I sure, am. I just filled up my tank with gas. I came to say goodbye. Just like I told you I would the first time I went to get gasoline," she said with a mischievous wink.

"Oh, Jenna, I'm going to miss you," she said, and went to hug her.

After their long embrace, Jenna said with tears in her eyes, "I'll miss you too. I can't thank you enough for all you've done for me over the past weeks."

"I was glad for your friendship. Now go and meet your sister. Before I start crying, too."

"Please tell Eduard thanks for me," Jenna said, starting to walk toward the door.

"You got it. Too bad Roy is asleep in his rig. He'll be sorry he missed seeing you off, and heartbroken you're gone," she said amusingly.

"I'm so sure. Tell him I said goodbye. And thanks for everything again."

"You're very welcome. Now you be safe out there, okay?" Lynn said.

Her memory kicked in gear, and she got the thirty-eight-caliber gun out of the trunk and put it in her jacket pocket. The box of bullets went into her backpack. She closed the trunk, got into the Mercedes-Benz, and tossed her backpack into the passenger seat. Just as she closed the door, she saw a New Mexico state trooper's car drive by the Phillips 66 station. With a wary expression on her face, she buckled up and started the car.

It was half-past twelve o'clock when she drove onto Highway 84 heading west. She welcomed the two-hour drive ahead of her, anxious to see her sister again.

Several minutes into her drive, something seemed different to her. The highway was fairly clear of debris. And several cars drove by under the speed limit. After all these months, if she didn't know better, she'd think that the epidemic was under control.

A mile or two later, she saw flashing lights in her rearview mirror. Three police cars pulled up behind her. She hoped the police wouldn't pull her over. Why would they? She didn't look like a criminal at all.

She had found the car abandoned in a parking lot. If they did pull her over, that was what she would tell them. She didn't steal the car. And even worse, she was packing a gun. She didn't steal that, either. No, she didn't have a license to carry it. She had found that, too. Conviction of illegal possession of a firearm could result in a prison sentence. The fact was, she was literally in possession of a stolen car and an unlicensed firearm. Could she be tempted to break any more laws?

The convoy of police switched lanes and sped past her. But just then two zombies came into view, walking along the shoulder of the highway. One of the cruisers slowed down. The officer in the passenger seat stuck his arm out of the window and pointed a gun at a zombie. As the zombies started to walk toward the car, the officer fired a bullet into each of their heads. The zombies fell dead to the ground. Then the cruiser sped up to catch up with the two other police cars.

The sensible thing to do was to press the brake pedal, lowering her speed by a good ten miles per hour. There she was, driving at forty miles an hour, keeping a reasonable distance behind the police cars. Not long after, they dropped out of sight altogether, and she waited five minutes for good measure.

Now was as good a time as any for her to push a button, lowering the passenger-side window. She checked her rearview mirror and the side mirror on the driver's side for the tenth time in the past two minutes. Reaching into her backpack, she pulled out the box of bullets and tipped it out of the window onto the shoulder of the highway. Next, she pulled the revolver out of her jacket pocket. Pointing it upward, she opened the chamber, emptied the bullets into her hand, and flicked them out the window. She pulled out a napkin from her backpack and wiped her fingerprints off the gun. She looked in the rearview mirror to see nothing, then hurled the gun out the window onto the shoulder, where it clanked as it bounced down into a ditch.

No way did she want to remember how it had felt to wrap her hands around the cold steel of a pistol, to pull the trigger. She would never tell anyone that she had used a gun. As hard as it was to keep a secret from Hannah, this was a secret she would take to her grave.

She pushed a button and the passenger's window rolled up. Increasing her speed, she passed an off-ramp. Her adrenaline peaked quickly, and all of her feelings for her sister surfaced. She was so close to Dulce she could taste it.

Chapter 67

VERY EARLY THIS MORNING, I woke up with a big yawn. Something was pressing on my mind, something I had to complete. I sat up in bed, ready to finish what I had started. It was time to record the final episode of this long, drawn-out video series I had created about the viral outbreak.

First, I went to the bathroom to brush my teeth and wash my face. Then I hopped into the shower. Uncomfortable at the thought of having to make an impromptu speech, so many times, I thought about what I was going to say. After I got dressed, I set up the camcorder on the dresser in the bedroom, hit Record, and started talking.

"Day 176. I've got good news for a change. A preventive vaccine against the virus has been developed at Biogenetics & Disease Control. Thanks to the hard work of our resident virologist, Dr. Julie Mehta. Most fittingly, it is called the Never-

DEAD vaccine. The vaccine causes the body to develop antibodies. These proteins destroy invading pathogens in the blood. The person has immunity, meaning that the immune system acquires the ability to resist the disease. Helicopters with medical teams aboard will deliver syringes and vials of the vaccine to hospitals and health centers all over the northern hemisphere, including Canada and Mexico.

But the sad news is that anyone infected must be killed. There is no cure for the virus once it establishes a foothold in the bloodstream, a pathogen invader the body's immune system can't overcome. Once infected, the virus causes too much damage to the body.

According to TV news reports, order is being restored in the United States. Law enforcement agencies have responded, with the military sweeping through neighborhoods, eliminating the infected, cremating or burying their dead bodies. SWAT members are in full tactical gear with helmets, shields and rifles patrolling the neighborhoods as well.

Last year, according to the ancient Maya civilization, the world was supposed to end on December 21, at the hour of the Winter Solstice. Even many scientists predicted that a polar shift would likely occur on December 21. It's just a theory, but I think it has some merit. Especially with what ended up happening.

Already, recovery is underway. I'm hoping my sister will show up. All this time, I'm perfectly comfortable living underground beneath the city of Dulce. But one day, I hope to return to the surface."

"Come here, you. That's right, I'm talking to you," I said to Mim, who was sitting on the bed watching me.

She looked at me with her soft blue eyes. Putting on an innocent face, there was no doubt she was good. Still, she looked puzzled as I took her in my arms while the camera was recording.

I waved goodbye to the camera, then said, "Mim, let's say bye-bye."

"Meow, meow," she said to the camera, looking amused.

"Hannah Winter signing off."

Mim was part of this story, too. I had to squeeze her in this last recording. And she handled it very well. She meowed on cue and without any rehearsals.

After pushing the Stop button on the video camera, I set Mim down on the bed and she ran off. My little cat was confused. That cluelessness was part and parcel of what made her precious to me.

Now that my video diary series was canceled, I wondered if I had captured the full story of the epidemic because there actually was something I had wanted to do a couple of months ago. At first, I planned to plug the digital video camera into a computer in the security room. This way I could record the live feed of the zombies huddled around the gated entrance. Knowing Lucas, he probably would have let me do it.

At the last minute, I stopped myself, just lost my nerve.

In truth, I didn't want to take advantage of his kindness. And if Ken Langtry caught me doing it, that could have landed him in serious trouble.

And so, I had come up with another plan to get footage of the zombies. With my expertise, I could have hacked into the security system from any computer. Security might never have found out that the system had been hacked. Once the video camera was plugged into the computer, it would have been so easy to record the feed from the surveillance cameras at the gate.

Once again, I chickened out.

What if Ken Langtry had discovered it? Because of my technical expertise, I would have been the first person he came to. Plus, who else could possibly want footage of zombies? He would have been disappointed in me. I could have lost my job. Then I would have been thrown out on the street with the zombies.

Then came a plan to ask Ken outright. That thought didn't last very long. I just knew he wouldn't let me record the zombies outside.

In the end, I gave up on the idea altogether. It was all too complicated.

If only I had gotten the footage I wanted of the zombies. Surely, I could have made a prize-winning documentary on the subject of the outbreak out of it. But now the chance was lost.

I slipped the SD memory card out of the camcorder and put it in its case. Inside a dresser drawer, I dug out the two memory cards that held my other recording sessions. I put them in an envelope and sealed it. Afterward I found a black Sharpie pen and wrote: WINTER'S TALE OF THE NEVER DEAD. I wanted a catchy name for my project, and the only thing that came into my mind was The Winter's Tale play by William Shakespeare. What made me think of that? I must have read it when I was in high school. The last thing I did was deposit the envelope on the top shelf of my bedroom closet.

Before leaving for work, I pet the cat for a few minutes, rewarding her with affection. Mim was curled up on the sofa, her head on a pink throw pillow. She was purring happily, so swept away, she had her eyes closed.

"She knows that she is loved. Yes, she does," I said endearingly.

There was no meow in response, not that I expected a response. I knew she was napping. It was only a short amount of time, but it felt good to have spent some quality time with my cat.

"I'm going to work, so you be good," I said as I walked out the door.

Chapter 68

A LITTLE BEFORE three o'clock, Jenna saw the sign for Dulce on 64. She was more than a little relieved. Tears of joy formed in her eyes and started to roll down her cheeks. No sooner did she wipe the tears off her face with her jacket sleeve, she saw the turn-off to the Biogenetics & Disease Control facility.

She slowed the vehicle to a stop and sucked in a breath of air, before turning left onto County Road 352. Approaching the BDC facility, she couldn't help noticing the half dozen security guards with Century Arms AK rifles slung over their shoulders deployed around the grounds. She stopped the car near the open gate with a sign hanging that read NO TRESPASSING.

Jenna was noticed immediately by Chloe Park, who was standing in front of a white medical tent. The Korean security guard with long hair, holding a rifle, began to walk toward her. Jenna thought she looked a little rough around the edges. She pressed the button, rolling down the window next to her, and cut off the engine.

Chloe Park, who was chewing a wad of bubble gum, approached the car. "Ma'am, this is a restricted area. What brings you here?"

"I'm here to meet my sister — Hannah Winter. She works here," Jenna said.

"Do you have identification?"

Jenna grabbed her backpack from the passenger seat and dug inside it. She took out her wallet and pulled out her Texas state driver's license and handed it to her.

She glanced at it, and then handed it back to her. "Hello, Jenna Winter. Welcome, my name is Chloe Park."

"Hello, how are you?" Jenna asked and gave her half a smile.

"I'm doing well, thanks. Now, if you'll wait just a moment."

"Yeah, sure. Be happy to."

Chloe lifted her walkie-talkie and spoke, "Ken, I have a Jenna Winter here to see her sister Hannah Winter. What do I tell her?"

Langtry's voice came over the radio, "Hannah Winter? I didn't know she had a sister. Send her for a medical checkup now to ensure that she is disease-free. She must get the vaccine. I'll send Lucas to get Hannah Winter."

"Copy that," she said, and clipped the radio back on her belt.

Chloe asked in a serious tone, "Can you step out of the vehicle, Jenna? A medical assessment is required."

"I'll be happy to."

Jenna had nothing to worry about. Thanks to God, she was free of the virus. Just as she was about to grab the door handle, it crossed her mind that she didn't need the car anymore.

"Where do you want me to park the car?" Jenna asked, sitting in the driver's seat.

"I don't know exactly. Let me ask the boss."

"Ken Langtry?"

"Do you know him?"

"No, I've never met him, but I've heard of him."

"You have?" Chloe asked, popping her gum.

"Yeah, my sister is Hannah Winter. Remember?"

"Jenna, just hold on tight for a few minutes."

Chloe radioed Langtry again. "Ken, where do you want Miss Winter to park?"

"Chloe, tell her to park her car behind the medical tent. And tell her to meet you in front of the medical tent," his voice crackled over the radio.

"Got it. Loud and clear," she said to him, then turned and said to Jenna, while pointing in the direction of the medical tent, "You can park your car behind the medical tent. I'll meet you at the entrance."

"Yeah, I heard him."

Jenna started up the car, drove the short distance and parked where she was told. After turning off the engine, she left the keys in the ignition. She unbuckled the seat belt, slipped her backpack on, and exited the car. Chloe was waiting for her when she arrived at the entrance of the medical tent.

"This way," she said to Jenna.

A call came over Chloe's radio, telling her to go somewhere else.

She put away the walkie-talkie and said, "Jenna, I have to go. Someone will meet you inside."

Before she could reply, Chloe walked off in another direction. She stepped inside the tent and saw a young black woman with almond shaped eyes seated behind a table. She wore a lab coat over blue scrubs, rubber gloves, an ID badge pinned to her lapel, and a had a surgical-type mask hanging around her neck.

"Welcome. How are you feeling today?" asked the woman.

"I'm feeling fine."

"Are you infected?"

"I am certainly not infected," Jenna said with conviction.

"Have you been vaccinated?"

"No. I didn't know about the vaccine."

"Well, now you know. The vaccine is mandatory. Please fill out this form," the woman said, and handed her a clipboard.

Jenna checked the appropriate boxes on the form. The questions pertained to her overall health and family medical history. It didn't take her long to complete the form and she signaled to the woman when she had finished.

"Walk over to that cubicle and Genevieve will assist you further," the woman said, taking back the clipboard.

"Take off your jacket and roll up your shirt sleeves. Then have a seat and I'll check your vitals," she told Jenna.

Genevieve, a tall, short-haired woman in her late fifties, dressed in a white blouse and white pants, appeared to be a nurse. In the exam cubicle, she wrapped the blood pressure cuff around Jenna's upper arm and began pumping it up. Jenna opened her mouth and received the thermometer under her tongue. Jenna's neck and arms were checked for bite and scratch marks. There were no visible signs of infection. She was satisfied that Jenna didn't have the virus.

"I'm merely giving you an injection of the vaccine. You may feel a little prick," Genevieve said, holding a syringe and squirting a little liquid out of the needle.

"Okay. I'm ready."

Jenna flinched as the needle slid into her arm. Genevieve put a Band-Aid over the spot the needle had entered. As Jenna grabbed her jacket and backpack, Chloe came into the room.

"She's all clear," Genevieve told Chloe.

"Good. Let's head out," Chloe said to Jenna.

Once she was escorted through the gate, Jenna wouldn't let herself cry. She was about ten feet from the elevator when Chloe stopped, turned and told her to wait. Jenna sensed what was coming next, she would soon see her sister. She smiled to Chloe, her expression anxious.

Chloe raised her walkie-talkie to her mouth. "Ken, I'm standing near the elevator with Hannah's sister."

Langtry's voice was heard over the radio. "Standby. Lucas will be there with Hannah soon."

Chapter 69

SITTING AT MY DESK, I was wondering what I was going to do over the weekend. Out of the blue, Lucas appeared outside my office, walking down the hall toward me. My heart sank. He wouldn't be here unless there was a problem. As he drew nearer, my mind jumped to conclusions too soon. I played out the scenarios in my head. Had the zombies broken through the doors? Was he here to evacuate me? Was there something wrong with the vaccine? As he burst through my office door with a rifle draped over his shoulder, no less, I was about to find out.

Lucas came up to my desk. "Hello, Hannah."

"Hello, how's everything going?" I asked reluctantly.

Keeping my head low, I knew I hadn't done anything wrong. Nothing that I was aware of, but at the same time I felt I was in some kind of trouble. I didn't carry out my plan to hack into the security system to record the zombies who had been hanging around the gate. If he only knew.

"It's going good, thanks."

Still suspicious, I kept my eyes down. "I'm glad to hear it."

"Let me tell you why I'm here. Ken Langtry sent me here to escort you to the ground-level entrance. You have a visitor waiting to see you. Will you come with me, please?" he stated softly but with an official ring in his voice.

I didn't get it at the time — I had to ask him, "Yes, I will come, but who's waiting for me?"

"It's your sister, Jenna. You knew she was coming, didn't you?"

Without saying a word, I froze for a second and then blurted out, "Yes, of course I knew."

How strange it was to know Jenna was truly here and that I would be seeing her shortly. There were no words for what I was feeling. Almost fainting with surprise, I could only thank God in my heart.

"Come on," he said.

"I'll just grab my purse," I said with tears springing to my eyes.

Moving quickly, I followed Lucas out the door. Approaching the elevators, I slowed my pace down to a brisk walk. I tried to appear nonchalant but was failing miserably. He could see right through me. Obviously, I was eager to see my sister.

Inside the elevator, I noticed he had a look of concern in

his eyes. Several times I caught him staring at me when he thought I wasn't looking. It was understandable as he could easily tell my emotions were a jumble. There was no way I could've known Jenna was coming today. No, I was aware she was coming but I didn't know when — or if — she would arrive. Oh, heck, I was confusing myself.

"Doing all right there, Hannah?" he asked.

"Yes, well, thanks," I said, a bit jumpy.

With a thud, the elevator stopped at the main level, and we got out. He walked me down the hallway to the elevator that led to the outside, ground-level entrance. Walking past him, I pushed the button for the elevator.

"I do not wish to keep her waiting too long," I explained.

What followed was the longest three minutes of my life. I paced around a little. The best way to deal with this, I told myself, was to remain calm and keep still. There was no need to worry because Jenna was here now. But that was wishful thinking. And the worst of it was, I began embarrassing myself, babbling trying to cover up my nerves.

"I don't know what I was thinking. When I asked you, who was waiting for me? I feel so silly. I should've known. Who else could it be?"

"It's okay, Hannah. I understand," he said with kindness in his voice.

I started thinking to myself. He looked good today in his security uniform. But I didn't flirt. The timing wasn't right. It wasn't like I had a crush on him. I thought of him as a nice person. Still, I couldn't help but wonder if he had a girlfriend tucked away somewhere. What were the chances he was single? I wasn't going to ask him.

The elevator finally arrived, and we hopped on. The car rose rapidly to the ground-level above. In the interim, I didn't speak. In my mind, many things were still jumbled and twisted as a knot of yarn. I was trying to sort it all through. Was I prepared for this? Many months had passed since I'd last seen her. Would I even recognize her? Stay calm, I told myself again.

The elevator chimed, and the doors opened. All I could see in the distance was Chloe Park, who I hadn't seen in a few months, dressed in a security uniform, rifle, and all. She used to work with her mother Linda in the Lotte Market. Now I find out she had gone all commando.

When I stepped out of the elevator, I could only focus on one thing: seeing Jenna. Everything else was a blur. After a few steps, I saw her standing next to Chloe. Even with her slightly tattered green jacket on, she looked skinnier than the last time I'd seen her, but there was no mistaking her. I ran to her and she fell into my arms.

"I was so worried about you," I said, hugging her tightly.

As she cried on my shoulder, it was impossible not to feel for what she'd gone through to get here. I tried to say something else, but when I opened my mouth to speak, nothing came out. I was just so caught up in the moment. Just as well. Some things were better left unsaid. We were together and safe, and that was all that really mattered.

We held each other for some time before Jenna said, "I've got so much to tell you."

Epilogue

THERE was still so much to be done, as it wasn't over yet. Cleanup would take months, a year, or longer. Dead bodies had to be buried or cremated. Abandoned and damaged vehicles, and debris needed to be removed from the roads. Now, at the end of July, the television news reported that the threat of the zombies had been contained. Only small numbers of the infected were still lurking about and could appear out of anywhere. It was going to be a while before the infection was completely eliminated from every corner of the Earth.

In my apartment, I set Jenna up on the sofa with a spare pillow and blanket. She even made a new friend, Mim, who slept with her now. I wasn't jealous. Though she still suffered from the occasional nightmare, she seemed to have fully recovered her old self in this post-pandemic phase. Most days, she spent lounging around the apartment reading and watching DVDs.

Jenna seemed to get along with most everybody at Biogenetics & Disease Control, and had one friend in particular, Chloe Park. Given their unique personalities, it was no surprise to me. She told me that Chloe had told her that last December during the Christmas holidays, when the virus broke out, she had been staying with her mother, Linda. The instant her mother saw the outbreak reported on the TV news, she told Chloe to stay put. She started helping her mother in the Lotte Market. However, there was no challenge in it for her. So, she volunteered to work in the security department. To the contrary, Jenna didn't want to work here.

Dr. Julie Mehta's work in developing a vaccine against the virus earned her a nomination for a Nobel Prize in Medicine. I think she could win it hands down, because the Never-DEAD vaccine saved millions of lives in the northern hemisphere alone. Most people weren't so lucky and had fallen victim to the virus. On a sad note, Vivian Wheeler confirmed that her husband and two sons, had become infected and their whereabouts unknown to her. The same fate fell on Ken Langtry's daughter Dana, who had been given up for dead. Unfortunately, Ken was left with no choice but to accept his daughter had succumbed to the virus. And Jenna was upset that her ex-boyfriend Kevin Flannery, became infected. As silly as it sounds, knowing him the way Jenna did, she was sure that if he was alive, he would have a phone.

Earlier in July, both the telephone and the Internet were working again. Jenna immediately dialed up the monsignor of a church in Abilene, Texas she had been sheltered in. She was pleased to find out that all of the staff were still there and safe. Whereas I was wandering around online and found a website for Coastal Airways. I scrolled down a page and found information about Flight 238. The wreckage of the plane was found in the Gila National Forest of New Mexico. There were no survivors. Nevertheless, Henry Winter was listed as one of the passengers aboard the flight. It was only telling me what I already knew — that my father was gone.

Jenna had planned to move into our late father's house in Albuquerque, as soon as possible, probably this September. For the next year or two, she would use the time to regroup. After all that had happened, she wasn't ready to pursue a career in fashion design, didn't know what she wanted anymore. I was going to be there every step of the way for her, visiting her on weekends in Albuquerque. That was one thing she could count on. From this point on, we were going to stick together.

Last Friday, I received a memo from the management stating that "BDC employees are allowed entry to the ground-level parking garage. They can access their vehicles." The next day, Saturday, Jenna and I rode the elevator to the parking garage level. It was a strange feeling, seeing my blue Subaru Outback wagon. It looked exactly the same as the last time I'd seen it. It was like I had stepped back in time, and it was December 2012 again.

"Shotgun," Jenna exclaimed, hopping into the passenger seat.

I started the car and turned up the air conditioning. Jenna rotated a dial on the radio and a blurt of static came from the speakers. She slowly turned the knob. The radio squawked with the voices of a multitude until she found an all-news station. The top story was the post-pandemic. A man with a deep, rough voice spoke about how the vaccine was being administered at a hospital in Santa Fe. Then he announced a Walmart had opened in Albuquerque.

Pretty soon we were bored stiff, listening to the same news over and over. Jenna reached for the radio and fiddled with the dial. She stopped on a station playing music, Katy Perry, one of her songs called "Part of Me." We sang along to the parts we knew, dancing in our seats, and soon we were laughing. It was the first time I'd seen her laugh since she'd been here. We had so much fun.

"You're a good pal," Jenna said to me.

"I agree with you on that," I said, cracking a smile.

"Is that all you're going to say? Am I a good pal, too, or what?" asked Jenna.

"Well, now that you said it. There's no reason why I should."

"You think you're funny, don't you?"

"Whatever do you mean?" I responded, pretending confusion.

Jenna glared at me. "If you're going to be like that. Forget it."

"Oh, you know I'm just playing with you."

She gave my arm a nudge and laughed. I laughed too.

Looking at Jenna, I was very impressed, so full of vigor, after what she'd been through. She had grown up very quickly in her time on the run from zombies, no longer the fragile, college dropout anymore. To think she had outwitted the never dead for months — making friends along the way, was remarkable and would likely stay with her for the rest of her life. From the stories she had told me, as much as I hated to admit it, I couldn't have done it on my own.

Considering all that had happened, I now felt the best decision I ever made was taking a job at Biogenetics & Disease Control. The better part was the staff of people that I was proud to call friends. For certain, I could see myself working here for my five-year plan.

Should the virus mutate and become resistant to the vaccine, I worry about it happening again. Would I survive it a second time? I couldn't help but wonder. In all actuality, the pandemic wasn't something I wanted to remember, but at the same time, I couldn't forget. I witnessed a world-changing phenomenon. The rise of the dead. It started with tragedy and ended with joy and elation.

ABOUT THE AUTHOR

ANN GREYSON's writing credits include poetry for *The Muse* literary & arts magazine, and theatre reviews for *Talent Magazine*. She has a passion for creating fictional characters for television, acting in the programs: *i Citizen*, *SpaceWoman Light-years Apart*, *Birdwatcher*, *The Lonely Vampire*, *The Out World*, and *puRR*. Ann portrays Hannah Winter in the *Never-DEAD* short television program with inclusion in the 2016 MystiCon Independent Film Festival. She is the producer of *Pompilia* broadcast on Anne Arundel Community Television, and *The Watchers*, a nominee for a VOLLIE Award for Best Local Documentary from Community Media Center TV of Westminster in 2014.

With many dancing credits on stage, she also sings and acts in the music videos: *Shine*, *O Christmas Tree*, *House of the Rising Sun*, *Motherless Child,* and *Buffalo Gals*.

Ann Greyson has an Associate of Arts degree in English from Howard Community College. She is a member of Actors' Equity Association, SAG-AFTRA and the Alpha Alpha Sigma chapter of Phi Theta Kappa.